ONE MORE LIE

BOOKS BY SHERYL BROWNE

The Babysitter

The Affair

The Second Wife

The Marriage Trap

The Perfect Sister

The New Girlfriend

Trust Me

My Husband's Girlfriend

The Liar's Child

The Invite

Do I Really Know You?

Her First Child

My Husband's House

We All Keep Secrets

Keep Me Safe

ONE MORE LIE

SHERYL BROWNE

bookouture

Published by Bookouture in 2024

An imprint of Storyfire Ltd.
Carmelite House
50 Victoria Embankment
London EC4Y 0DZ

www.bookouture.com

Storyfire Ltd's authorised representative in the EEA is Hachette Ireland
8 Castlecourt Centre
Castleknock Road
Castleknock
Dublin 15 D15 YF6A
Ireland

ISBN: 978-1-83525-964-1
eBook ISBN: 978-1-83525-963-4

For my fabulous readers.
To those of us who are in or who have suffered within a manipulative relationship, never lose your sense of self.

Betrayal may shatter our faith in others, but it should never shatter our faith in ourselves.

Unknown

PROLOGUE

'Stop,' I beg him shakily.

'The tap was dripping, plop, plop, plop.' He emits a short, scornful laugh. 'It was enough to drive a person out of his mind.'

'Please,' I murmur, fear crackling through me like ice as he moves towards me.

He pays no heed to my pleas. 'The body wasn't swinging, but I swear I could hear the rope creaking.'

'Stop!' I scream, pressing the heels of my hands to my ears. I'm still holding the knife in one hand. I drop it back to my side, my knuckles tensing as I clutch it more closely.

He simply stares at me. His face tight, white. His eyes drilling furiously into mine.

Deep visceral fear settles in the pit of my belly. 'What are you going to do?'

He blinks, a deep furrow forming in his brow. Then, 'I've no idea,' he answers with a shrug. 'It wasn't part of my plan to fall in love with you.'

What? My heart booms, nausea swilling through me as I realise he actually is insane.

He takes another step towards me. I take another step away,

only to realise my back is almost to the wall. 'I couldn't tell you,' he goes on ridiculously. 'I knew you wouldn't let me anywhere near you if I told you. I'm not going to hurt—'

'Get *back!*' I raise the knife. My hand shakes. My whole body trembles right down to my bones.

'Woah.' He stops, holds his hands up. 'You need to put that thing down.'

'I said get back!' I scream, as he moves again towards me.

He falters, his head tipped to one side, his expression a mixture of confused and cautious. Then, 'Jesus.' He blows out an astonished breath. 'You really do think I'm going to hurt you, don't you?'

'Back away,' I warn him, looking feverishly past him for a means of escape.

'Christ, I'm not going to hurt you. I would *never* hurt you.' He shakes his head in bewilderment. 'You must realise—'

'Liar!' I yell. 'You hurt my friend. You *killed* her.'

ONE

BECKY

Now

My throat closes, tears wetting my cheeks as I drop my rose onto the casket. We've chosen yellow roses – Emelia, Tom, Richie and I – to signify friendship. It's our shared secret that binds us, bringing us together occasionally over the twenty years since our university days, the weight of which lies so heavy in my chest I sometimes feel I can't breathe. There should be five of us, each of us carrying our secret to the grave. Now there are four. Clearly overcome as the minister delivers the graveside eulogy, Jodie's ex-partner emits a heartbroken sob, and Richie, my husband, a kind, caring man, reaches to place an arm gently around her shoulders. 'Why did she do it?' Kelly murmurs as he eases her to him.

Richie's gaze as it glides to mine is filled with the same uncertainty I feel, and I have to look away. As a sprinkle of earth rains down on the lid, I close my eyes, attempting to slam the door that opens in my mind, to block out the sounds of the long ago day that will haunt me into eternity: the shrill craw of a solitary seagull, waves crashing against the shore, the beach littered with shingle, the view interrupted by something that doesn't belong. It takes me a moment to register that the blueish white mound that lies there is her, her body exposed to the elements, her limbs and torso pale and naked, apart from the algae. It looks as if someone has placed it over her to preserve her dignity, I think obliquely. Then come the blood-freezing screams, Emelia screeching, hysterical, 'She's *dead*. She's fucking dead! What the hell was she *doing* out here?'

Tom's shocked voice, bobbing somewhere between adolescence and manhood, 'We need to go.'

Emelia stammering, teeth chattering, 'B-but we can't just leave her.'

'We need to get out of here!' Tom clutching her arms, spinning her towards him, shaking her. 'Emelia! We have to go! *Now!*'

Richie, less emotional, more decisive. 'He's right. This is nothing to do with us. She wasn't even supposed to have come. She said she was going home for her mum's birthday. There's nothing we can do for her now. We should just get out of here.'

How did he know she'd been going home? I wonder again now, as I have a million times since that day. I'd been aware that Pippa was going home for the mid-term reading week. It was her mother's birthday, she told me, and she felt obliged to go. How would Richie have known, though? He'd said he'd only ever spoken to her on the one occasion we were all together in the pub. I hadn't pressed it back then, panic driving me, driving us all to follow his lead as he shepherded us away. He'd been the person who'd kept his head when we were all losing ours, reassuring us we weren't to blame. Once the investigation was over, I tried to stuff the memory of the tragedy that plagues me deep down. It didn't work. I think about her every day. Remember her in my nightmares, when the sea regurgitates her body over and over and I wake wet with sweat as the pale limbs twitch and the dead eyes spring open.

'Becky?' I start as I realise Richie is talking to me. 'They're moving off to the reception.'

I follow his gaze as he nods towards the others walking sombrely away from the open grave. We should go too, but I hesitate. It's going to seem odd my asking him after all these years, but being here is such a sharp reminder of the events that led up to Pippa's death. A rush of raw emotion crashes to the surface as I see him in my mind's eye, dancing with her, his eyes locked on hers as he smiles encouragingly at her, and I blurt out the question that's been burning inside me, 'How did you know, Richie?'

He looks at me askance.

'That Pippa was supposed to be going home? You said she wasn't supposed to have been at the beach party when we found her. Remember?'

'Becks.' He sighs and threads an arm around me. 'I thought we'd all agreed not to dwell on all that? It only upsets you.'

'I know—' my eyes flick guiltily away and back '—but I can't stop thinking about it, especially now. We were all there at Pippa's funeral too, yet we never said a word about the way we'd treated her.'

'What good would it have done, though, Becks? It couldn't have brought her back, could it?' His tone is tinged with a mixture of sadness and despair. 'Look, I get why being here has brought it all back. It was so long ago, though, I honestly can't remember when it was I spoke to her. I think I was standing next to her in the refectory queue. Now's not the time to dredge it up again, though, is it?'

Giving my shoulders a reassuring squeeze, he encourages me on. He's right, I realise. We'd all agreed to bury it, never to talk about it, but surely with this devastating reminder of our own mortality, we must each individually be searching our consciences? If it had been someone else who'd run off after being taunted the way Pippa had, wouldn't one of us have gone straight after her? Why had we left her to wander around on her own? And why hadn't we gone to her when we discovered her lying on the beach like a lonely mermaid spat out by the sea? I've been plagued by that image ever since, more so since finding the seashells on the decking in our garden shortly after we'd moved into our new house, the slimy wet seaweed in the hall. Richie had said my imagination was running away with me, that hormones due to my pregnancy and misplaced guilt were making me neurotic. Still, though, I feel as if someone or something is haunting me, haunting us.

The police thought she'd had sex, news that had shocked us all. 'But she couldn't have,' I'd blurted. It was inconceivable to all of us that Pippa, the girl who was so socially awkward she would flush bright scarlet if a boy even looked at her, had had sex hours before she died. With whom? When? The beach Jodie had suggested was in a beautiful, secluded little cove, accessible only by foot or boat. There'd been a lot of dog walkers along the coastal path during the day, but they'd dwindled to just a few after sundown. As far as we all knew, it was just our group partying on the beach that night, Jodie and her then girlfriend, Zoe, Tom and Emelia, Richie and me. Also Dylan and Sophie, who weren't really inner circle and had left early. Pippa was house-sharing with Jodie and Sophie and had overheard us talking about the party. I'd felt obliged to invite her. As she'd said she was planning to go home and also tended to be a bit of a loner, I hadn't thought she'd come, but she'd turned up late in the afternoon, telling me her mum had plans for the evening. I dearly wish she hadn't.

The detective who'd been taking our statements had squinted at me curiously. 'You seem surprised,' he'd said.

'I am,' I'd mumbled, thoughts still firing through my mind as to who it might have been. 'I mean, I didn't realise she was seeing anyone,' I'd added, attempting to collect myself.

'She didn't have a regular boyfriend,' Emelia had inter-vened. 'Although there was someone she saw a few times.'

'Do you know who?' the detective had asked.

Emelia had shaken her head. 'No, sorry. I saw him once when she met him outside the pub, but only from a distance. I never got to meet him. Did you, Becks?'

'No.' I'd glanced from the detective to Emelia, whose face was a picture of innocence. This had been news to me.

Once the detective had left, having explained that they would know more after the post-mortem, I'd asked her if it was true. She'd insisted it was. There was something about the way she wouldn't quite meet my eyes, though, and apprehension had prickled through me. Had she been thinking the same as me? That it might have been one of the boys in our group Pippa met? Tom considered himself irresistible and was the obvious suspect, but he and Emelia were an item by then. Surely he wouldn't have cheated on her so soon into the relationship? I had considered whether it might be Richie, who'd rivalled Tom in the looks department, both tall and dark. Personality-wise, though, Richie was nothing like Tom, who was full of himself, flexing his muscles on the beach, very aware of his own attrac-tions. Richie was less confident, quiet and bookish. Also kind, which is what attracted me to him. I didn't know Dylan well, but it had been obvious he was besotted with Sophie and didn't strike me as the sort who would mess around. They'd been superglued to each other, in any case, before they'd decided to walk back into town, preferring a warm bed to a damp ground sheet. The only alternative was that she had met up with some-one. It was possible, I'd supposed, but given how self-conscious Pippa was, it seemed unlikely.

The relief had been palpable when we'd learned there was no evidence of force. Also, no semen found, the assumption being that a condom was used. Any other possible DNA evidence they might have been able to collect from her clothes, which had been located on the beach, had been washed away, the detective had informed us. I imagine that, nowadays, with the advancements in DNA technology, they might have found something more concrete.

The news coverage had been scant, a request for anyone who might have met with her or have any ideas about her last movements to come forward. No one ever had. She was asthmatic, but as she'd been face down in the sand and her lungs had been filled with water, the cause of death was eventually deemed to be drowning due to over-consumption of alcohol.

'How come they never found her inhaler, though?' Jodie had asked as we'd walked away from her funeral. 'They found the lid from it lying not far away from her,' she'd pointed out.

Richie had suggested it had probably been washed out to sea.

'Odd, though.' Jodie had frowned in contemplation. 'That the lid should have become separated from the chamber, I mean.'

TWO

Emelia, Richie and I sit awkwardly around a table at the funeral reception while Tom goes off to the bar to fetch drinks. 'So, how's things, Em?' Richie asks to fill the silence.

'Not bad.' Emelia smiles. 'Although Tom's pissed off with a potential client, hence his moodiness.'

'Because?' Richie asks.

'The usual.' Emelia sighs. 'I'm sure they think investment bankers earn a fat commission for sitting on their backsides. It's so unfair when he works so hard. We were almost late coming here, thanks to him having to tweak some analysis or other – and then the client had the nerve to call him while we were on our way, would you believe?'

'I suppose it must have been important,' Richie ventures.

Cue a roll of the eyes from Emelia. 'Obviously. When is work *not* important above everything else is what I would like to know? He's always late home nowadays. I wouldn't be surprised if he was late for his own bloody funeral.'

Richie glances awkwardly at me, and I guess why. She's talking loudly and animatedly, inappropriately, shooting daggers in Tom's direction. Tom, who's standing at the bar with his back to her, seems completely oblivious.

'Apparently they want him to meet further with the company directors. I've no doubt that will be at the weekend over a round of golf.' Emelia sighs again dramatically. 'It drives me mad, I swear. I feel like a golf widow half the time.'

I can't help feeling annoyed with her now. She hasn't changed since our university days. If there's a gathered audience, I'm sure she thinks she has to play to it. At uni, her undeniable beauty and extrovert personality attracted people. Students were desperate to be part of her coveted circle. And she thrived on it. She loved being 'top girl'. Confident and outgoing, she never had time for people who were less so.

'So how are the kids?' Richie asks, clearly attempting to steer the conversation onto something less controversial.

'Good.' Emelia brightens. 'No thanks to the nanny. She was a complete waste of space, I swear.'

I bury a sigh of my own and decide now would be a good time to excuse myself and go and speak to Kelly. 'Won't be a sec,' I say, getting to my feet.

Emelia stops talking mid-flow. 'I'll come with you,' she says, grabbing her bag. 'It's cold enough to freeze the balls off a brass monkey out there. I'm dying for a pee.'

'I'm actually just going to have a quick word.' I nod towards Kelly.

'Oh, right.' Emelia plops back down again. 'Give her my condolences, won't you?' Her brow creases sympathetically, briefly, before she turns her attention back to Richie, her urgent need for a 'pee' apparently forgotten. I've noticed the last couple of times we've met, a New Year's party and again six months ago for Tom's fortieth birthday, that she seems to have taken to grabbing her chance to talk to Richie alone.

Richie, for his part, looks a little desperate, and I can't help feeling relieved that, despite the fact that she attracts appreciative male glances wherever she goes, he appears not to want to spend time in Emelia's company. Unlike some women, pregnancy doesn't suit me. Far from radiant, I look pale and washed out, and Richie's a good-looking guy. With a melancholic Jake Gyllenhaal look about him – mesmerising ice-blue eyes, thick lashed and incongruous with his dark hair – he definitely turns female heads.

I try not to judge Emelia as I head off. It's just the way she is. She thrives on attention because she didn't have much as a child, she'd once confided. Her mum drank like a fish and her dad was largely absent in her life. Whenever her parents were together, they would do nothing but argue, violently sometimes, Emelia caught in the middle of it. I'm sure she doesn't mean to be quite so insensitive.

As I pass Tom coming back with the drinks, orange for me as I don't drink, beers for himself and Richie and a large white wine for Emelia, I note the bottle of wine also on the tray and suspect Emelia's conversation will be becoming more animated as the afternoon wears on. 'All right?' He smiles.

'As well as I can be under the circumstances.' I give him a small smile back, but don't linger. Tom and I also have a shared secret and I'm sure he'd rather I keep a little distance between us.

Kelly looks up as I approach her. She's devastated, clearly. She and Jodie had split up a few months before Jodie's death and she's undoubtedly blaming herself. 'I'm so sorry, Kelly.' I squeeze her into a hug as she stands.

'Why did she do it?' Easing back, Kelly searches my eyes. Hers are tortured and my heart breaks for her.

'I don't know.' I sigh in sympathy, though I suspect that I do. Like me, Jodie struggled with what happened on the beach on that long ago day. *She haunts* me, she'd confided when we met up just a few short weeks ago, which jarred me. So often I've been jerked from sleep in the small hours, the image of Pippa standing silently over me seared so vividly on my mind, I would swear I could reach out and touch her.

'She seemed so well lately.' Kelly's forehead creases into a troubled frown. 'So upbeat. It just doesn't make sense.'

'Perhaps she was trying to hide how she was feeling because she didn't want to upset you,' I suggest, unsure what else I can say.

'No, I mean it *really* doesn't make sense.' Kelly's tone is adamant. 'We were going to get back together. Get married. We'd even told the children. I don't believe she would have done this to them. I just don't. What was it she was keeping from me, Becky?'

That catches me off guard. 'I'm not sure. I don't think there was anything.' I feel my mouth run dry as I deliberately lie.

'Oh, but there was.' Swiping a tear from her cheek, Kelly fetches her bag from under her chair. 'Look,' she says, producing an envelope and handing it to me.

As I realise it's Jodie's suicide note, my heart constricts sharply. It almost folds up inside me as I read it.

Dear Kelly,

You were my heartbeat. You gave me everything, shared yourself completely. I let you down. There was part of me I could never share with you. I so wish I could have. Just know my choice now is not because of anything you did. You were the light in my darkness. The best part of me. Shine brightly, my lovely. I'm so sorry. Please try to forgive me.

I love you,

Jodie

'What was it, Becky?' Kelly asks wretchedly again. 'Was it

something that happened before she met me? It took me ages to get her to open up to me. She never did, though, did she? Not completely?'

'I honestly don't know,' I mumble. 'I'm so sorry, Kelly.' If it's possible to feel any worse than I did when I heard the news about Jodie, than I did all those years ago when we'd found Pippa, in this moment, I do. The thing Jodie couldn't share could only be the secret we all kept, the thing that haunted her. What scares me is that she'd meant it, literally. She was convinced there was something, something intangible she couldn't see, right there in her bedroom with her. Everything pointed to her death being by suicide. She'd left the letter. It was eloquent, heartbreaking. Yet it was typed on a PC and printed off, which seemed awfully impersonal considering it was addressed to Kelly. I daren't say anything to the others but, after what Jodie had said, I can't help wondering, *had* there been someone there with her the night she died? Had it been suicide? Or had someone killed her?

THREE

Tears rising so fast I struggle to hold them back, I hurry across to our table, where Emelia is still holding court. She's hanging on to Tom's hand, as she tends to in public, while singing his praises, telling Richie what a brilliant father he is, despite the demands on his time. 'The kids are absolute angels, though,' I hear her now expounding her children's virtues, 'which is obviously down to good parenting, hey, Tom?' She looks at Tom expectantly.

'Undoubtedly.' Tom gives her a smile, but I can't help noting it's a touch cynical.

'Did I tell you that Charlotte played the lead role in the nativity play last year?' Emelia asks Richie. 'She was amazing. She's obviously gifted. Tom and I are thinking of enrolling her in dance and drama classes, aren't we, Tom? There's a Stagecoach Performing Arts school quite close...'

She stops as Richie half stands when I reach my chair. 'How is she?' he asks, catching hold of my hand and giving it a supportive squeeze.

'Devastated,' I answer, grateful that he's so caring, there for me when I need him to be. 'Did you know they were getting back together?' I glance around, note the surprised looks, and gather they didn't.

'Shit, that's rough.' Tom takes a swig of his beer. Richie looks gutted for Kelly, while Emelia widens her eyes, her expression a mixture of bafflement and surprise, and I'm hugely relieved she refrains from commenting.

'So she has no idea why she might have...' Tom falters. 'You know,' he adds with an awkward shrug.

I hesitate before answering. 'She showed me the note she left. Jodie mentioned there was something she couldn't share with her.' I reach for my orange to wet my dry throat.

'Shit,' Tom mutters again.

'*Tom*,' Emelia chastises him. 'Language. We're at a funeral.'

'Yes, right. Sorry.' Tom nods. 'So, do you think she meant to...?' Again, he trails off.

'I have no idea.' I take the tissue Richie offers me. 'According to Kelly, she seemed happy. Upbeat.' Kelly's right, I realise. It doesn't make sense. Jodie had said she was seeing a counsellor when I'd last spoken to her on the phone. She'd said he was really nice and totally trustworthy. She'd even said I should consider talking to him. She *had* seemed more posi-tive. Why would she then suddenly decide to end her life? And the way that she had? Jumping from the cliff not far from the beach we'd been partying on was a terrifying echo of the past.

'She was quite emotionally volatile, though, wasn't she?' Emelia offers up her opinion, to receive a scathing look from Tom. 'What?' She blinks innocently. 'She was. She was always getting herself in a state about some issue or other. Cruelty to animals. Women's rights. LGBTQ rights. Climate change. She was usually banging the drum about something.'

Richie and I swap disbelieving glances. 'It doesn't make her volatile, Em,' he points out.

'Well, no,' Emelia concedes, 'but she did like her wine,

didn't she? She was knocking it back at that New Year's Eve party, do you remember? She was certainly volatile then.'

I look at her askance as Emelia picks up her glass, tips her wine back and reaches for the bottle, which appears to be going down fast. 'We were all drinking too much,' I remind her, a spark of anger igniting inside me. 'As I recall, *one* of us fell over on the dance floor and had to be helped into a taxi.'

As I shoot her a pointed look, Emelia looks contrite, momentarily. 'I meant she drank a lot generally as far as I could see,' she clarifies with a pout. 'I just thought it might be a factor, that's all. Drinking that much, she was bound to have mood swings.'

Tom looks at her with a mixture of surprise and disbelief. He doesn't say anything, but the weary shake of his head speaks volumes.

'She was obviously depressed,' Richie offers in the intervening awkward silence. 'I mean she must have been, mustn't she?'

Enough to have done this, though? I still can't believe it. I'd been more in touch with Jodie than Emelia had over the years, because she and I both carried guilt over what we'd done. I know she'd struggled with her guilt more at one point when Kelly's daughter was coming up to university age, but she hadn't seemed depressed, not then, or when I spoke to her before her death.

'Aren't we all?' Emelia sighs. 'I mean life *is* depressing sometimes, isn't it, but you just have to deal with it, don't you?' She places her glass down, folds her arms across her chest and actually looks pious.

My mouth almost drops open. Surely she can't be *that* insensitive.

'Perhaps she couldn't move on from what happened,' Richie suggests hesitantly. 'I mean, it's always there, isn't it? In the back of your mind.'

'So dwelling on the past and drinking heavily was going to

help?' Emelia eyes the ceiling, picks up her glass and swills the contents back. 'She should have got married, thought about having children. Properly, I mean.' She reaches again for the bottle, clearly oblivious to the astonished glances all around. 'Tom and I have been a tight unit since our children came along, haven't we, Tom?'

Tom doesn't answer, taking another swig of his beer instead.

Richie looks annoyed, unusually. 'That's a little out of order, Em,' he points out.

'I'm just saying that having a family focuses you on the future,' Emelia goes on, oblivious. 'We don't have time for regrets or reminiscing about what might have been, do we, Tom?'

He kneads his forehead tiredly, while I stare at Emelia, flabbergasted. She knows very well that Jodie thought of Kelly's children as her own. Looking to the future was precisely what Jodie had been trying to do, but the past kept dragging her back, just as it did me. I suspect that's why her relationship had floundered in the first place. Richie and I had each other. We didn't talk about it much, usually only when the nightmares plagued me. When we lost the baby I was carrying just weeks after Pippa's death, he'd understood the grief and guilt that had driven me to my bed for a whole week. I didn't believe I should have the things in life Pippa had been denied. My hand goes protectively to my tummy and the precious life I'm carrying now. I still don't. Yet here was Emelia acting as if nothing had touched her. Everything in her life perfect.

It's not true. According to Jodie, who took Kelly's youngest to and from school, Emelia's kids are wild, cared for mostly by their nanny. Emelia is doing what she's always done, painting a glossy veneer over her life. But then she is a beauty therapist and image consultant. Glossing over imperfections is what she does. Tom, though, is definitely not as perfect as she wants everyone to believe. He might tick all the boxes, successful, tall and classically good looking, but I would be very surprised if he'd given up his womanising ways. I love Emelia. I've always felt she needed to be loved, and I realise I'm being judgemental, but it's *really* hard not to be right now.

'Tom?' Emelia presses him when he doesn't reply.

'Er, not many regrets, no,' he answers quietly, his eyes meeting mine across the table.

'I mean we'd all like to go back and change the past, but we can't, can we?' Fuelled by the alcohol, Emelia trundles on.

'We would,' Tom agrees, his eyes still holding mine.

I avert my gaze, feeling it over: the nauseating panic I felt back at university when I'd been cornered at an end of term party by a man who thought himself so hot no woman could resist him. A man who, though clever enough to be taking advanced mathematics, simply couldn't get his head around the word no.

Anger swells afresh in my chest as I recall the look in his eyes then, confident and cocky. His smirk and his beer breath as he nuzzled his face into my neck. 'Come on, Becks. You know you want to,' he mumbled, one hand sliding up my thigh, his other cupping my buttocks. The more I squirmed to try to get away from him, the harder he pressed his body against mine. When he gripped my face and thrust his tongue into my mouth, I pressed the heels of my hands against his chest and shoved him away hard.

He was shocked. Laughing, bewildered. 'I thought you were up for it,' he said, his look one of bemusement as he righted himself on his feet. 'You were all over me half an hour ago.'

I was not *all over* him. I danced with him. *He'd* been all over me until Emelia cut in, thankfully. Did I send out the wrong signals? I stared at him. I didn't. I know I didn't. 'You're a complete *bastard*,' I spat, wiping my arm across my mouth, wiping him off. 'I have no idea what Emelia sees in you.'

Cold fear constricted my stomach as I watched his cool grey

eyes darken, his pupils so wide as to almost obliterate his irises. 'Do not breathe a word of this to Emelia, Becky,' he seethed. 'I'm warning you.'

What was he warning me? My panic escalated as I realised he was between me and the door. Relief crashed through me as Jodie burst through it a second later. 'Em's drunk too much,' she said, oblivious to what was happening. 'She's in the loo being sick. I'm just grabbing her a glass of... What's up, Becks?' She stopped halfway to the sink, the expression on my face clearly alerting her to something.

'Nothing.' I forced a smile as she looked cautiously between us. 'Tom was just wondering where Em was actually. Weren't you, Tom?'

I shot him a look of ice-cold contempt as I walked past him. I never did tell Emelia. Because I knew she was besotted with him. Because I was confused, part of me wondering whether I actually might have sent out the wrong signals, part of me knowing I hadn't. As time went on, I figured she would find out what he was like. Had she? Might that be why she drinks so much? Because she knows what he's capable of? The more terrifying question that burns inside me is: Did Pippa find out what he was capable of?

FOUR

I glance at Tom as he pushes his chair back. His expression is pensive as he stands, picks up his glass and heads to the bar. What's going through his mind? I wonder, though I'm pretty sure it was the same thing that had just gone through mine. Or rather, his version of events.

'Cheers,' Richie says, picking up his empty glass and looking bemusedly after Tom.

'His mind's obviously elsewhere,' Emelia mutters. I note she's watching Tom narrowly over the rim of her glass as he approaches the attractive woman serving at the bar. She's half Tom's age, probably a student, and I wonder now what Emelia's thinking.

'I'll go grab another.' Richie gets to his feet. 'Would anyone else like one? The wine bottle seems to be empty.'

'No. Thanks, I'm good,' I decline as he glances pointedly from the bottle to Emelia.

'Oh dear, so it is.' Emelia plucks up the bottle and shakes it, then plonks it down with a sigh. 'I'll have a large white wine, please, Richie.' She picks up her glass, drains the dregs, then hands it to him with a smile.

I'm growing worried for her. She's already drunk far too much. I notice her gaze settle back on Tom, and I wonder whether she does know about him, whether she has for a long time. I cast my mind back to Sophie and Dylan's wedding six or so years back when she'd very nearly caught him in the act. He'd fancied his chances with one of the female guests at the reception, accosting her on the first-floor landing of the hotel. I'd been coming up the stairs, Emelia behind me. Even with his back to me, I could see he was doing more than saying hello to the woman. When I'd called back to Emelia to be careful on the stairs, warning him for her sake, Tom had stepped hurriedly away from the woman. I'm not sure whether she'd been a willing participant, but she'd disappeared into the hotel room behind her pretty swiftly, while Tom hurried towards where Emelia emerged onto the landing. I'd never told her about that either. How could I with her about to give birth to their youngest?

I turn my attention to Richie who's joined Tom at the bar, cutting any flirtations he might have been attempting short. Over the years, Richie had been teased about being quiet and studious. Tom had often ribbed him about becoming a boring accountant. I'd rather have caring and boring, though, than gnawing uncertainty.

'God, honestly, I wish Kelly would get a grip.' Emelia sighs audibly, and I look back at her and then to Kelly, who, clearly distraught, is being comforted by her daughter, Anna. 'It's not like they were a proper couple, is it?' Emelia goes on, a disdainful look in her eyes.

I'm immediately irked. 'They were together for ten years, Emelia,' I point out sharply. 'Jodie was there for a good chunk of Anna's life while she was growing up.'

'Yes, but they'd split up, hadn't they?' Emelia argues.

'And they were getting back together,' I remind her. 'They were going to get married.'

'Oh.' Emelia widens her eyes in surprise. 'Well, I didn't realise that, obviously.' I see a flash of contrition and feel I'm definitely being too judgemental. My charitable thoughts evaporate as Emelia goes on, 'Everything in their garden can't have been roses, though, can it?' she says with a sage nod. 'Or they wouldn't have split up in the first place.'

Now I'm utterly stunned. And perplexed. 'Do you really not know what was eating away at her?' I ask, working hard to keep my voice down. 'What eats away at me? At Richie?' I can't speak for Tom. He appears to be a man with no conscience.

Emelia picks up her glass. Finding it empty, she looks more concerned about that than anything else.

'Don't you ever think about that day at the beach, Emelia?' I stare hard at her. 'Don't you have even a smidgen of guilt about what happened?'

She doesn't even have the good grace to look uncomfortable. She looks more indignant, indifferent. 'Why should I have?' She averts her gaze, groping to collect her bag from the floor. 'I wasn't responsible for what happened to her.'

'But you *were*, Em. We *all* were,' I remind her forcefully.

FIVE

PIPPA

Then

The music was loud, a mixture of R&B and reggae. Sitting on the damp beach, Pippa hugged her knees to her chest as she watched the others laughing and dancing. The smells: salt and sea and wood burning reminded her of the campfires she'd hated sitting around as a child. She never was very outdoorsy, a big disappointment to her dad, who only ever showed her minimal affection. Scratch that. He never showed her any, more seemed to tolerate the fact that she existed at all. 'Try to look as if you're enjoying yourself, Pippa,' he would often say with a tight smile. 'You're spoiling it for everyone else.' Everyone else being her uncle and aunt who they would go on camping holidays with, proud parents of twin boys, both of whom were sporty. The twins had been in their element doing boy stuff, climbing, canoeing or playing football. Her brother not so much. Older than her and the twins, Adam was more into his music and computer games. He tried to look out for her, telling her to ignore their father.

Their dad was hard to ignore, though. He was always putting her down, telling her to comb her hair, stop biting her nails, stop eating so much, stop being so introverted and join in. She tried, but whenever she did join in, her cousins would jostle her, making sure she never got the ball. And she hated all the water-based stuff. She couldn't swim for a start. She'd been petrified when they'd gone swimming in the river on one such happy holiday and her dad had nodded towards the water and said to her mum, 'There's one way to teach her.' If her mum hadn't plucked up her courage, threatening to take Adam and her and go home on the train if he dared throw her in, Pippa was sure he would have.

He was a bully, always trying to toughen her up, insisting she sat around the campfire until the smoke ended up choking her. She'd been glad when he'd left. Her mum had too, even though he'd left her in a financial mess – and with her confidence shattered, Pippa realised later. His going off with someone half her mum's age and half her size who was into glamping, rather than camping, preferably in the South of France, would have done that. The woman might find glamping a little less glam when her dad decided it was his prerogative to run her down if she put on a bit of weight, or to punch her if she ever dared really annoy him.

Pippa had stopped eating so much eventually. In an attempt not to be different because of her weight, she'd stopped altogether for a while. Now she counted the calories as if her life depended on it, taking the daily suggested intake for a female and halving it. She never did manage to stop biting her nails.

Chewing on a ragged thumbnail now, she turned her attention back to the 'in crowd'. They were smoking marijuana. She could smell it thick on the humid air, along with the pungent smell of cheap beer and cider. She glanced towards Becky, who she liked and sensed might like her a little. She'd invited her here, after all. They might even be friends, if only Becky wasn't influenced by Emelia, who she was always hanging out with, and who was a complete bitch. The rest of the group were indifferent to her, hardly noticing she was there, as evidenced by Jodie passing the spliff to her girlfriend who then passed it to Sophie who passed it on to Dylan before it went back to Jodie. Pippa didn't want a toke anyway; she would only cough her guts up, end up having an asthma attack and then die of embarrassment with everyone watching. It would be nice not to be so obviously overlooked though.

She looked back to Becky, who was busy dancing with Richie. Pippa liked him. He looked at her when he spoke to her, which made her feel seen, which felt nice. Becky was definitely into him. You only had to see the way she looked at him to know she really fancied him, but Pippa didn't think they'd slept together yet. Becky wasn't a slut, like Emelia, who was currently wearing two triangles covering her nipples, bikini bottoms that wouldn't even qualify as dental floss, and was snogging heavily with Tom, who she was definitely sleeping with, much to her previous boyfriend's dismay when he'd found out before they split.

Feeling like a spare part, she wondered whether to make some effort at conversation with the others. Jodie, though, who was studying history and philosophy, was deep in intellectual conversation with her girlfriend, and Sophie and drippy Dylan had got to their feet, giggling as they headed towards the sand dunes, which they were no doubt about to disappear into to make out.

Sighing, Pippa began to doodle in the sand. She wished someone would notice her instead of making her feel like she didn't exist. A minute later, she almost died when someone did. 'Fancy a dance?' Offering her his hand, Richie smiled down at her.

Pippa glanced from him to Becky, who she thought might not be very pleased. Becky looked surprised at first, but then she smiled and nodded.

Pippa wasn't sure it was a good idea, though. She was as rubbish at dancing as she was every other activity that required any coordination.

'I don't bite, promise.' His mesmerising blue eyes holding hers, Richie smiled again in that endearingly boyish way he did, and Pippa's tummy flipped right over.

Just do it. She summoned her courage and, with her dad's words of 'toughen up' ringing in her ears, reached to take his hand. She was so nervous as he helped her up and led her to the patch of sand they were dancing on she almost fell over her feet before she got there.

They were playing reggae, 'Red Red Wine', an oldie most people would be familiar with, but Pippa had no clue how to move to it. Glancing at Becky, who'd joined Emelia and Tom now they'd managed to tear themselves away from each other, she began to emulate her moves. Tom was watching her, she noticed after a moment. She wished she could be more like Emelia, confident. Look like her, sexy and natural.

Feeling she was getting into the rhythm a little, she smiled at Richie as he smiled at her, then almost had heart failure as he reached to take her hand and pull her to him. *Relax, for God's sake. It's just a dance.* Chastising herself, she leaned into him and followed him around in a circle – and that was when she really wanted to die.

'Oh my God! You have to be kidding,' Emelia screeched behind her. 'For fuck's sake, Pippa, have you been sitting in dog shit or something? It's all over your backside!'

Mortified, Pippa pulled away from Richie and scrambled back to her tent.

Desperate to be on her own, away from all of them, she grabbed her inhaler, and scrambled out again. It was the toilet roll Emelia threw after her that crushed her. Her dad had humiliated her in many ways, but nothing was as soul-crushingly humiliating as this. With Emelia laughing hysterically behind her, her heart wedged up somewhere near her throat and a wheeze rattling her chest, Pippa fled.

SIX

BECKY

Now

Folding her arms across her chest, Emelia scowls at me. 'What on earth are you on about, Becky?' she asks. '*How* were we responsible, exactly? We didn't *force* her to do anything.'

'But we *did*, Em.' I search her face for a speck of remorse and find none. She really doesn't get it, does she? 'If we hadn't all stood by and watched while you were so bloody awful to her, she would never have run off.'

'So, now you're blaming me?' Emelia stares at me in astonishment. 'This is bloody unbelievable.'

'No. That's *not* what I'm doing.' I sigh in despair. 'I think we have to own some of the blame, though, Emelia. We knew she was nervous and we could have tried to be a little more understanding.'

'Oh for God's sake.' Rolling her eyes, Emelia shoves her chair back and jumps up. 'Do you know something, Becky? You're getting quite boring. Richie's goody-two-shoes influence rubbing off on you, no doubt. She was a *grown up*,' she imparts angrily. 'Supposed to be. She didn't need babysitting. Why can't you just let it go?'

Staggered, I watch as she strides past me and stalks off, reeling into a chair and almost falling over it as she heads for the corridor leading to the loos. I can't help feeling furious with her. Surely she must realise that we did have a responsibility towards Pippa? She was vulnerable. She'd been mortified after the bitchy comment Emelia made, that's why she was out there in the dead of night on her own. I'm not trying to point the finger at Emelia. *Am I?* It occurs to me that maybe I am – to ease my own conscience. And now I feel awful. Emelia is clearly emotionally fragile and I've obviously upset her. I didn't mean to do that. I just wanted her to realise that some of us still struggled with what happened, that Jodie had.

Guiltily, I go after her. 'Em?' I call, going through the toilet door. There's no sign of her, and, after checking the cubicles, I go out again, suspecting she's probably outside having a quick vape. She never had quite managed to give up her nicotine addiction.

Heading towards the exit to the car park, I stop in my tracks as someone calls behind me. Tom, I realise as he calls again, and I spin around, apprehension creeping through me as he hurries towards me. 'I'm glad I caught you,' he says, stopping a yard or so away, his expression uncertain.

'Did you want something?' I respond stiffly.

'Just to apologise,' he answers with an awkward shrug. 'I should have done it years ago, when I...' he falters. 'I behaved like an idiot. I'm sorry.'

Actually, like a sexual predator, I'd like to point out, but this is not the time or the place.

'I was way out of order,' he goes on as I study him, wondering whether his remorse is genuine. I guess it must be since he's showing a side of himself he rarely does. I've never seen him anything but full of himself. Had Jodie's death prompted him to examine his conscience? 'I'm really sorry, Becks. Can you forgive me?' Smiling hopefully, he reaches to place a hand on my arm. 'I've been tearing myself apart ever since— *Shit.*'

Trepidation crawls over me as he snatches his hand away, closing his eyes and visibly wincing.

Slowly, I turn around – and almost die.

'Well, this is cosy, isn't it?' Emelia's gaze swivels suspiciously between us.

'We were just talking. Catching up,' Tom says quickly.

'I gathered.' Emelia locks her eyes on his. 'What is it she has to forgive you for, Tom?' she asks.

SEVEN

'I, er, nothing,' Tom answers nervously. 'It was years ago. I acted like a bit of a dick, and—'

'I bet you did,' Emelia seethes and spins around towards the exit.

'*Shit.*' Tom's eyes dart worriedly to mine as he hurries past me to follow her. 'Em, wait.'

Uncertain what to do, I hesitate. Guessing going after them won't help, I sigh in despair of myself and turn around to head back to the lounge. What on earth is wrong with me? Do I need everyone else to feel guilty to make myself feel better, is that it? Well, Jodie had, hadn't she, and it had killed her. With my own guilt now eating away at me and my mind on what explanation Tom might come up with to appease Emelia, I don't notice the man approaching the swing doors from the lounge until I almost hit him with one.

'Whoops. Almost got me,' he says, catching the door and moving to one side to let me through.

'God, I'm so sorry,' I apologise, flustered. 'I was miles away.'

'I gathered.' He smiles warmly. 'Jack.' He introduces himself. 'Jack Evans.'

'Rebecca Shaw—' I reach to shake the hand he's offering me '—but everyone calls me Becky. I'm a friend of Jodie's. Was,' I add, and swallow.

'Nice to meet you, Becky,' he says, filling the second's heavy silence.

'Likewise,' I say, composing myself. 'So are you a friend, or...'

'I was Jodie's counsellor,' he provides. 'I thought I should pay my respects.'

That was nice of him.

'Jodie spoke highly of you,' he goes on, with another warm smile. He has kind eyes, I can't help but notice, deep hazel with warm flecks of cinnamon, earnest and open. 'I gather you were all at university together?'

'That's right.' I nod, my gaze wavering as I wonder how much Jodie might have told him. Recalling what she'd said about him being caring and totally trustworthy, I relax. She'd definitely seemed more optimistic after talking to him.

'I'm detaining you,' he says. 'I'm sure you want to get back to your husband.'

'No hurry. He's talking to Kelly—' I nod towards where Richie and Kelly are deep in conversation '—about her financial affairs, I think. Richie did the accounts for the café she and Jodie ran together. It's probably best to leave them to it.'

'Would you care to join me while you wait?' Jack indicates an empty table where he appears to have a drink.

My hand goes to my bump where my lively little foetus is practising his kickboxing. I don't normally flag so early in the day but after all that's happened, I feel suddenly overwhelmed with tiredness. 'I'd love to. Thank you.'

He gives me another smile as he hurries to pull a chair out for me. 'Can I get you anything?' he asks as I sit. 'A drink or some food possibly? You look as if you've had a long day.'

I shake my head. 'I'm fine, thanks. Just tired. I'm afraid pregnancy doesn't seem to come naturally to me, whereas Emelia sailed through hers. She's also a friend from university, by the way. She's here somewhere.' I look around, hoping Tom and she have come back in, but I don't see them and worry gnaws away at me. Emelia was right. I should have left things alone. Emotions will already be running high without me stirring things up. I hope she's all right. That she and Tom are. They have two children. Their marriage is clearly precarious. I couldn't bear it if this causes further trouble between them.

'Is she okay?' he asks as he sits down opposite me. 'I couldn't help but notice her argument with the chair.'

'A bit emotional,' I confide, now feeling protective of Emelia. Her propensity to drink too much is inherited from her mother, I suspect, exacerbated by the fact that she's obviously unhappy. I really wish now that I hadn't chosen today to dredge up the past.

'It's an emotional time.' He nods understandingly.

'Jodie's partner feels terribly guilty,' I confide. 'I think she thinks she should have seen the signs. She's says that Jodie seemed happy, though, upbeat, which is why it's come as such a shock to her.'

'It's often the way,' he says. 'People tend to be racked with guilt when a life ends so tragically, wondering what they could have done to prevent it. The thing is, people often hide the fact that they're not coping because they feel ashamed that they're not. If someone is intent on taking their own life, they can seem happy because they feel a sense of relief that they've made their decision, if that makes sense. They don't want to alert anyone to the fact in case they try to talk them out of it. I doubt there was anything anyone who knew Jodie could have done to stop her.'

His demeanour is serious yet gentle, his voice deep, yet soft and reassuring, and I feel somewhat comforted by that. 'Can I ask you something?' I eye him cautiously. 'Jodie, did she tell you whether there was something worrying her?'

He hesitates. 'It would be unethical of me to disclose anything that goes on in the therapy room but, yes, she did allude to something.'

That jolts me. 'But she didn't say what?'

'Unfortunately, no.' He sighs, a flicker of disappointment crossing his face. 'We were due to talk it through at our next session, but... To be honest, I'm carrying a certain amount of guilt myself. I had to reschedule our appointment due to a family crisis. I can't help feeling that, if she'd been able to talk more, it might have helped her state of mind.'

Jodie was right. He clearly is caring. 'You shouldn't,' I try to reassure him.

'Rationally.' He nods. 'As a counsellor, you're not responsible for people. They've allowed you into their deepest thoughts, though, shared their pain with you. You'd have to be heartless not to take that away with you.'

I nod, understanding.

'You shouldn't blame yourself either,' he adds, a concerned furrow creasing his brow. 'Obviously, I couldn't know Jodie well in the short time we spent together, but she did mention you. She said you'd asked her to be a godmother to your child. She would want you to move on and embrace life, I think, for the sake of that child. Dwelling on the past doesn't allow us to do that.'

'No. I know.' I swallow tightly, my thoughts shooting back to Pippa. The children she might have had. The life she would never embrace. How painful and lonely her last moments on this earth must have been. How does one move on from that?

EIGHT

PIPPA

Then

Pippa dropped down on the sand, drew her knees to her chest and watched the sun go down, a huge golden disc, painting the sky with a breathtaking array of colours, from bright reds and oranges to soft pinks and purples, before it slipped silently beneath the edge of the ocean. As its last ethereal rays disappeared, she felt it acutely, the absolute loneliness of being alone.

She wasn't sure how long she'd been walking aimlessly around. She'd heard the thump of the music up until an hour or so ago. It had seemed to resonate through the sand and up through the soles of her feet. They'd obviously partied on in her absence. They were probably as high as kites by now. She didn't care. At least she wouldn't end up throwing up and feeling like death warmed up in the morning. She tried to console herself with that thought. It didn't work. She still felt like a social leper. As if there was something fundamentally wrong with her that she couldn't fit in no matter how hard she tried. It had taken every last ounce of her courage to come here tonight. She shouldn't have. Even wearing what she thought were the right clothes, which she'd spent her last penny on: frayed denim shorts and a strapless bikini top she'd been terrified she would fall out of, she still felt excluded. She'd dyed her hair from boring brown to bleached blonde in the hope of blending in with the crowd. It was awful, as brittle as straw and more like candyfloss in the damp sea air than the sexy, just-got-out-of-bed look Emelia effortlessly wore. It was coming out, too, in clumps. Her mum said it was because her body was lacking essential nutrients. Pippa knew she was right. She'd promised her she would eat a healthier diet, but the thought of putting on weight and being ridiculed for that was enough to put her off food for life. She didn't want to worry her mum, though. Or her brother. And she knew they were worried.

Picking up a handful of sand, she let it spill idly through her fingers as she wondered what to do. Now the sun had gone down, it was growing colder. She felt the cold. Her thighs were already an unsexy shade of mottled blue. She should have thought to grab a sweater. She wished she hadn't come tonight. It was a bloody stupid idea. She wished she hadn't come to university at all and just got a job. Any job. It was her brother who'd persuaded her to apply. He'd said she was talented, unique. She was definitely the latter. She would never be one of the crowd. He'd told her she needed to have more faith in herself. Pippa had snapped at him, telling him it was easy for him to say. He took after their dad – in looks only, thank God. People were attracted to him. Girls swarmed around him like bees to honey, and blokes were best mates with him because he was the cool guy to be seen with. Actually, those weren't his only attributes. He cared about her. Tried to look out for her. For their mum too, getting a part-time job to help out financially, buying her flowers to cheer her up. Pippa didn't think there were many guys his age who would be that thoughtful. She wished she hadn't snapped at him.

Sighing, she pulled herself to her feet, the damp patch on

her backside reminding her of how pathetic she was. Picking up her bag, she began walking to try to keep warm. It was even colder on the wide expanse of the beach, a bitter wind blowing in from the sea, but she wasn't going back, not until the others were in their tents anyway and wouldn't notice her. She doubted she would be missed, other than to provide the entertainment. But then she'd probably provided enough already to keep them going all night. She would bet they were crying with laughter, especially that cow Emelia. What did Tom see in her, that's what Pippa didn't get – apart from the obvious attributes, of course, a perfectly honed and tanned body and huge breasts.

Aware of her own less abundant attributes, she wiped a hand under her nose and wrapped her arms around herself. Goosebumps popped out all over her body as icy sea spray spat spitefully at her, compounding her misery.

She'd walked a few yards, not sure where she was going, not much caring. Then stopped, sure she saw something moving. *Hell.* Were there foraging animals out here? It hadn't occurred to her there might be.

Panic blooming in her chest, she scoured the scrub and tall weeds at the edge of the beach, and her heart jolted as she saw a shadowy figure climbing down the rocks towards her.

NINE

BECKY

Now

I smile at Richie as he glances at me from where he's talking to Kelly. He smiles back and mouths, 'Two minutes,' and I remind myself how lucky I am to be with a man who's attentive and caring. I'm not sure how I would have survived without him in the dreadful days after we'd found Pippa. He'd been the glue that held me together. He'd held everyone together. It was as if he'd grown from an adolescent into a man that day, remaining calm and in control while everyone around him was in danger of falling apart. *We didn't lie to the police*, he'd reminded us. *We were vague about her movements, that's all. We were in shock, traumatised.* We'd been ashamed of our actions, the cruel way we'd treated Pippa, that was the unspoken truth. I certainly was, which is why I couldn't let it go. A combination of booze, weed, and my own morning sickness, which came on at all times, meant none of us were thinking clearly, but I do feel we need to own our actions. I always will.

Richie had stopped drinking so much after the beach party. I was grateful for that, that he was someone I could depend on, for the solidity between us, but I wish he would realise that we needed to talk about what happened, properly. No one had ever asked the question outright: Was it one of our group who'd been with Pippa that night? Once we got back to our tents, Richie had fallen fast asleep. As far as I knew, he hadn't gone out during the night. I was outside myself in search of the loo when I saw Tom standing staring at the sky. He'd been sucking on a roll-up, swigging back yet another beer. Swaying slightly, I noticed. What had he been doing out there? I've wondered over and over since. At the time, I'd thought that, like me, he couldn't sleep, but was it possible he'd been contemplating what he'd done? I was judging Tom based on his reputation, and I shouldn't be, but if only we could *all* just talk about it, then maybe I wouldn't be. What good would it do though? It couldn't undo anything. You can't take the stone back after it's thrown.

'I hope I'm not boring you?' Jack jars me back to the present.

'Sorry, what?' I shake myself.

'I asked if this was your first?' He nods towards my bump.

My breath catches as my mind shoots back to the baby I'd lost two short months after Pippa's death. I'm sure now that stress had played a part in why I had. She'd been so tiny, I could have held her in the palm of my hand, yet, to the eye, fully formed, ten tiny fingers and toes, a tiny button nose. We called her Angel, because that's what she looked like, a perfect, peaceful angel. I think of Richie, how I'd caught him quietly crying, his head bowed as he'd stood in front of the little second-hand cot we'd assembled in the bedroom of the flat we rented. We'd bought her clothes too, all pre-loved, babygros and bootees. It had broken our hearts to part with them. Richie's more. That's what had sealed my love for him. 'No,' I answer vaguely. 'It took us a while. How about you? Do you have a wife? Children?'

'I do, on both counts. Two children, a boy aged six, a girl coming up to eight, and a wife I love very much.'

'That's a lovely thing to say.' I look at him in surprise.

'Don't get me wrong, we have our ups and downs. It's not all plain sailing, juggling jobs and kids,' he sighs, 'but we make it work.'

I can tell by his fond smile that he's happily married. I can see why. Also why he's a counsellor. He has a way of making the conversation flow and he obviously relates to people. I'm about to ask him how Jodie came to be consulting him, when Emelia walks, or rather weaves, in our direction.

'Whoops,' she says, backstepping precariously as she passes us. 'Well, well, you really are a dark horse, aren't you, Becks?'

I feel my cheeks heat up as she looks insinuatingly between Jack and me. 'Now, *he...*' she leans forward, almost falling into Jack as she extends a finger and prods him in the shoulder, 'most definitely doesn't look boring. Ditch the accountant, I would.'

'Em.' I glance apologetically at Jack. I'm half on my feet, thinking I should help her, hold her up, attract Tom's attention, something, but Emelia stumbles onwards.

'Musht dash,' she says, slurring her words and waving a hand behind her. 'Have to see to my little darlings in the absence of a husband who gives a shit.'

Oh no. I squeeze my eyes closed. There's obviously trouble between them. I glance in the direction of the bar, to see Tom swilling back what appears to be a whisky, and my heart sinks. This is not my fault, I know it's not, but still I feel responsible.

'Excuse me.' Giving Jack another apologetic glance, I go after Emelia. I'm halfway across the floor when Richie catches up with me. 'She drove them here,' he says, worried, clearly.

My stomach lurches as I get the gist. She obviously has the car keys.

'I'll go after her.' Richie moves past me.

As he hurries towards the exit, I swallow back my racing heart. Why couldn't I have just kept my mouth shut? I should have spoken to Emelia alone, somewhere she had no access to alcohol. If anything happens to her, I will never forgive myself.

TEN

Seeing Jack on his phone when I go back to the table, I mouth, 'Sorry,' and point to the exit, indicating I'm leaving.

He nods, gives me a sympathetic smile, and goes back to his call.

I'm halfway to the door when I bump into Tom talking agitatedly into his phone. 'That was Richie. He's taking Emelia home,' he says, smiling tersely as he finishes the call. 'Good old Richie, hey? Always reliable. Always there in a crisis. I have a lot to live up to apparently.'

Shaking his head cynically, he strides off, and I feel my eyes filling up all over again. Wiping my cheeks, I head on out, only to realise that Richie has taken our car, meaning I have no way to get home. Sighing, I pull out my phone and call a taxi.

My mind on Emelia and how that exchange between Tom and me outside the loos had probably contributed to her drinking, it takes me a moment to realise it's Jack who's pulled up in front of me.

He winds his window down and leans across. 'Do you need a lift somewhere?' he asks.

'Thanks, but I'm fine,' I assure him. 'I've called a taxi. It shouldn't take too long to arrive.'

'You sure?' Jack frowns and checks his watch. 'It's coming up to rush hour.'

I waver. He's right, I realise. 'As long as it's not too far out of your way,' I say, deciding to accept his offer.

'I'll let you know when you tell me the address.' He smiles, amused. 'It's really not a problem. I don't have anywhere pressing to be and I'd rather know you got home safely.'

'Thank you.' I climb gratefully in. I'm dead on my feet, and worried sick about Emelia. I hope Richie gets her home safely.

'I hope you won't feel I'm speaking out of turn—' Jack glances hesitantly at me, once we're underway '—but I'm a bit concerned about how Emelia's husband spoke to you. Also, the way he looked at you. It's probably just me being overprotective, my wife accuses me of that a lot, but I'm not sure I'd trust him.'

That takes me aback. 'What do you mean, the way he looked at me?' I study him quizzically. Tom was annoyed – with Emelia for stalking off, I assumed. There was some bitterness in his tone, because, to be fair to him, Emelia had often compared him to Richie. She had at the New Year's do. *'Why can't you be there for me, like Richie is for Becky?'* she asked him after they'd had words about his arriving home late, meaning they'd arrived late at the party.

'Because I have to work,' Tom had answered moodily. *'It pays for the luxuries, Em, in case you didn't notice.'*

Emelia had turned to stalk off that time too. *'I'm talking about emotionally, Tom,'* she retorted tearfully over her shoulder. *'As you very well know.'*

Jack frowns pensively. 'I'm not sure. It might just be me slipping into counsellor mode, but it wasn't kindly. It could be because of the amount he's drunk, but I can't help thinking the man has issues.'

ELEVEN

'He works long hours. He gets tired and Em gets frustrated because he's never there,' I offer in Tom's defence. I know from experience that Tom does have issues, though. Issues I've never mentioned to Richie either, for Emelia's sake.

'Ah.' Jack nods. 'Drinking doesn't help, though, does it, when emotions are already fraught?'

'No.' I have to agree with that. It certainly hadn't on the night of the beach party. There'd been far too much alcohol flowing. I'd been the only one capable of coherent thinking. Yet I'd gone along with the others, agreeing that Pippa would be fine when she obviously wasn't. I will never forgive myself for that.

'I was probably too quick to judge,' Jack says. 'He was obviously upset about his wife going off. I don't think he should have been taking his frustration out on you, though.'

I ponder that. Tom was out of order. Richie would have pulled him up if he were there. Tom would have been annoyed about that too. 'Your protective gene kicking in?' I ask.

'It gets me into trouble.' Jack sighs. 'Apparently, I'm assuming women need rescuing when they actually don't. If I go into counsellor mode around Katie, I'm duly despatched to the dog house.'

I laugh, despite everything. 'And are you allowed back in?'

'Eventually. But only once I've seen the error of my ways. If you ever meet my wife, don't let on I slipped up whatever you do.'

I find myself laughing again, which is definitely therapeutic. 'I won't,' I promise.

'Good.' He smiles in my direction.

'I'm just glad Richie doesn't drink much and was able to go after Emelia.' A shudder runs through me as I think of what might have happened if Emelia had climbed behind the wheel. 'He gave up over-indulgence years ago at uni,' I add, 'thank goodness.'

'Student excess making him see the error of his ways?' Jack enquires.

I hesitate, an image of Richie dancing with Pippa flashing so vividly into my mind I feel myself reel inside. I can smell the sea air. Hear the music, 'Red Red Wine', and my stomach turns over. Before that night, I'd thought nothing could touch us. But it had. It would never leave us. 'Definitely.' I shake off a shudder. 'He gets labelled boring, probably because he's also an accountant, but I'd rather have him that way, especially now with a baby on the way.'

'Reliable.' Jack nods understandingly. 'And what about you? Do you work, or...?'

'I do, though I'll be on a sabbatical shortly, obviously. I'm a speech and language therapist.'

He looks impressed. 'And do you enjoy it?'

'I love it. It wasn't what I intended to do,' I go on, glad to steer the conversation away from Tom. 'I was toying with the idea becoming an art therapist and then my mum had a stroke. Her swallowing and speech functions were impaired.' I falter. I can never tell anyone everything. How awful things were, even before then. How badly my mother's mental health had deteriorated. Only Richie knows all of it. He's the one person I felt able to trust enough to tell. 'It got me thinking, wishing I could do something to help her, you know?'

He glances again at me. 'I'm sorry. That must have been difficult.'

'Thank you. It was,' I hurry on. 'By the time I'd completed my training, it was too late to help Mum, she died from a heart attack two years into my training, but I do get a lot of satisfaction from helping other people, especially children whose speech might be slow to develop because of physical or learning disabilities, sometimes both. It can be a challenge, but I suspect life is a lot more of a challenge for my patients.'

I stop, realising I'm doing all the talking. Jack has an uncanny knack at making me want to. I'm sure, if Jodie had managed to confide in him about the way she was feeling, that he would have been able to help her. Having lived with mental illness, been aware how moods can swing suddenly and sometimes catastrophically to extremes, I can only imagine her depression must have spiralled suddenly.

'I get that,' he says. 'I think it was losing my parents quite close to each other that pushed me towards counselling.'

'Oh no. I'm sorry, Jack. That must have been devastating for you.'

'It was a low period in my life,' he concedes after a moment. 'Mum had a rare brain tumour. It was hard watching her waste away and being able to do nothing. More so for my father. He was diagnosed with advanced liver cancer six months later. He couldn't cope with knowing what it would do to him, so he saved up his tablets and...' He trails off with a telling shrug.

'Oh, Jack.' I stare at him, shocked. 'I'm so sorry.'

'Me too.' He smiles sadly. 'I started making poor choices after that, drinking too much, which I guess is why I get so reactive when I see other people making the same mistake. I figured it was the best way to drown my sorrows. Needless to say, it wasn't. Finally, I realised I was in a downward spiral and took myself off to counselling. The rest, as they say, is history. I decided I wanted to try to help others overcome loss and bereavement and the resultant inevitable anxiety. I offer various types of therapy now. It's something people need, even though sometimes they don't realise they do, and I enjoy it, so I guess it all worked out in the end.'

'You're pretty amazing, do you know that?' I say, impressed. 'Turning things around like that, I mean.'

He smiles. 'I'll take the compliment,' he says. 'I think we have a lot in common. I get the impression you're a kind person, Rebecca Shaw,' he adds, surprising me.

I drop my gaze to my lap. I have no idea how to respond. He only sees the outside, the superficial me. He doesn't know the real me.

'I just wish I could help everyone who comes through my door,' he says reflectively.

I glance at him. His gaze is fixed forward. I gather he's thinking about Jodie and I feel for him.

'Is this it?' he asks, as my mind drifts back to Pippa, how I could have done more to help her, and wish dearly that I had.

'Sorry, miles away. Yes, this is it,' I confirm, realising we've reached my house. 'Number eight on the right.'

'Nice house,' he observes.

'We like it. It needed some work, but we're getting there slowly.' It actually needed a tremendous amount of work inside and we were stretching ourselves financially to do it. Richie and I had poured all of our savings into it, meaning our budget was tight, but we'd thought it was worth it. A semi-detached with large bay windows, coved ceilings and a feature fireplace in the lounge, it was full of character. Before we moved in, I pictured the whole painting walls and rollers thing, imagining christening every room. The less romantic reality was we'd been too exhausted to do anything but eat takeaway and fall into bed. We love it now that we're making it our own, though. Modest it might be, but we're thinking it will be our forever home.

'Nice location, too.' Jack glances around as he pulls up outside.

'I thought so.' One road back from the beach was close enough for me. We wanted to be within walking distance. Looking out over the sea, though, would have evoked too many memories. Not that I needed much to evoke them. 'Thanks for seeing me back here.' I smile and unfasten my seat belt.

'My pleasure,' he says. 'It's been nice talking to you.'

'Likewise.' I reach for my door.

'Becky,' he stops me, 'if you ever want to talk more – about Jodie or anything else, please feel free to call me.' He reaches in his top pocket for a business card and passes it to me. 'I'm told I'm a good listener.'

Smiling, I look down at the card and trail my thumb contemplatively over the embossed lettering on it. 'I will.' Looking back at him, I see the sincerity in his eyes and so wish I could talk to him. He's definitely easy to talk to, but I doubt he can help salve my conscience. There are no excuses for the awful thing we did to Pippa, making her feel so bad about herself, she'd fled and ended up dying such a lonely death. I don't think any amount of talking would make the guilt go away. I also doubt I could ever bring myself to admit to the worry that gnaws constantly away inside me: Who was it Pippa had been with that night?

TWELVE

I sense something's wrong the second I walk through the front door. The smell of perfume that lingers on the air, musky jasmine and vanilla, isn't mine. It's Emelia's. Her signature perfume. She'd been wearing it in abundance yesterday when she'd come over to discuss the joint wreath we decided to buy. I was out on an appointment. She and Richie had been in the kitchen when I'd arrived home. Emelia had grabbed her bag and hurried towards me as I'd gone through the door. 'Running late,' she'd said, looking flustered. 'I'm supposed to have collected Josh from a birthday party five minutes ago.'

'I thought she had a nanny,' I commented, going back to the kitchen after seeing her out and waving her off.

'She let her down, apparently,' Richie provided from where he was making coffee. 'Emelia dropped by on the way back from seeing a client to say she's paid for the flower arrangement.'

'Really?' I widened my eyes, more surprised by her rare display of actually caring than her generosity. With Tom's income, money was no object to Emelia, and she tended to spend it like it was going out of fashion.

'She thought Jodie deserved something tasteful.' Richie smiled over his shoulder.

'Conscience money,' I'd muttered, my mind going to Pippa, where it had been constantly since we'd learned of Jodie's death, the awful, lonely way she'd also died.

'Don't, Becks.' Richie sighed, clearly exasperated. 'Just leave it. Dredging up the past isn't going to help us deal with this, is it?'

I'd felt guilty, again. Told myself he was right. But he's not. If we don't talk about it now, when will we ever? Burying it, as we've tried to, isn't going to make it go away.

Seeing no sign of Richie now, I drop my bag on the hall table and head towards the lounge. Then stop, frozen in confusion as I hear him, his voice panicky, 'Em, come on, pack it in. Becky could walk in at any minute.'

'Then we'd better be quick,' Emelia drunkenly purring, her voice full of implicit meaning.

What the *hell*? Shock giving way to incandescent fury, I launch myself at the partially open lounge door, crashing it so hard against the adjoining wall, my *friend* and my husband shoot apart as if they've been electrocuted.

Richie appears too stunned to speak, his face blanching as I stare at him in astounded disbelief. But then he recovers himself. 'Jesus, Becks,' he emits a nervous laugh, 'you almost gave me a heart attack.'

'Only almost?' I growl, dragging a derisory gaze over him. 'Pity.'

'Becks...' He takes a step towards me.

I step away, my gaze swivelling to Emelia, who has the actual temerity to be standing in *my* lounge fastening the buttons on her fucking blouse! 'Get out!' I seethe, hot tears of hurt and humiliation rising so fast I can't stop them.

'Bloody hell. Becky?' Richie moves fast, catching hold of my forearms as some primal thing inside me propels me towards her. I want to rip her perfectly balayaged blonde hair out by its roots, scratch her big blue eyes out. How *dare* she?

Richie wraps his arms tightly around me as I struggle to be free of him. 'Becky, just stop!' he begs, his voice thick with shock. 'This is *not* what it looks like.'

I emit a short, hysterical laugh. 'She has her tits out!'

'She was upset,' he babbles, tangible fear now in his voice. 'She's had too much to drink. She—'

'*Upset?*' Now I'm utterly staggered. 'What the *hell* is she *doing* here?'

'She felt sick.' Richie scrambles for an explanation, looking pretty sick himself.

Contempt spiralling inside me, I say nothing.

'Our house was closest to get to,' he adds less stridently. 'I could hardly throw her out to be sick in the gutter.'

For a second I waver, but I flatly refuse to discuss this with *her* looking on, having no doubt achieved what she wanted to. 'Get her out of here.' I look her over in disgust and then away.

'She's drunk, Becks.' Richie glances at her and then imploringly back to me.

That only fans the rage burning inside me. 'Oh, right, yes. That explains it then, *obviously*.' I spit the words out. 'It explains every despicable thing she's done, doesn't it? What she did to Pippa, it explains *that*.'

Richie pales further if that were possible. 'That's not fair, Becky,' he says tightly, as if I should be considering her feelings. *Unbelievable.*

'Not *fair?*' I almost implode. 'Get her *out* of here! *Now!*' Yanking myself away from him, I spin around and stride out. I can't bear to look at her, standing there, her expression bewildered, tears plopping down her face. Did she cry for Pippa after her initial hysteria? *No.* Did she shed anything but crocodile tears for Jodie? No, she did *not*. But now she cries, huge, fat tears of self-pity. The woman's pathetic.

THIRTEEN

Why had my instinct been to fly at her and not him? I wonder as, unable to be anywhere near them, I retreat to the bedroom. He's as guilty as she is. How could *he*, right here in the house that was supposed to be our forever home? How could he do that to me? To us? My hands go protectively to my tummy, where my tiny baby's limbs flail energetically, as if he senses my distress. *It's okay, sweet pea. I will never let anything hurt you. Not ever.* The tears come, hot tears spilling down my face as I sit on the bed where, after years of trying, we'd finally made our precious baby together. Where we'd lain together, limbs entwined, holding each other through the good and the bad times like we would never let go. It meant nothing, did it? To Richie, our marriage, our baby, meant nothing. I didn't think I could bear it. *Why, Richie?*

I choke back a ragged sob and go to the window as a car horn beeps outside. Seeing Richie helping her down the path to the waiting taxi, her reeling into him as he does, I'm consumed with such sudden visceral hatred, it shocks me. Can he not see what she's doing? That, drunk or not, she *knows* what she's doing? She's using him, trying to play him off against Tom as if we were all still back at university. What is *wrong* with her? Insecure she may be, but in what world does she consider that justifies doing this to me?

Hearing him on the stairs minutes later, I wipe quickly at my cheeks and turn from the window. I have to force myself to look at him as he appears in the doorway.

'It wasn't how it looked, Becky,' he says, his tone wary. 'Tom was being a dick. She drank too much. You know she did.' He looks at me appealingly. 'She was upset, and...'

I say nothing as he trails off, folding my arms across my chest and waiting to hear the lies he will spin me instead. Tom and Emelia have problems, obviously. And, I've no doubt that Emelia was upset, as evidenced by her swigging back the wine. Distraught, however, wasn't how she'd sounded just now. And would Richie really have responded so lamely to her stripping off in front of him, telling her to *pack it in* because I might walk in. Wouldn't he have been shocked? Furious?

'He cheats on her. You know that, right?' he goes on, as if that's any kind of excuse.

I look him over scornfully. 'So she thought she would make him jealous by cheating on him? With you? Or were you just trying to help her with her self-esteem issues?'

'Okay.' Richie sighs. 'It doesn't suit you, Becky, but I get why you would be so scathing. Would you please just calm down and listen to me, though?'

I narrow my eyes. Does he realise how dangerously he's stoking the fire?

'I am *not* cheating on you,' he insists. 'Christ, Becky, I would never do that.'

I take a second. 'You had your arm around her,' I point out, *calmly.*

'I was comforting her,' he says, as if it was inconceivable he would be doing anything else.

'Ah, right.' I nod. 'By stroking her breasts.'

'Oh for fu...' Richie bangs the heel of his hand against his forehead. 'I was trying to do her bloody buttons back up. I was trying to stop her.'

'What? Making a fool of herself?' I suggest, my tone caustic, however much it *doesn't suit* me. 'Because naturally *good old Richie* would turn her down, wouldn't he?'

'Yes!' He glares at me. 'Okay, I give up.' He throws his hands up in despair. 'This is obviously a complete waste of time. I can't talk to you when you're like this.'

'Like what?' I stare after him in disbelief as he turns away.

Richie stops. 'Over emotional.'

'Over emotional?' I laugh, flabbergasted.

Richie draws in a tight breath. 'Yes, over emotional,' he repeats, clearly trying to turn this into something I'm supposed to have done. 'You get like this. You have a sudden attack of the guilts and there's just no talking to you.'

I almost choke. 'Right, and you have nothing to feel guilty about, do you, Richie? You're as pure as the driven snow, aren't you? Never put a foot wrong in your life.'

Richie's shoulders stiffen. He doesn't answer for a second. Then, 'You know something,' he says, his voice tight as he turns slowly back, 'I reckon you want me to have been cheating.'

'What?' I baulk, now truly astonished.

'Fine. Think what you like. Ask yourself one question, though, Becky.' He tips his head to one side, eyeing me questioningly. 'Could you blame me?'

That hits me like a body blow.

'You're obviously miserable, aren't you?' he goes on, bitter accusation in his tone. 'With me, with our life together, constantly banging on about the past, determined to drag everyone into your misery with you instead of appreciating what we have, here, together.'

I gasp out an incredulous breath. 'Are you saying I make

you miserable?' I search his face, willing him to say no, to *not* be doing this.

'Frankly, yes,' he says crushingly. 'We can't all live our lives consumed with guilt, Becky. You might want to, imagining you're paying some bloody penance, but I *don't*.'

Staring after him as he walks through the bedroom door, I listen to the broken remnants of my marriage crash to the floor around me. Up until then, I might have been persuaded to believe him. If he admitted there was an affair, I might even have been able to forgive him, but not now. Because it strikes me painfully, it doesn't appear that he wants me to.

FOURTEEN

Numb inside, I stay where I am. Then, fury and hurt kicking ferociously in, I race along the landing after him. He's at the front door, car keys in his hand. 'Don't you *dare.*' I warn him. 'Don't you dare twist this around and then walk out. If you do, I swear I'll change the locks.'

Richie hesitates and I start angrily down the stairs, then stop suddenly, my heart almost stopping with me as I stumble.

'What the?' He spins around as a yelp of fear escapes me. Panic crossing his face, he bounds upwards as I clutch the handrail. 'Are you all right?'

'As if you care,' I retort childishly. I feel like a child, so badly in need of someone to comfort me and tell me everything is going to be all right. But it's *not.* Everything went wrong the night of the beach party and things will never be right because what we did was wrong. What I did was *wrong.* I need to talk about it, but every time I bring it up, Richie shuts me down. Would I believe what he had to say if we did talk, though? I realise I wouldn't. And that terrifies me.

'Of course I bloody well care.' Richie blows out a frustrated sigh. 'Look,' he wipes a hand over his face, shaken, clearly, 'just let me help you down. I'll make us some tea and—'

'That will fix everything, won't it?' Fighting back my tears, I push on past him. 'Why don't we invite Emelia while we're at it? We could have a nice cosy threesome.' My tone *is* scathing. And it's *not* me, but what am I supposed to be exactly? Apologetic? I won't be that.

'This is pointless,' Richie mutters, as I carry on to the kitchen.

'My thoughts entirely,' I throw back.

He emits another heavy sigh. 'Makes you wonder why we kept trying for a baby, doesn't it?'

My heart jarring, I turn warily to face him as he follows me. 'What's that supposed to mean?'

Richie shrugs disconsolately. 'I thought it would make you happy, but you're not happy, are you? Not really. You don't think you deserve to have good things happen. That we do.'

'That's ridiculous.' My chest fills up. 'This is turning into a character assassination of me, and it's absolute rubbish.' Swallowing hard, I whirl around and stride to the sink.

'Are you sure about that?' he asks.

'Why are you doing this, Richie?' My hand trembling, I fill a glass with water. I can't drink it. 'Why do you want to hurt me so much?'

'I don't want to *hurt* you.' His voice is filled with exasperation. 'I just want you to have a life. For *us* to have a life.'

I glance at the ceiling, blink hard. 'It appears to me you want to have a life without me.'

'That's not true,' Richie answers tiredly. 'Becky, will you *please* just forget all this crap about Emelia and me and listen?'

'*Forget?*' I crash the glass down and turn to face him. 'You mean pretend it didn't happen? Just like I've tried to pretend all these years that Pippa didn't happen?'

'For pity's *sake*.' Richie's voice rises. 'Will you just forget about Pippa for one bloody minute and *listen* to me. I do *not* want a life without you. I want a life *with* you.' He glares at me. 'The you I used to know.'

Who is he? Because this person is most certainly not the man I used to know. 'Which means what?' I ask, my breath stalled in my chest.

Richie kneads his forehead. 'You used to be fun,' he says tiredly. 'Carefree. Now, you're... Well, let's face it, Becks, you're becoming neurotic.'

I stare at him, astounded.

'Always going on about being cursed by what happened years ago. Can't you see it's self-fulfilling prophecy? We're not bloody well being punished or haunted by Pippa's *ghost*. You need to let it *go*.' He echoes Emelia, and I feel what's left of my heart crack. They've clearly been talking about me. After sex? I wonder, an image of them lying together crashing excruciatingly into my mind.

'We *deserve* to be haunted,' I argue, my anger rising. 'We were responsible for what happened to Pippa that night. *All* of us. *I* was, but at least I have the balls to own it, Richard.'

'That's crap, Becky,' he snaps. 'Bordering on paranoia.'

'Really?' I eye him coldly. 'Well, for your information, *Dr* Shaw, Jodie felt exactly the same way. She took her own life because *she* couldn't live with it. Meanwhile, you and Emelia, who's never given a damn about anyone but herself, are happily shagging behind my back, behind Tom's back, as if you haven't got a care in the world.'

'I am *not* having an affair with Emelia!' he yells. 'And since when did you give a damn about Tom, hey? You want to know something, Becky?'

'More home truths? I'd be ecstatic.'

'One of the reasons Emelia was upset?' Richie's face is tight, rigid with anger. 'Because you going on and on about that night reminded her that Tom had been missing after Pippa took off.

She thought he'd gone to the toilet. Apparently, he was gone ages. When she looked for him, she said she saw you creeping back to our tent.'

'What?' I shake my head, trying to keep up. 'I wasn't creeping anywhere. I'd been to see if I could see any sign of Pippa and then I went to the loo. I saw Tom on the way back. He...'

'Were you with him, Becky?' He eyeballs me furiously. 'Is that what this obsessive guilt is all about? Why you're so down on Emelia?'

I feel as if he's just slapped me. 'Why are you doing this?' My tears explode with a mixture of hurt, confusion and anger. 'Have sex with Emelia, if that's what you want. Do what you like, but don't do this.'

'For the last time, I am *not* having sex with Emelia,' he shouts. 'I feel sorry for her, but I don't bloody well *fancy* her. I never have. For your information, since we're back there – not that we're ever *not* back there, I liked Pippa. Your grief wasn't exclusive, you know, Becky. Nor is your guilt. We all feel it. *I* do. It doesn't mean we have to live the rest of our lives in fucking purgatory.'

He'd liked her. My mind flies back to the conversation after Pippa had gone off, Tom's immature taunts aimed at Richie. Richie's uncharacteristic response. He'd been furious then. Defensive. Not like Richie. Different.

FIFTEEN

BECKY

Then

'We should go and look for her.' I glance towards where Richie's sitting glugging on a beer. 'It's getting dark. I'm worried about her.'

Richie glances towards me, one eye closed. 'I suppose.' He sighs and takes another swig from his beer, then gets to his feet. He's had a lot to drink, I realise as he sways a little, but we have to try and find her. We can't just leave her out there. I look around for Jodie, but I guess she and Zoe have gone to their tent. They were both pretty wasted.

'I wouldn't worry too much about it,' Tom says, lighting up yet another spliff. 'She'll turn up. She's probably gone off sulking somewhere, as you girls do.' Inhaling sharply, he drops to his haunches and blows smoke high into the sky.

I stare at him, incredulous. For a moment there, I thought he was having a decent human emotion. I'm on the verge of saying something when Richie catches my arm. Shaking his head, he gives me a look and I get it. Starting in on Tom isn't going to help anything.

'I'll go grab my trainers,' Richie says, giving Tom a despairing glance as he walks past him.

Tom's oblivious, I notice, unsurprisingly. I look from him towards Emelia, who emerges from their tent looking bored as she glances at her fingernails and then idly around. 'She's not back then?' she observes.

'We're just going out to look for her,' I say, thinking she might offer to come with us.

Instead, Emelia rolls her eyes and sighs. 'I bet she's doing it deliberately to attract attention,' she imparts and proceeds to pick at her nail polish.

'Em?' I stare at her in astonishment.

Emelia shrugs, marginally contrite. 'Well, you have to admit, she is a bit weird,' she mutters – and I'm really struggling now not to lose it.

'She's definitely that.' Tom lies back, propping his head up with his arm. 'Pity.' He takes another tout on his spliff. 'She's actually not bad looking, if only she'd loosen up and stop taking things so seriously.'

Emelia shoots him a surprised glance. 'Don't tell me you fancy her?' She laughs in disbelief. I note the flicker of nervousness in her eyes though and I wonder if she's aware that Tom might not be quite so invested in their relationship as she is.

'Nah.' Tom screws up his face. 'Not my type. A bit too bookish. I reckon Richie fancies her, though, don't you, Richie boy?' Amusement dancing in his eyes, he swings his gaze in Richie's direction as he returns from our tent.

'Don't I what?' Richie eyes him warily.

'Pippa,' Tom exhales with a smirk. 'I was saying how you fancy showing her what she's missing.'

'Piss off, dickhead,' Richie growls.

'Temper, temper.' Tom tsks. 'Seems like I might have rattled your cage, mate.'

'It might have escaped your notice, *mate*, but some of us can control our sexual urges,' Richie retorts, looking him over contemptuously.

'Sure about that, Richie boy?' Taking another draw on his rollie, Tom looks him over languidly. 'I mean she fancies you, doesn't she? You can see it a mile off. And you can't deny you were giving her the eye while you were *slow* dancing.'

Making inverted comma signs with his fingers around the words slow dancing, he gives Richie a wink, and Richie's look is thunderous. 'You're a prat, do you know that?' He drags his disdainful gaze away.

There's something in his eyes as his gaze flicks to mine, though. Embarrassment? Guilt? No, surely not. Richie doesn't fancy Pippa. He's angry, that's all, as he should be with Tom who is a prat, if only Emelia could see it. Richie's just not the kind to mess around. My hand strays to my tummy.

SIXTEEN

Then

'Rich?' I whisper, after staring at the roof of the tent for what seems like hours. Realising he's still fast asleep, I ease away from him and find the zip on the sleeping bag we're both squeezed into. After fiddling with it and finally unzipping it, I wriggle out. It's early, barely past sunrise and freezing cold, but much as I would like to stay snuggled up with him, I can't. I've had about an hour's sleep. I'm worried to death about Pippa. Emelia and Tom had joined us searching for her in the end, albeit begrudgingly, Emelia mumbling something about it being pointless and that she'd probably walked up to the coastal road, called a taxi and gone home. With nausea churning my stomach, and feeling grindingly tired, I'd left them to it after a while. Now, though, the enormity of the situation is hitting me. I can't just lie here.

Quickly tugging on my jeans and fleece, I hurry to Pippa's small tent, shivering as I go. 'Pippa?' I call, aware I'm probably waking the others, but my now overwhelming sense of dread won't let me leave it. There's no answer, and I reach for the Velcro strip on the bottom of her door flap and pull it up. The first thing I see once I crawl inside is her purse lying on her sleeping bag and my stomach turns over. Finding her key inside it and her dead phone a second later, panic blooms inside me.

'Richie!' I'm yelling almost before I've crawled out again. 'Tom! Em!'

Richie appears in seconds, bleary-eyed but clearly concerned. 'What's up?' he asks, glancing warily past me to Pippa's tent.

'She didn't call a taxi. She hadn't got her purse or her phone.'

'Christ.' Richie looks down at the items I have in my hand then worriedly back to me.

Tom joins us a minute later, still looking half-wasted. 'What's happening?' he asks, squinting and holding a hand up to block out the first blinding rays of the sun.

'Pippa went off without her purse and phone.' I glance from him to Jodie, who emerges from her tent, half-hopping as she tugs a plimsoll on. 'Her front door key is inside it.'

'So she couldn't have called a taxi,' Jodie murmurs, looking as shocked as I feel.

'She could be anywhere,' I murmur, an image flashing through my mind of her lying out there on the cold beach, her badly bleached hair splayed about her face, her eyes frantic. The same image that had floated into my dreams when I had managed some sleep. 'It would have been pitch black on the cliff edge in the dead of night. She was only wearing her shorts and bikini top,' I remind them, now feeling sick to my soul. 'She might have frozen to death out there. Anything could have happened.'

Richie locks eyes with mine for a second and then nods decisively. 'We need to split up and go back out and look for her,' he says. 'Jodie, can you and Zoe check the coastal path?'

Jodie's face is as pale as alabaster, but she clearly gets the urgency. 'On it.' She nods and goes to grab Zoe.

Richie turns to Tom. 'Tom, do you want to come with Becky and me and search the beach?'

Tom frowns. His complexion is ashen, I notice. Clearly he's thinking something must have happened to her too. 'Right. Yeah, no problem. Give me a sec. I need to throw some clothes on and grab my boots.'

'Is Emelia okay?' I ask, as he turns back to his tent.

'Out for the count. Crashed out as soon as she hit the sack. She was well stoned,' Tom answers with a despairing shake of his head.

I catch Richie's eye and I can see he's thinking what I am, that she probably wouldn't stir herself anyway.

'Keep your phones on,' Richie calls as he hurries to get dressed. 'I don't think there's much of a signal so we'll meet back here in an hour.'

'Got it,' Jodie calls back as she and her girlfriend hurry towards the coastal path.

An hour later, Richie and I head back to camp. Hoping for a miracle, I check Pippa's tent again. She's not there. Fear slices through me like an icicle and out of nowhere a more blinding image assaults me: Pippa lying still and cold. So lonely. 'She's dead, isn't she?' I murmur. Richie doesn't answer, but I feel his tension as he threads an arm around me.

Emelia's still in her tent, I realise. 'She has her fucking *radio* on.' I look at Richie in complete disbelief. 'What the *hell* is wrong with her?'

'She probably doesn't realise what's happening.' Richie squeezes my shoulders, stilling me as an urge to smash the radio almost overwhelms me.

At last Jodie and Zoe appear, approaching from the foot of the coastal path. 'Anything?' Richie shouts across to them.

'Nothing,' Jodie calls back, her face grim. 'We searched the cliff edge and followed the path as far as the road. There's no sign of her.'

I look across to Tom, who's on his way back after searching the left of the beach while Richie and I took the right. 'Tom?'

'Nope, nothing.' Tom sighs, pulling a rollie from his top pocket and lighting up.

I glance at Richie, petrified. 'We need to call the police.'

He takes a sharp breath. Nods. We need to get our stories straight first.

SEVENTEEN

BECKY

Now

Had Richie been *eyeing Pippa up?* His denials had been swift and vehement. Alarm bells scream loud in my head as I note the thunderous look on his face is exactly the same as it was then. He'd denied ever speaking to Pippa, yet he had. He'd been the one who'd urged us to make sure we could all account for our movements before reporting what we'd found. He'd changed after than night. Stopped drinking, apart from the odd social drink. He'd never been overly emotional but since then he'd kept his emotions carefully in check. It was almost as if he was afraid of losing control. But he *is* losing control. He's palpably furious, vigorously denying everything now, just as he had then. What's his anger really about?

Cold trepidation chills me to the bone as I look him over and realise I don't recognise him. 'Was it you who had sex with Pippa?' I ask him outright, my heart thudding. 'Were you there on the beach with her?'

'Oh for crying out *loud.*' Richie eyes the ceiling. 'Were you?' He snaps his gaze back at me, his eyes blazing. 'Is that why you're so racked with guilt, Becky? Were you jealous? Did you bloody well follow her out there and *kill* her?'

'Get out!' I scream. 'Just *go*.'

Richie draws in a deep breath. 'I have nowhere to go,' he says eventually. 'Look, I'm sorry.' He closes his eyes, some of his anger seeming to dissipate, then walks towards me. 'I said some things I shouldn't have. We both have. Can we not just rewind this and—'

'You can't take it *back*. You can't *unsay* things. *Or* undo them.' I look him over in disbelief. I don't know him, do I? Fear settles icily in the pit of my belly. I thought I did, but I don't. His cool, calm exterior, his caring nature, it was all an act to hide who he really is. 'You're as heartless as Emelia,' I whisper. 'You need to go.'

Richie stares hard at me for a long, blood-freezing moment, and then turns around and heads for the stairs.

I hear him in the bedroom above opening cupboards and drawers. Minutes later, he comes back down with an overnight bag. 'I'll be in the office,' he mutters, yanking the front door open.

Still reeling with shock, I stay where I am as he slams the door shut behind him. I tell myself I don't care where he goes. But I do. What happened? One minute we were looking forward to the birth of our baby, our future together as parents, the next we were mourning the death of our friend, and now our marriage is disintegrating. I feel as if I'm on a rollercoaster, my life turned violently upside down.

Had I overreacted? He'd been adamant he and Emelia weren't involved. But I know what I saw. *And* what I heard. My stomach churns as Emelia's sultry, slurred suggestion plays through my mind: *Then we'd better be quick*. If they haven't been having an affair, they'd been on the brink of it, I was sure. And if he had cheated on me with her, who else might he have cheated on me with?

Am I paranoid? I don't believe I am, but Richie certainly wants me to think so, twisting things around the way he had, blaming me, insisting I'm obsessed with the past. Has his life with me really been so miserable?

With my heart like a stone in my chest, I go upstairs, change quickly into my pjs and crawl into bed, curling up under the duvet where I want to stay until the pain goes away. I don't think I can do this without him. I don't want to. My hand strays to the empty space where my husband should be, where only last night he'd held me, reassuring me he would always be there for me, the dependable person I thought I knew, right up until he turned into someone I didn't.

I can smell him, the reassuring scent of his aftershave, citrusy and spicy, mingled with essence of man, my man. My throat closes, tears sliding silently over the bridge of my nose as I reach for his pillow and clutch it to my midriff. Is he where he says he was going? I picture him there in the office he'd bought as an investment when he'd expanded his accountancy practice, finally finding himself in a position to be able to take on an assistant. It was important to have a presence, he'd said, much of his commercial business coming from local referrals, but the location, in a tiny side street close to the town centre, had taken priority over comfort. The old Edwardian building is badly insulated and still has single-glazed windows. Even in milder weather it's cold and drafty.

My mind drifts again to Pippa, how cold she must have been in her last hours on that beach. I can almost hear the wind gusting, the sea lapping hungrily at the shore, creeping closer to her prone body. How long had she lain there before the sea reached her?

Shivering, I double the duvet over myself and burrow down deeper. Hours tick by, and no matter how hard I try to push thoughts of Pippa away, she's still with me. As my mind drifts, I swear I can hear her, *Becky, please help me*. But I don't help her.

Instead I stand by, watching her chest rising and falling as she gasps for life-giving breath, and suddenly it's me who's struggling to breathe, the damp night air seeming to clog my throat, pushing down on me like a cloying grey blanket. Panic spiralling inside me, I blink against the suffocating dark, heavy and oppressive all around me.

Becky! she calls again. Frantic. I see her, her hand outstretched on the beach, her chest rattling as she draws her last breaths. *Becky!*

'Pippa!' I cry out as a bang, loud against the silence, jerks me upright. Disorientated, sweat wetting my body, I blink hard. Realising I'm in my bed, not out there in the unfriendly dark of the night, that the weight I'm wrestling with is just the bunched up duvet, relief crashes through me. I'm about to climb out of bed and go to the bathroom, when I hear the distinct sound of wood creaking. I freeze. There's someone here, climbing the stairs. 'Richie?'

There's no answer, nothing but the frenetic thud of my heart. Then comes another sound, one I can't place at first. When I do, fear rips through me. With the cobwebs of my dream still clinging to my mind, I tell myself I'm mistaken. Being paranoid. Praying I am, despite my fervent conviction I'm nothing of the sort, I swing my legs out of bed, and freeze as it comes again, a rasping, rattling wheeze.

Stilling my own breaths, I strain to listen. There's nothing now but silence. As I press my feet to the floor and pull myself unsteadily to standing, it comes again, a high-pitched wheeze. Laboured breathing. Unmistakable. 'Who's there?' I murmur.

It's not real. I'm still dreaming. I have to be. *Please let me be.* My hand trembling, I reach for the bedside lamp and snap it on, blink rapidly as the light temporarily blinds me. Goosebumps rise over my skin as I try to think what to do. My instinct is to run and hide, curl up in some dark corner until the nightmare is over. But there is nowhere to run. Nowhere to hide. Whoever is out there, *whatever* is out there, knows I'm here.

Even as I tell myself that Richie was right, that I am neurotic, obsessed by the thing that haunts me, I know I'm not. Jodie had said *she* was being haunted. This isn't neurosis. This is real. But it's not a ghost. It's *not*.

Apprehension crawling over me, I search for my phone, then squeeze my eyes closed, cursing silently as I realise it's still in my handbag downstairs. Indecisive, I hesitate, and then make my decision. Hesitantly, I venture forward. 'I've called the police,' I shout. 'Whoever you are, you need to leave. *Now*.'

I wait, nausea swirling inside me. There's no answer. '*Please*,' I murmur, pressing my forehead against the door. 'I'm pregnant.'

Why did I say that? I know if something terrible happens to me, they won't be able to save my baby, and now I feel as if I've put him in danger. I feel as if I'm going out of my mind. Or else being driven out of it. 'What do you *want*?' I scream.

My whole body trembling, I stay where I am. Still I hear nothing. Praying hard, reasoning that if they'd wanted to come in, they would have easily by now, I press the door handle down and inch the door open. Finding no one on the landing, I venture further out. Then fly to the top of the stairs as I hear another bang. A door slamming? *Richie*. It has to be.

Gripping the stair rail tightly, I tread carefully down, scanning the hall as I go. My heart thrumming a rat-tat-tat in my chest, I reach for the front door latch, then stop, whirling around as there's a crash from the lounge.

'Who's there?' I grab up the porcelain statue we keep on the hall table. Torn between going forward or fleeing through the front door, I hear it again. Not a crash, more a thwack. As I creep forward, a cool, salty breeze brushes my cheek, and I take another tentative step. Relief floods every cell in my body as I glimpse around the lounge doorway to find one of the side windows open and flapping in the wind.

I'm dashing to secure it, trying to convince myself that that would explain everything, the wood creaking, the wheezing and rattling – it was the wind blowing, the old house settling – when I stub my toe painfully on something. As I glance down my reassurances to myself evaporate. Bending to pick it up, I recognise the faces looking back at me through the splintered glass in the photo frame that doesn't belong to me: Tom and Emelia, Richie and me, sitting cross-legged on the beach. Behind us, Jodie and her then girlfriend, Zoe, along with Sophie and Dylan. On the periphery of our circle, her knees drawn to her chest, sits a sad, solitary figure: Pippa.

It had been taken by a passer-by earlier in the day using the camera Pippa had brought with her. We'd wanted a group photograph. What struck me as odd about it, apart from Pippa sitting in lonely isolation, is that Richie isn't looking at the camera. He has his arm around me, but he isn't looking at me. He's gazing at Pippa. Tom's taunts spring back to mind, '*I mean she fancies you, doesn't she? You can see it a mile off. And you can't deny you were giving her the eye while you were slow dancing.*' Richie's aggressive, defensive reaction. His mood had changed as if a switch had been flipped, just as it had tonight.

Studying the photograph more closely, I swallow back a sour taste in my throat. Pippa's gaze isn't on the camera either. She's looking at Richie.

EIGHTEEN

PIPPA

Then

Pippa squinted up at the rocks. Still she couldn't make out who was there, nothing but a tall, dark silhouette climbing slowly down. It was definitely a man. Her heart jumped as he reached the far side of the beach and started walking towards her, and then clunked unsteadily back into its mooring as he got closer. 'I'm glad it's you,' she said, relief sweeping through her. 'I couldn't make out who you were up there.'

'Sorry.' He smiled. 'I didn't mean to scare you.'

'You didn't,' she assured him, her cheeks heating up as he ran his eyes over her.

'Are you okay?' he asked, his forehead creased in concern. 'I was worried about you out here all on your own.'

Pippa felt a thousand butterflies take off in her tummy. She couldn't quite believe he cared enough to come out and search for her. She'd been a little frightened of him at first. He'd smiled in her direction a couple of times but she'd never spoken to him until he stopped her that time as she came out of the lift at uni. He'd placed his hand on the wall to the side of her, between her and the door exiting the lift area. She could hardly duck under his arm, but she couldn't help but be a bit wary about why he would want to talk to her. No one ever stopped to talk to her on their own, particularly the guys, who would probably be worried they would be taunted by their immature mates for fraternising with the clumsy university pariah. He didn't appear to be bothered, though. The truth was, she was probably more nervous about tripping over her tongue than she was of him, but still he was going out with one of the prettiest girls in their year, and she couldn't help but wonder why he would waste his time talking to her. He'd asked her how she was then too. Suggested she should come to the pub just off the campus and get to know a few people. It had hardly been an invitation to join him personally but she couldn't help but be quietly thrilled that he'd noticed her. No one normally did. She might as well be invisible sometimes. She obviously wasn't to him.

'I'm okay, you know?' She shrugged now, as if she didn't feel totally humiliated, not least by her own childish reaction, running off and no one appearing to care that she'd gone. He cared, though. Clearly. She felt her spirits lift a little.

'That was a shitty thing Emelia did back there. She can be a real cow sometimes.' He sighed, his eyes twinkling in the moonlight as they softly caressed hers. 'Sure you're okay?'

'Sure.' She nodded and gave him a small smile.

'Good.' Cupping a hand to her face, he smiled warmly back.

He studied her intently, grazed a thumb over her mouth, and Pippa's pulse rate picked up. She could feel the burn of his eyes, his breath, hot on her cheek. And suddenly his lips were on hers, moist and warm against hers, his tongue gently parting her lips, and it felt nice. Right.

Ignoring the niggle of guilt gnawing away at her, she reciprocated as his tongue found hers, softly exploring her mouth. A jolt of electricity shot through her as he eased away to kiss his way hungrily down her neck.

'I want you,' he murmured, his voice husky, his mouth finding her breasts. His hands suddenly all over her, he made short work of her strapless bikini top, shoving it down.

More exposed than she'd ever been in front of a man, Pippa was beginning to feel uncomfortable. Her stomach turned over as he found the buttons on her shorts, popping it and sliding the zip. She squirmed as he hooked his thumbs over the waistband, pressed her hands to his torso. It was too much. Too quick. It didn't feel right any more.

Panic blooming inside her, she tried to pull away, but now his mouth was hard against hers, his tongue forcing its way into her mouth. The word 'no' was stuck in her throat, and she tried harder to get away, but he was holding her tight, one arm forcing the breath from her body, his free hand fumbling inside her shorts.

Stop. Her panic spiralling, she bit down hard. He yelped, recoiling away from her, and Pippa took her chance. With her heart booming and the salty taste of his blood on her lips, she whirled around and ran.

She gone barely two yards before she was face down, winded, gritty sand in her mouth, in her nostrils. A heavy weight bearing down on her, she couldn't move, couldn't breathe past the debilitating wheeze constricting her chest.

NINETEEN

BECKY

Now

Sleep deprived and tearful, unable to believe I'd spent a hellish night on my own in what was supposed to be our forever home, I wander listlessly down to the kitchen to make tea – and stop dead. This time there's no mistaking it. I'd checked every door and window in the house before I'd gone back upstairs so I know that, despite the howling wind outside, it couldn't have blown in. It hadn't been walked in. The seaweed, thick, slimy green algae, has been placed here deliberately, all over the kitchen floor. How?

Fear prickling icily over my skin, I spin around to go back upstairs for my phone which I'd made sure to take up with me, then curse as I step on something. Frowning, I crouch to pick it up. It's a broken shell. There are more, pieces every-where, scattered all over the hall floor, the intention clearly to cause injury. But *why* would Richie do this? It has to be him, given no one had broken in. Is he trying to convince me I *am* neurotic, paranoid, all of the things he said I was. Is it some terrifying attempt to shut me up, because he's scared I might

try to talk to the police about what I'm growing sure
happened that night on the beach? Is he trying to get *me* to
take my life, just as poor Jodie had, which would certainly
make sure I stayed quiet? Even as I think it, I know it's
preposterous. Richie might have acted out of character, but he
would *never* do this. It was more than him simply acting out
of character, though, wasn't it? He said I was miserable. That
I made him miserable. He probably does want me out of his
life. Perhaps he wants to make a new life with Emelia? One
with no financial commitments and money in the bank from
the sale of the house? Emelia is used to a luxurious lifestyle.
She won't have that without Tom's substantial income to
fund it.

My mind shoots feverishly back to the photograph, the way
Richie had been looking directly at Pippa. *Giving her the eye.*
That photograph had been left to draw attention to that fact.
The thought hits me like a thunderclap. It was Tom who'd left
it. It has to be. Emelia had told Richie he'd been gone ages after
Pippa had fled. I saw him coming back along the beach towards
our camp. Like Emelia, I assumed he'd been looking for the loo.
I'd seen him later, staring at the stars as if deep in contempla-
tion. About what he'd done? Why would he have left the photo,
though? To deflect blame from himself? Point the finger at
Richie, presumably hoping to shut me up in the process?

Someone had gone after Pippa that night. I'm more sure of
that now than I've ever been. Someone had had sex with her
and I don't believe it was some random person she met. Was
that because they were on a promise? Because they 'fancied'
their chances? That kind of conceited cockiness better
described Tom than Richie. Might Tom have been having a
relationship with Pippa? I remember how he'd said, *She's actually not bad looking, if only she'd loosen up and stop taking
things so seriously.* Emelia had been upset when she suspected
Tom fancied her. I'd seen it in her eyes. Did she challenge Tom?

I wonder. She'd laughed his comment off but, knowing Emelia, she would have been consumed with jealousy.

Pippa hadn't simply lain down and drowned. She'd met someone, perhaps argued with someone. I'm sure of it. Possibly had a debilitating asthma attack. Either way, her death would have been an excruciatingly painful one.

And what of poor Jodie? My mind races. Was it possible her death really wasn't suicide? That someone might have been scared she might start digging things up? There *had* been someone here last night. Just as Jodie had insisted someone had been in her house. Had they been hoping I would try to climb through the bedroom window and fall – with the help of a sharp shove from behind? Or else blunder out onto the landing, as I actually had, and fall down the stairs? They might need to finish the job, but...

My thoughts trail off as I realise what I'm doing: kneeling on the hall floor surrounded by broken seashells being as neurotic as it was possible to be. This is what Richie sees, what he's tried to live with: a woman who's driving *herself* paranoid, in so doing, driving him to despair. He was miserable because of me. He was miserable because I didn't trust him. I'd driven him into Emelia's arms.

I pull myself to my feet, try to calm myself, but I can't. Panic seems to have taken root inside me and it won't let go. I feel as if I'm going insane. I really do, as if my nightmares are becoming my reality. Tears almost blinding me, I tread carefully over the debris and fly up the stairs to grab my bag. My hands tremble as I dig into it. The phone's not there. Where *is* it? It was here last night. I'd fetched it. Had someone taken it? *Stop!* Pressing my hand to my forehead, I go to the bed and tip the contents out. No one's taken it. Attempting to slow the rapid beat of my heart, I take a deep breath, then snatch my phone from where I'd placed it, right where I could reach it on the bedside table, retrieve the card Jack had given me and key the number into it.

'Jack Evans?' he answers immediately, and I've never been so relieved in my life. I'm growing truly frightened now. Of myself.

'Jack, it's Becky. I'm sorry to bother you so early. I was hoping I could talk to you,' I almost babble the words out.

'You're not bothering me. Are you all right?' he asks, a curious edge to his voice. 'You sound a little stressed.'

'I am.' I choke back a sob. 'Sorry. I don't know what's wrong with me.'

'No apologies necessary,' he says kindly. 'Just take your time. I'm not going anywhere.'

'I feel like I'm being haunted,' I blurt it out, realise just how mad that sounds and backtrack. 'Not by an actual ghost. At least, I don't think it's an actual ghost.'

Jack is silent for a second, and I clutch my phone tight to my ear. 'Jack?'

'I'm here,' he says, sounding reassuringly calm. 'Go on.'

'I think someone means me harm.' Taking another breath, I continue falteringly. 'Things keep happening. Strange things. Things being left in the house. Someone's been here, while I was in bed. Jodie's death, I can't help thinking that was strange too. No one else does, but I do. She thought...' I stop, wary now of sounding completely unhinged.

'Is Richard there, Becky?' Jack asks, clearly concerned.

'No, he... We... I'm scared, Jack. I need to talk to you. Can I see you?'

'Give me an hour,' he says. 'Then come to my office. The address is on the card. Will you be okay until then?'

'Yes.' I nod, relief surging through me. He will help me. Objectively. Non-judgementally. He will be my voice of sanity.

TWENTY

EMELIA

'For God's sake! Charlotte, what on earth are you *doing*?' Jarred from semi-consciousness by her six-year-old daughter leaping on top of her, Emelia wasn't in the best mood.

Straining her neck, she squinted through grainy eyes, to see Charlotte looking at her with rather less jubilance than she'd obviously had when she'd launched herself at her.

'I came to show you my seashells,' the little girl said, clearly crestfallen. 'Daddy collected them for me while I was eating my Coco Pops.'

'Oh. Did he?' Feeling immediately guilty, Emelia forced her face into a smile, then glimpsed at Tom as he came into the room behind her. 'Well, they're lovely, sweetheart,' she assured her, as Charlotte shuffled over to give her room to sit up. Which was a bad idea in retrospect. Her head felt like it was being squeezed in a vice, pinpricks of sharp light forming behind her eyes telling her the excruciating pain in the base of her skull wasn't going to go anytime soon.

As he walked towards them, Tom gave her a look – *that* look, the one that told Emelia he wasn't impressed with her. 'They're for her school art project. The one you forgot about,' he said, holding her gaze pointedly as he tucked his hands under Charlotte's arms and swung her down.

'She didn't tell me about her art project.' Emelia frowned and tried to kickstart her sluggish brain.

'I did, Mummy.' Charlotte looked at her worriedly from under her eyelashes. 'I brought you a letter. You put it on top of the microwave. Didn't she, Daddy?' She looked at Tom, as if she needed him to back her up, and Emelia felt dreadful, like the worst mother ever.

'She did,' Tom answered, giving Charlotte an encouraging smile. 'Go on, sweetheart.' He nodded her towards the door. 'Go and brush your teeth. And tell Josh he needs to get his skates on or we'll be late for school.'

'Hell, I forgot.' Pressing a hand to her forehead, Emelia shoved the duvet back and eased herself unsteadily to her feet. Then reeled dangerously as her head swam. *Ugh.* She waited for the walls to slow down. *Never again.* She promised herself, but part of her knew she would break her promise.

'We gathered.' Tom bent to retrieve a stray shell from the floor and then stood to face her. 'I won't ask how you came to be falling out of a taxi last night when you left the reception with Richie. Or why Becky sounded so pissed off when she rang just now to say she was on her way over. You'd better get your story straight though, Emelia. And get your damn act together, will you, for *all* our sakes.' His dark eyes pools of pure contempt, he looked her angrily over, then turned to stalk to the landing.

Oh no. Nausea swirled inside her. What had she done? But she knew, with mortifying, sickening clarity it came back to her. She'd ruined her friendship with Becky forever. Becky had looked as if someone had punched her when she'd walked in on them. As she would, faced with her so-called friend attempting to bare her breasts to her husband. Groaning inside, Emelia squeezed her eyes closed. Then snapped them open as Josh mumbled, 'I'm coming. I'm coming,' in answer to Tom calling him.

Attempting to hide the fact that she had a hangover from hell, Emelia headed to the landing. 'Bye, sweetheart,' she said, plastering a bright smile on her face as Josh emerged from his bedroom. Her heart plummeted as her son, a miniature replica of his father in so many ways, answered with a scowl and then, averting his gaze, almost pushed past her.

'Josh?' Emelia spun around after him – also a bad idea. 'Don't I get a hug?' she asked, her arms outstretched.

Reaching the top of the stairs, Josh swept cool eyes over her, then clumped down without uttering a word – and Emelia felt her heart drop to the depths of her soul. She loved her children with her bones, but Tom was winning them over. And she was losing them, because she was losing her grip.

TWENTY-ONE

'I have a late appointment this evening,' Tom called up the stairs after gathering the children ready to leave. 'Can I assume you'll be well enough to collect them since you dispensed with the nanny's services?' he asked dryly.

Before you serviced *her*, Emelia would like to have shot back. She had no doubt his *appointment* was with a woman, probably the poor innocent he'd been chatting up at the bar yesterday. You'd think he would have managed to restrain himself at a funeral. Oh no, not Tom. The more challenging the conquest, the more it turned him on. He would pursue a bride at her own wedding, she would swear. Her conscience pricked painfully, though, as she remembered her own abysmal behaviour.

'Bye,' she called back. Then wiped away a tear when no one answered but her daughter. She did have to get her act together, she thought, angry – with herself. And she would, despite Tom.

Right now, she had to get dressed and work out what on earth she was going to say to Becky. As if Becky would be in any mood to listen. With her throat parched and her head now feeling as if someone was pounding through it with a jackhammer, she was making her way gingerly towards the bathroom to quench her thirst and take a quick shower, when the doorbell rang. *Shit.* Becky, it had to be. Should she just not answer it? Emelia debated, a bubble of panic rising inside her. She didn't have much choice but to, she realised. Tom had just left with the children, and her car was on the drive, which would give the game away. She would have to go down and face her. She would have to sooner or later anyway.

Heading to the bedroom door, she pulled her dressing gown from the hook. Catching her reflection in the wardrobe mirror as she tugged it on, her heart sank to a whole new level. She looked like death warmed up. Scratch that. She looked like death full stop. Why had she drunk so much? Why couldn't Tom just stop torturing her and be there for her, like Richie was for Becky. And why the bloody hell couldn't Becky stop banging on about Pippa, as if it were only her whose life had been affected by her death? She should try Emelia's life on for size. The timid little mouse had followed her around like a shadow back at university. She was still following her around now. Did Becky realise, she wondered, that that timid little mouse had claws. Claws she was all too ready to sink into Tom, or Richie, come to that. She might have been sitting there demurely in her denim shorts and tiny strapless bikini, but she'd been eyeing them up. It was obvious she was. Becky really was too forgiving sometimes.

Emelia just hoped she would be able to forgive her, though she seriously doubted it. The urge to kill the women Tom messed around with was so overwhelming sometimes, she struggled to restrain herself. She couldn't blame Becky if she wanted to do the same to her.

Hurrying down the stairs, she paused, wondering again whether to just not answer the door. Becky had been so consumed with rage last night, Emelia suspected she actually might have killed her if she'd reached her before Richie had intervened. She was obviously still fuming. She realised she couldn't avoid the inevitable, though, when clearly spotting her through the opaque glass, Becky hammered on the door, then yelled, 'I know you're in there, Emelia. You'd better open up, because I'm coming in one way or another.'

Nerves knotting her stomach, Emelia clutched her dressing gown more tightly around her, braced herself and reached for the door latch. 'Becks, I am so, so sorry,' she said as she pulled the door open. 'I know what you think of me, and I don't blame—'

'Were you at my house last night?' Becky snapped.

Emelia blinked at her, confused. 'I...' she started and stopped. She had no clue how to answer.

'Well?' Becky demanded, her sharp green eyes blazing.

'Yes,' Emelia replied warily. 'You know I was, but I didn't mean to hurt you, Becks,' she added quickly. 'I know I have, and—'

'I'm not talking about then.' Becky shook her head impatiently. 'Later.'

Emelia knitted her brow. Was she on something? She'd thought *she* looked like death but Becky didn't look much better. Normally groomed and perfectly made up, she was glaring at her now through a mad tangle of auburn hair that plainly hadn't seen a comb, and she wasn't wearing a scrap of make-up. She was livid, that much was clear. She also looked a little bit mad – as in, crazy, rather than outraged. Could jealousy do that? But it could. Emelia knew it could.

'Is the question too difficult?' Becky asked facetiously. 'I mean, I'm assuming you must be stupid to have initiated sex with my husband in my house with me about to walk in – unless you'd planned for Richie to get caught in the act, of course; I wouldn't put that past you.'

'Becky...' Emelia was taken aback. This wasn't the Becky she knew. Her friend was kind, annoyingly so sometimes – she couldn't seem to see the bad in anybody. She was hardly ever hurtful or sarcastic.

'I'll rephrase it, shall I?' Becky went on. 'Did you come to my house while I was in bed on my own, due to the fact that you couldn't keep your hands off my husband, and try to scare me out of my mind?'

'*No.*' Emelia looked at her with a mixture of shock and dismay. She obviously was out of her mind, halfway anyway, with grief and anger obviously. 'Why on earth would you think that?'

'Ooh, now let me see.' Becky pressed a finger to her chin, making a great show of thinking about it. 'Because you've set your sights on Richie, possibly? Clearly you don't give a damn about the trifling little fact that I'm carrying his baby. That I *love* him,' she snarled, her eyes a glistening sheen of pure hatred.

'Becky?' Tears sprang to Emelia's eyes. She'd hurt her. Of course she had. She'd crushed her. But she hadn't meant to. 'Please listen to me. I'm *sorry*. I didn't mean for any of this to happen. I'd drunk too much. I was upset, because of Jodie. Because of the way Tom was behaving. I never did find out what you two were whispering about at the reception. Tom said it was nothing. But he always says that when he's been messing around and I thought... Oh I don't know *what* I thought, but—'

'So is *that* why you went after Richie like a bitch on heat?' Becky stared at her, incredulous. 'Because you thought there'd been something between Tom and me?'

'*No.*' Emelia was growing more flustered by the second. 'Becky, just stop. *Please.* It wasn't like that. I didn't do anything of the sort. And I know there was never anything between you and Tom. You're not like that. I know you're not.'

'No, Emelia, I'm not. I'm your friend.' Becky held her gaze. Hers was as cold as the Arctic Ocean. 'Was,' she added pointedly.

Wrapping her arms around herself, Emelia dropped her gaze.

'Are you and Richie having an affair, Emelia?' Becky asked. 'I think you owe it to me to tell me the truth.'

Emelia shook her head hard. 'No,' she whispered, forcing the word past the knot in her throat.

'But you would have done, had Richie been willing?'

Emelia didn't answer. There was absolutely nothing she could say. No way to redeem herself. She wished she could die.

'You really are a selfish cow, aren't you?' Becky growled. 'You'll stop at nothing to get your man, will you, whoever that might be? You'll stop at nothing to keep him, will you? As Pippa would attest to – had she been allowed to live to tell the tale.'

Emelia snapped her gaze back to her. 'What the hell is that supposed to mean?'

Becky said nothing. Dragging a disdainful glance over her, she turned away.

'You're so determined she was wronged, aren't you?' Emelia shouted as she walked to her car. 'Poor picked on little Pippa, sitting there all on her own, looking sorry for herself. It's *you* who's wrong, Becky.'

Becky's step faltered.

'She wasn't the little Miss Innocence she pretended to be,' Emelia blurted. 'Trust me on that.'

Becky turned slowly back. 'And you know this how?'

Emelia wasn't about to answer. She'd said enough. Swiping at her tears, she gave Becky a meaningful look instead, stepped back and closed the door.

TWENTY-TWO

BECKY

Arriving at the address on Jack's card, I press the buzzer and take a breath, attempting to calm the confusion of emotion churning inside me: Anger, so raw I can taste it. Grief, as I realise I've lost my friend as well as my husband – even if Richie wanted to come back, would I want him back? And Emelia, could I ever forgive her? Drunk or not, she would have gone through with what she'd intended, meaning she didn't give a damn about our friendship, about me, about my baby. Guilt, now so heavy I don't think I can bear it. I should never have let what Emelia had told the police about Pippa having a boyfriend slip by unchallenged. I should never have colluded in the awful treatment of her. I could have intervened. I could have been a friend to her. I could have saved her.

The damp drizzle on the morning air seeming to bite into me down to my bones, I press the buzzer again. Still there's no answer. Shaking with cold and fear, I step back and glance up at the old, red-bricked building. There's a Costa coffee shop on the ground floor and I assume Jack's renting an office on one of the upper floors, but there doesn't appear to be any sign of activity. I have no idea what to do. Richie has been my whole life. I don't have anyone else I can turn to. Now my life is unravelling, the home we'd built together, my hopes and my dreams crumbling. My marriage, broken. But I don't know that Richie *has* cheated. And if he hasn't? It's still broken. I'm making him miserable. According to him, I'm neurotic. Paranoid. The thing that terrifies me is, I think he might be right. I really do feel as if I'm losing my mind.

Tugging the flimsy jacket I'd grabbed on my way out tightly around myself, I turn away, though I have no idea what I will do or where I will go. I can't go home. I don't feel safe there, and the unbearable reality is, with Richie there, I think I would feel less so.

I've gone a few yards when I hear someone behind me. 'Becky.'

Jack. Feeling he's my one shred of sanity amid the madness, relief sweeps through me.

'Hey,' he smiles as he reaches me, 'how are you?'

'I'm okay.' I attempt a smile back.

He knits his brow, his deep hazel eyes clouding with concern as they search mine. Clearly he's gathering from my bedraggled appearance that I'm not okay. 'Sorry about the delay answering the door,' he says. 'My PA's off sick. It's a security door and I couldn't figure out how to release it from upstairs. I'm pretty rubbish at anything technical, but better at counselling – and my coffee making skills are acceptable, I'm told. Shall we?'

I nod and smile and, out of nowhere, my eyes fill up all over again. 'I'm sorry. I don't mean to be so emotional,' I mumble, wiping at my wet cheeks with my fingers.

'No apologies necessary.' He hesitates, then threads an arm around me. 'Come on, let's get you inside where it's warm,' he says, steering me back towards his office.

Moments later, I'm sitting in a comfy chair, a box of tissues placed before me on the table, while he makes coffee.

'Black and sweet and not too strong, as requested,' he says, carrying it across.

'Thanks.' I accept it gratefully. I'm watching my caffeine intake but after the night I've had, I need this.

'Pleasure.' He sits down opposite me. 'I'm glad you came.' He eyes me thoughtfully as he places his mug on the table. 'I could sense you were struggling with some things when we spoke at the funeral.'

He's obviously astute as well as kind. I was wary coming here but then I'd reminded myself that Jodie had trusted him. Now, seeing his level 5 diploma in counselling displayed on a wall, a framed photo of his wife and children on his desk, potted plants and tasteful pieces dotted around the room – a raggedy rabbit I assume is one of his children's amongst them – I feel safe with him.

'Take your time.' Leaning back, he steeples his hands under his chin, smiling encouragingly over them. 'Just go at your own pace. There's no rush.'

I stare down into my coffee. 'I'm not sure where to start.'

He's quiet for a moment. Then, 'You said you thought someone meant you harm,' he prompts me gently. 'That someone had been in the house. Do you have any idea who it might have been?'

I glance up to see him watching me contemplatively. 'You mentioned Richard wasn't there when I asked,' he goes on. 'Was he there when whoever it was entered the property?'

I shake my head.

'Or when these things you spoke of were left in the house?'

'No.' I swallow and place my cup down, the coffee untouched.

'Are you able to tell me what these things were, Becky?'

I take a tremulous breath. 'Seashells, seaweed. A photograph. They might seem fairly innocuous items, but...' I trail off.

'They're not, I take it?'

Again, I nod.

He waits.

'I can't say why.' I look away.

'That's okay.' He assures me. 'Anything you say here is strictly confidential, but you don't need to tell me anything you're not comfortable with.'

'Thank you.' I smile shakily, feeling perilously close to tears again.

'I'm assuming the person who left these items shares this knowledge?' he probes gently.

I nod and fall silent. 'Richie wasn't there because we argued,' I confide after a moment.

He raises his eyebrows slightly but doesn't comment.

My gaze drifts away again. 'After you dropped me off last night, I found him and Emelia... well, let's just say, in a compromising position.' I quickly look back at him. 'I don't think they...'

'But you suspect they might have, had you not arrived when you did?' Jack asks carefully.

'I don't know,' I answer. I realise then that I'm clinging to the possibility that Richie isn't involved with Emelia, that somehow he will make all of this go away, however naïve that might make me.

'Tell me about this photograph,' Jack urges me on. 'I presume it was significant?'

'Extremely,' I confirm, feeling more at ease with him. Because he's listening, I realise. Because he's not judging me. 'At least I think so. It's an old group photograph: Richie and me, Tom and Emelia, Jodie and her girlfriend, not Kelly. She was seeing someone else back then. Also a couple of other friends, but they weren't really close. It was taken at a beach party years ago, back at university.' I hesitate. I've never breathed a word of this to anyone.

'And the significance is?' Jack encourages me on, his demeanour serious yet gentle. I can see how people would feel comfortable opening up to him. How Jodie would have, had she lived.

'There was another girl there. Pippa.' My throat closes as I think of her. 'We weren't very nice to her. We excluded her. It was a bloody awful thing to do, she was obviously lonely, and...'

'And?' he says gently.

'She died.' I catch a sob in my throat. 'That night on the beach.'

Jack's expression remains neutral. 'I see,' he says, with a small incline of his head. 'And?'

'I encouraged her to dance with Richie. She didn't really want to,' I force myself on. 'And Emelia... She was horrible to her, making fun of her. Pippa was mortified. She ran off, and...' I stop as the tears come.

Jack reaches to push the box of tissues towards me. 'Take a moment,' he says.

I swallow, tug a tissue out and press it hard to my eyes.

'Okay?' he asks after a pause. 'We can stop if you want to.'

I shake my head. 'No, I'm okay.'

'How did she come to die, Becky?' he asks, once I've composed myself. 'It's clearly something that's been eating away at you.'

'It has.' I breathe deeply. 'The police concluded it was an accident,' I go on falteringly, 'that she died from drowning after drinking too much, but...'

'You're not convinced?' Jack finishes.

'No,' I answer with a firm shake of my head. 'I'm not. She was asthmatic. I'm sure that must have been a factor,' I press on, trying to explain why I can't *let it go*. 'She'd had sex with someone apparently. I can't help wondering...'

'Whether it was with one of your group?' Jack picks up when I can't bring myself to voice the thought that squirmed its way into my mind back then and has niggled away at me ever since.

I nod, relieved on one level that I've finally been able to say it out loud. On another, petrified of saying too much. 'She might have met up with someone. Emelia thought she might have been seeing some guy, but I don't think so. In fact, I think Emelia might have been lying. Pippa was so shy and awkward in company. I wish I'd done more to be a friend to her.'

'So, it's Pippa who haunts you?' Jack concludes. His tone is soft, his expression impartial, but still I can't quite meet his eyes.

'She haunted Jodie too,' I murmur.

Jack nods. 'She did allude to there being some kind of tragedy but, as I mentioned, we never got to talk about it.' He pauses, his steady gaze faltering. 'We're obliged to contact the authorities if we feel there's a threat to life. I didn't feel that when I last saw her, but I can't help thinking I should have.'

I feel for him. 'You're not responsible for other people, Jack,' I say gently, reminding him of what he'd said at the funeral reception.

'No,' Jack concedes, pinches the bridge of his nose and pulls himself up in his chair. 'So, do you think it's possible that whoever was with Pippa might have had something to do with her death?' he asks, his eyes flecked with a mixture of concern and curiosity as he looks back at me.

'I don't know.' I sigh. 'I wish I could talk to the others about it, but they're reluctant to. They think I should let it go. The thing is, I can't. Jodie clearly couldn't either. Richie called me neurotic. He thinks I'm obsessed because I'm stuffed full of guilt. He thinks I'm a lot of things, apparently.' I smile sadly. 'I couldn't believe it when he turned on me. But then, I would never have believed he would cheat on me either.'

Jack doesn't comment, diplomatically.

'I actually did start to feel neurotic at one point,' I go on with a shaky laugh. 'I thought...' I falter, looking him over uncertainly. 'You'll probably think I'm mad.'

'Try me.' Jack smiles.

I draw in a breath. 'I thought that maybe Richie was doing it. You know, so he would have an excuse to leave me. Who wants to live with a paranoid obsessive, after all? Then I thought it might be Tom. And then I wondered about Emelia, even whether she and Richie might be in it together, trying to scare me into doing something drastic. It would certainly shut me up if I did, wouldn't it?'

Jack doesn't reply immediately. From the pensive look on his face, he appears to be deep in thought.

'Well, do you?' I urge him. 'Think I'm mad?'

He hesitates. 'I don't normally offer opinions. My job is to guide people to reach their own conclusions, to provide strategies to help them cope with whatever they're struggling with. However—' he kneads his forehead, then looks back at me, looking troubled '—after your friend's suicide, I feel obliged to. No, I don't think you're mad, Becky. I might be wrong, but I suspect, given all you've told me, that your husband *is* trying to scare you. I actually think the things he said to you could be deemed to be gaslighting you.'

'Gaslighting?' I stare at him, stunned.

'Trying to make you believe that you're going out of your mind,' he clarifies. 'Maybe, as you say, to drive you into doing something drastic. I also think, and I really hope I'm wrong about this, that it is possible that he, or maybe this Tom character, could have played a part in that young girl's unfortunate death.'

He's echoing my own disjointed thoughts, but still I feel the blood drain from my body. 'And Jodie's death?' I whisper.

Jack's eyes are cautious as they scan mine. 'It's possible,' he says eventually, clearly reluctantly.

'But what about the note?' I remind him she'd left one.

'I gather it was typed on a PC. Conceivably anyone who might have gained access to her cottage could have typed it,' he points out, again echoing my own thoughts.

He pauses, studying me carefully before continuing. 'In my experience, people who lie, pathological liars, narcissistic personalities, will often go to terrifying extremes to avoid having their lies exposed and the truth coming out. I know it's not what you want to hear, Becky, but I'm concerned you might be in danger.'

TWENTY-THREE

'Narcissists find it difficult to truly connect with people on an emotional level. Their focus is on themselves and their own needs,' Jack goes on to explain when I look at him in astonishment. 'They may seem distant or reserved, appear calm in a crisis. Often, they will use the pretence of emotion to control others when, in reality, they fear intimacy because they believe it makes them vulnerable.'

'But that's not Richie.' I laugh, bewildered. 'He's not over-emotional, but he doesn't try to control people.'

'Are you sure about that, Becky?' Jack furrows his brow thoughtfully.

'Yes,' I reply, adamant. 'No. I...' My mind shoots back to the day I can never forget, when we'd found poor Pippa. Everyone's emotions were raw. Emelia was hysterical. Tom was shocked. Richie, though, was the calm in the storm. Decisive. He'd taken control, urged us to make sure we got our stories straight. No. Jack's wrong. He *has* to be. Richie was trying to look out for us, that was all. That wasn't narcissistic behaviour. If anyone is focused on themselves, it's Tom.

'People with narcissistic tendencies will also try to deflect blame if they feel caught out,' Jack continues as I study him uncertainly. 'They might say you're "this" or "that" in a situation, an argument, say, to deflect blame from themselves. Turning the tables frees them from responsibility. It also leaves you questioning yourself.'

That's crap, Becky. Bordering on paranoia. I am not having an affair with Emelia! And since when did you give a damn about Tom? Were you with him? I hear Richie's voice in my head, his furious accusations, and my chest tightens. *Is that what this obsessive guilt is all about? Why you're so down on Emelia? You used to be fun... you're becoming neurotic.*

'I have to go.' I grab my bag and jump to my feet.

'I've upset you.' Jack stands, following me as I head for the door.

'No. I'm okay. I just...' I falter. He's right, isn't he? I'd tried to give Richie the benefit of the doubt, to convince myself those cruel comments were thrown out in the heat of the moment, but he had left me questioning myself. Questioning everything. 'I have an appointment,' I explain. 'A young man with a traumatic brain injury. I had to reschedule because of Jodie's funeral. He struggles with depression, I can't let him down again.'

It's true. I don't want to let him down, but I also need some space. I need to process all that's happened, all that Jack has just said. 'Oh, I have to pay you.'

Placing a hand gently on my arm, Jack stops me as I delve into my bag. 'No need,' he says. 'We can discuss costs going forward, assuming you'd like to come and talk to me again? I hope you do. I think you need to explore your emotions a little more, Becky. Repressing them isn't healthy.'

'I know.' I swallow back the hard knot wedged in my throat. 'Can I call you?'

'Anytime,' he assures me, opening the door for me. 'Where will you go?'

'Home,' I answer with a sad shrug. 'I don't have anywhere

else.' I recall how hard I'd worked decorating the house and making it our own. How I'd agonised over the colour in the lounge, eventually deciding on calming soft pink walls with pops of red, which worked with our blue suite. I'd decided on warm neutrals for the nursery. I'd pencilled in time off to decorate it. 'It is my home, after all,' I add more decisively, while trying to dismiss the unbearable reality that I might find myself there alone, 'my baby's home. I'm not going to be scared out of it.'

'I'm glad you're determined to fight.' Jack nods approvingly. 'Do you mind if I offer a little advice?'

'No.' I eye him cautiously.

'It's just a suggestion, but you might want to consider getting the locks changed and some window locks installed.'

I glance at him in alarm. Surely he's not thinking that Richie would be physically violent?

'It might be that this will all blow over,' Jack adds, clearly noting my expression. 'Richard might regret the things he said. We all say things in the heat of the moment. He might have nothing to do with the strangely appearing items you mentioned but he does have access to the house, and as you're so uncertain about his involvement... If I were you, I would err on the side of caution, at least until you've had the chance to talk together honestly.'

But will I know if he's being honest? Is it possible he really is using the pretence of emotion to manipulate me? Into what? Letting it go? *We can't all live our lives consumed with guilt, Becky. You might want to, imagining you're paying some bloody penance, but I don't.* What guilt was it he didn't want to live with? If he did have a narcissistic personality, was he even capable of feeling guilty? Why would he say all of those hurtful things unless to 'turn the tables'? The man who'd been so agitated isn't the Richie I know. Perhaps I've never really known him? I can't believe he'd *pretended* to have emotions for me, pretended to love me, but then there hadn't been much love in his eyes last night. Did I really think it was him who'd crept back to the house and left those things, though? The window had been open when I'd found the photograph. But what about the seashells?

'Will you report last night's events to the police?' Jack asks, walking with me out onto the landing.

I scan his face, unsure. 'Do you think I should?'

He hesitates. 'Given all you've told me, I suspect you might be reluctant to, but I would advise you to, nevertheless.'

He's right, but then I would have to tell them everything, going right back to Pippa and the events around her death. The detective involved at the time had seemed almost apathetic. They might reopen the case. There would be no going back then. What would Richie's reaction be if I did? 'I'll think about it,' I answer.

Jack nods. 'You have my number. If you're worried about anything, call me. Anytime, day or night.'

I arch my eyebrows at that.

'My wife's okay with it.' He smiles, clearly having read my mind. 'She was struggling with some issues when we first met. She understands that out-of-office hours can sometimes be the loneliest.'

'Thank you.' I swallow back a tight lump of emotion. I can't know whether his wife was one of his clients, but I think she's a lucky woman to have met him.

TWENTY-FOUR

EMELIA

Emelia stood in the bedroom surveying herself critically through the wardrobe mirror. She was a mess. With yesterday's mascara cried all down her cheeks, far from a pulled together image consultant, she looked like a clown. A very lonely, sad clown, and one well past its sell by date. What happened? Once she could have had any man she'd wanted. At university they were falling over themselves to get her attention, and Emelia had played the field. Until Tom. It was a confidence thing. Gaining attention gave her that. She'd had precious little at home with her mum constantly sozzled and her dad largely ignoring her, unless to bawl her out for dressing like a tart and coming home late.

She and Tom had only been going out for a couple of weeks when, despite her promises to herself never to get stuck with one man and end up miserable like her mum, she realised she'd fallen for him, big time. Aware he attracted girls like bees to honey, she'd been desperate to hang on to him. Try as she might to be everything a man could desire, though: attractive, attentive, sparkly in company and hot in bed, she soon found herself competing for his attention. His eyes wandered. Even sitting right next to her in the pub his gaze would be elsewhere, on some pretty, naïve thing no doubt making eyes at him. Naivety seemed to appeal to him. Pippa's naivety had appealed to him, he'd made that obvious.

As the years passed, she had to try harder – she wouldn't be seen dead now without her make-up. He'd sapped her self-esteem with his cheating. He denied it, of course, but she knew he did – there were more damp squids than fireworks in the bedroom lately. He was clever, making sure never to leave his phone around unlocked. He didn't even bother to lie to her anymore when she told him she knew he was using his evening appointments with 'important' clients as a cover for his cheating. He would say nothing, simply give her *that* look, somewhere between pity and despair.

Then they would argue. 'A man doesn't have condoms in his pocket unless he's fucking around,' she would end up screaming at him, reminding him of the packet she'd found when they were at uni. They'd been an item by then and she'd been so humiliated. 'That was years ago!' he would yell back, and off he would go, stalking out of the house and slamming the door behind him, using *her* 'unreasonable behaviour' as an excuse to carry on crushing her.

He'd called her a drunken lush once. Could he blame her for drinking? Tears rising, she tore herself away from the mirror, which really wasn't her friend anymore, and headed back downstairs. Marching into the kitchen, she pulled the fridge open and retrieved the water bottle she kept topped up in there, poured a hefty measure of vodka from it into a glass and coloured it with fresh orange, then took a glug. After waiting for it to hit the spot, she took another. Then whirled around as Tom walked into the kitchen behind her. 'I spoke to Richie,' he said, looking from her to the glass and then derisorily back at her.

Emelia felt the blood drain from her body.

'Bad move, Emelia,' he muttered, and turned back to the hall.

Emelia went after him, catching hold of his arm. 'Nothing happened,' she said, a desperate edge to her voice.

Tom looked down to her hand clutching his sleeve, then back to her face. 'I'm not surprised,' he sneered, dragging another disdainful gaze over her. 'Enjoy your drink.'

Yanking his arm away from her, he headed back to the open front door. 'Oh, and you needn't bother collecting the kids from school,' he tossed over his shoulder. 'They're not there. I'm leaving you.'

Frozen with shock, Emelia stayed where she was for a second, then flew after him. 'You wouldn't *dare*,' she shouted.

As he pulled his car door open, Tom turned to face her. 'No?' He tipped his head to one side. 'I have news for you, Em. I just did.'

'I'll *ruin* you.' She followed him to the drive, careless of the neighbours, who were nothing but jealous because their house was the best on the road, because she had good taste and stylish clothes. 'I'll contact your clients and tell them all about you. I *swear* I will.'

'Really?' Tom surveyed her coldly. 'And what will you tell them, Emelia? That I loved you? That I kept trying to love you, despite your constant accusations, your drinking? I can't do it anymore, don't you get it? You want to drink yourself to death. Fine. Do it. I've had it.'

TWENTY-FIVE

BECKY

Going through the front door, I hurry upstairs to change out of my leggings and sweater. I can't let my client down no matter how exhausted I feel. He was only twenty-eight when he had his car accident, a good-looking man with a career in teaching, which he'd loved, ahead of him. Now, due to his brain injury and despite having no physical injury, he's unable to regulate his emotions or speak coherently. We were due to do an assessment to monitor his progress and identify areas we still need to work on when I'd had to cancel. I know he hangs on to the hope our meetings bring him. I can't just abandon him to wallow in my own misery. I don't want to. That would be like giving up and I can't do that. My future feels bleak, but I have my baby to think of, his future.

I've agonised over Jack's advice about going to the police and decided he's right. I do need to report what's been happening. I'll ring Richie first, tell him I'm going to contact them and listen to what he has to say. If it's a repeat performance of all he's already said, though, then I will know that that's how he really feels, assuming he's capable of feeling. I suppose in not calling or texting me, he's made that obvious anyway. Is there a way forward for us? I wonder. Do I want there to be? I realise I do. I want things to go back to the way they were. For Richie to be who I thought he was.

As I head for the bedroom, I pause, peering into the room that will be the nursery and picture it as I imagine it will be, my baby gurgling contentedly in his little white cot, his little limbs flailing as he gazes up at the starburst mural I intend to paint on the ceiling. I've bought one or two items I couldn't resist – a long-necked, polka-dot giraffe and a beautiful soft-fabric rocking horse, but I haven't started the decorating yet, purposely. Richie had asked me whether I thought I might be tempting fate. I am superstitious, yes, but if I'm honest, it's more that I feel we already have. Perhaps I've been waiting all these years for fate to catch up with me, with all of us. It's a good job I didn't admit that to Richie. I would definitely have been paranoid.

'Don't worry, sweet pea, Mummy will keep you safe,' I whisper, pressing my hand over my tummy, my love for my tiny baby already so strong it's almost overwhelming. I've never known an emotion so powerful. I've heard people say they would kill to protect their children, and I honestly believe that I would.

Walking on to the bedroom, I drop my bag on the bed, trying not to actually look at the space Richie and I shared, making love together, sharing our hopes and our dreams together. Had what I thought we had really been so different for him? So unbearable? If it had, then maybe he shouldn't have been too cowardly to tell me before we'd finally succeeded in getting pregnant again. I immediately reel that thought back. I want this child, fiercely. He might have fractured our marriage, made me question myself and my sanity, but he can't take this away from me.

Quickly I go to the bathroom to splash cold water over my face and run a comb through my hair. I'm not sure why I'm bothering. For pride's sake, I suppose. I don't want people to see me broken. I don't want Richie to think that I am.

As I apply my moisturiser, my phone rings. *Richie?* I hurry back to the bedroom, a surge of hope rising inside me, despite the fact that I think Jack might have been right about what he'd said about him. Trying to make me believe I was paranoid was gaslighting. His managing to twist around what I saw happening between him and Emelia with my own eyes, accusing me of having had sex with Tom on the night of the beach party, was cruel. If it was Richie who was responsible for leaving those things in the house, then his behaviour was petrifying.

Grabbing my bag, I find my phone and check the last call received. *Emelia.* My heart drops. I can't talk to her. Even as I think it, my thumb hovers over the call button. I don't feel I can ever forgive her, but still I'm worried for her. She obviously has problems, a drink problem definitely being one of them.

Seconds later, I receive a text: *Please call me, Becks. I'm desperate. Tom and I argued. He said he spoke to Richie. I don't know what Richie said but Tom's left me. I'm not involved with Richie, I swear I'm not. Please call me back.*

Oh no. My heart drops. Tom would have had questions about why she'd arrived home in a taxi having left the funeral reception with Richie. Of course he would. Recalling how furious I'd been on the phone when I'd called telling Tom I was on my way over there, I have a horrible feeling that would have confirmed any suspicions he might have had.

Where were the children? Charlotte and Josh would be in the middle of all of this. They will have been bewildered and frightened if their parents had argued violently and their daddy had ended up walking out. Might Tom have taken them with him? My heart jars at the thought that he might have, rather than leave them with a mother he considered incapable of looking after them. Emelia's not a bad mother, she loves her kids, but she's been drinking steadily, more and more over the years. She will be horrendously hungover this morning, no doubt in a terrible state emotionally, especially after I'd launched into her. Part of me thinks she deserves to be. Another part of me feels for her. I really don't want to talk to her, but I would never forgive myself if anything happened to her.

My mind goes to Jodie. Jack is clearly thinking along the same lines I am. Whatever happened to Jodie, though, whether she'd taken her own life or someone – I daren't linger on who – had coerced her into jumping to a certain death, she would have been desperate. She'd been home alone. Her cottage is isolated, high up on the cliff top. She'd possibly been preyed upon and subjected to the same psychological torment I had. I can't let that happen to Emelia. I don't believe she's mentally strong enough.

Bracing myself, I call her back. Trepidation twists inside me when I reach her voicemail: *Hey, you've reached Emelia Connor, image consultant and beauty therapist. Sorry I missed you. I'm super busy right now, but please leave your name and number and I'll get right back.* Her tone is upbeat, optimistic, more like the Emelia I used to know, and in sharp contrast to the woman I now know, whose natural effervescence seemed to have fizzled out, giving way to bitterness.

Unable to help but be concerned about her, I leave her a message to call me back. When she hasn't returned my call by the time I'm changed, I send a text message. She doesn't respond and I try her number again. I'm half expecting her phone to go to voicemail, thinking that maybe she's decided she can't face me, after all, when the call is answered. 'Emelia?' I say, when she doesn't speak. 'Em?' Still, she doesn't reply and now I'm growing extremely worried. Unsure what to do, I'm about to end the call and head over to her house, when a shrill scream launches my heart into my mouth.

TWENTY-SIX

When I can't get any answer at Emelia's front door, I lift the letter box flap and call through it. I can't see any signs of life inside, yet her car's still on the drive where it was earlier. 'Emelia?' I shout and wait, then drop the flap. With no idea what to do next, I pull my phone out and call her. A knot of panic tightens inside me as I hear her phone ringing. If she is inside, why isn't she answering? Apprehension prickling my spine, I step back to survey the front of the house. The curtains to the main bedroom are still drawn. I move to the side of the door to squint through the tinted glass in the long, floor-to-ceiling hall window. The hall's empty, the kitchen door at the end of it closed. I check the lounge window and, finding that room empty, go back to the door and rap hard again.

What if she's done something stupid? Dread clenches my stomach and, aware that the internal door of the garage goes straight through to the kitchen, I race that way. Finding it locked, I sigh in frustration. What's going on? Had Tom come back? Had they argued again and... My chest tightens as I imagine what might have happened. I have to get in there.

After trying the side gate and finding that bolted, I debate whether to climb over it, but common sense prevails. It's six foot high. I can't risk hurting my baby. Should I call the police? Are they likely to come out for a domestic, though, even if I tell them that my friend's not answering her door and that I'm concerned for her? My thumb hovers over the keypad but I decide to try Tom first. He doesn't pick up and, fear growing inside me, I call Jack's number. He's probably busy and might not want to get involved anyway, but with Richie highly unlikely to want to get involved either, given the circumstances, I can't think of anyone else who could help me gain access. Emelia has no one who gives a damn. She never has. I'm all she has and, as much as I hate her for what she'd done, I still care about her. I have to be there for her.

Quickly, I fill Jack in, my voice catching as I tell him about the scream I'd heard over the phone. 'Something's happened, I'm sure it has. She was so drunk last night. She and Tom argued.' Guilt rips through me as I recall again how furious I'd been with her. 'She could have had an accident. Anything might have happened. I can't just leave it, Jack. I have to find out if she's all right.'

'I'm already in the car,' Jack says. 'I'm on my way.'

Ten minutes later, he pulls up in front of the house and relief surges through me. 'Have you tried her phone again?' he asks, climbing out.

I nod. 'It's ringing from inside the house.' Sick trepidation grips my stomach and won't let go. 'I have to get in there, Jack.'

His gaze travelling from me to the gate, he nods decisively, and then heads towards it. He's up and over it in seconds. Praying it isn't padlocked, I wait on the other side of it. Another surge of relief crashes through me as I hear him drawing the bolt and I'm through the gate almost before he's opened it.

'It might be better if you check through the downstairs windows,' he suggests. 'She's unlikely to remember me from the funeral and I don't want to frighten her.' Leading the way to the back of the house, he tries the back door as I squint through the orangery room doors. There's no sign of her.

Jack steps back, his gaze sweeping the upstairs windows as I head to the kitchen window. 'Do you know if they have any ladders?' he asks. 'Looks as if one of the bedroom windows might be—'

'She's here.' My heart jolts as I see her. Her face buried in her hands, she's scrunched into a ball sitting on the kitchen floor. Petrified. Clearly. 'Emelia!' I shout through the window.

She scrunches herself tighter.

'*Emelia*,' I call urgently again and knock on the glass – and she's up in a flash, unfurling herself and flying towards the kitchen door leading to the hall.

'Emelia, it's me, Becky.' Frightened for her, I shout and slap my hand harder against the glass.

Seeing her face stricken with terror as she glances back before scrambling through the door, my heart turns over. 'She's scared to death.' I glance fearfully at Jack as he joins me. 'I have to get inside.'

'Do you want me to try and force the back door?' He nods towards it.

I debate. 'Shouldn't we call the police?'

'They might take a while,' Jack answers, looking as worried as I feel. 'Even then, they would probably have to be convinced there was a danger to life before breaking in.'

I curse inwardly. Why isn't bloody Tom answering his phone? Because he knows it's me calling, obviously. 'Do you think you can force it?' I ask.

'Depends whether it's bolted on the inside, but I can try.'

Making up my mind, I nod firmly. I'll concern myself with damage to the property later. Right now, my concern is for Emelia.

Jack nods in turn and, after sizing the door up, steps back, raises his foot and kicks at it hard. It appears to make little impression and he kicks at it again, and again. Finally, hearing the sound of wood splintering, he launches his shoulder at it, winces and emits a curse, and then tries again.

The lock gives on his third attempt. He shoves the door open and we're in. 'Thank you,' I breathe, moving swiftly past him to race to the hall. Glimpsing into the lounge to find it empty, I hurry on to the stairs. 'Emelia,' I call from the foot of them, 'it's just me, Becky. I only want to make sure you're all right. Please answer me.'

When she doesn't respond, I mount the first few steps. Then, hearing her sobbing, I fly the rest of the way up. Finding her sitting on the edge of her bed, her arms wrapped tightly around herself, her face tear-stained and streaked with mascara, I hurry across and crouch down in front of her. 'What is it, Em?' I can't help but address her kindly. She's clearly completely distraught. 'Is it because of Tom?'

'Was it you?' She stares at me, her eyes wild.

I frown in confusion. 'Was what me, Em?'

'The stairs,' she mumbles nonsensically, and now I'm becoming truly scared for her. Has she had some kind of a breakdown? She can't be drunk this early in the day surely? 'Did you put it there?' She scans my face, her expression guarded, but at the same time so beseeching it breaks my heart.

'There's nothing on the stairs, Emelia,' I say gently. 'Nothing I can see.'

Tightening her arms around herself, she doesn't reply for a second. Then, 'He was at the window,' she murmurs, her gaze swivelling from me to the door behind me, to the window, and then back.

I scrutinise her warily. 'This window?'

She shakes her head. 'Downstairs.'

'That was me, Em.' Icy apprehension prickles over my skin, and I'm thinking I should probably call someone. Her GP possibly. 'I was looking for you. I was worried about you.'

'No.' She shakes her head again hard. 'Before that. He came inside. He was here, in the house. I could hear someone walking around and I thought... I thought.' She stops and chokes back a wretched sob. 'And then he was there, on the stairs. Just standing there.'

'Who, Emelia?' Moving to sit next to her, I catch hold of her shoulders.

'I don't *know*,' she cries, tears streaming down her face. 'I couldn't see. He was wearing a mask and a black hoodie.'

Richie? My heart pumps with shock and fear. He has a black hoodie. He wears it when he goes out running. No. It's incomprehensible. He wouldn't. He would have to be a complete Jekyll and Hyde character to do something like this, terrify a woman alone in her own home. Why would he? Gripping Emelia's shoulders more firmly, I hold her gaze. 'What did this person do, Emelia?'

'He just stood there. I couldn't get past him. I thought he was going to *kill* me.' Emitting another choking sob, she swipes a hand across her cheek.

'And he didn't say anything?' I frown, unsure what to make of any of it.

Another shake of the head. 'No, he just turned around and walked down the stairs and out of the front door. That's when I saw it.'

'Saw what?' I scan her eyes carefully. 'What did you see, Emelia?'

'It's still there,' she answers tremulously. 'At least, I think it is.'

'Okay,' I nod, but I'm dubious. There was nothing on the stairs when I came up. Easing away from her, I get to my feet. 'Stay here. I'll go and check.'

Emelia catches my hand. 'You won't leave, will you?' she asks urgently.

'I'll be just a minute.' Giving her a reassuring smile, I

squeeze her hand and head back to the landing. I'm not sure what it is I'm going to look for. Her fear is real, palpable, but I can't help thinking she might be imagining it all. Whether the shock of Tom leaving combined with the amount of alcohol she's consuming is causing her to have some kind of hallucination. But someone came into *my* house, I remind myself, with the sole purpose of terrifying me. Had that same person gained access to Jodie's house too? Had she been so terrified she'd fled blindly into the night and fallen to her death?

My heart jars as I think of her. But why would anyone do this? Someone was clearly targeting us, the female members of our group. It could only be Richie or Tom, but Emelia would have recognised Tom, surely? Fear crystallises inside me as I recall the black hoodie.

With my mind a whirl of confusion, I don't notice it at first. When I do, I feel my world tilt violently. The photograph pinned to the crossbeam over the stairs – a group photograph, Pippa sitting in lonely isolation, Richie gazing right at her – is the same one that was left at my house.

Drawing in a breath, I descend the stairs and lift a trembling hand towards it. What's truly frightening, what had obviously petrified Emelia, is that her face has been viciously scratched out. As has Jodie's.

TWENTY-SEVEN

'Jesus.' Jack stares at the photograph, shocked. 'You need to involve the police, Becky. I don't think you have any choice but to now. This is clearly a threat.'

'No.' Emelia appears at the top of the stairs. 'We can't,' she says, looking pleadingly between Jack and me. 'It won't do anyone any good now. It's history.'

'Clearly not for someone,' Jack points out, his forehead creased in consternation as he studies the photo again. 'Who took this?' he asks.

'A passer-by,' I provide. 'We wanted a group photograph.'

'And the camera? It belonged to one of you, presumably?'

'Pippa,' I murmur, my heart twisting as I think of that day and how long Pippa had left to live after the photograph was taken.

Jack nods. 'The girl who died,' he says, the furrow in his brow deepening. 'Do you know whether her personal effects were returned to her family?'

'I suppose they must have been.' I try to recollect. 'The police held on to her phone to check her recent calls, but I think everything would have been returned eventually.' I stop as I

remember Pippa's mother, how distraught she'd been at her
funeral, so broken she could barely walk without support.

'But the film was developed,' Jack points out. 'Did someone
in your group go into town with it?'

'We were only there one night,' Emelia says, her face ashen
as she descends the stairs. 'No one left the party.'

'Apart from Pippa,' I add, my throat closing.

Jack gives me a small smile, as if attempting to reassure me. I
dread to imagine what he's really thinking. Of me. Of all of us.
'So it was definitely developed after she died,' he says, drawing
the same conclusion as me, 'but we've no idea who by and no
way of finding out without approaching the family.'

'We can't do that, though, Jack. Not after all this time.' I
frown uncertainly. Assuming we could find her, her mother's
unlikely to remember any of us. Why would she when we made
no effort to be friends to Pippa? It would be like a random
stranger turning up to ask questions about her long dead daughter. No, we can't. It would be far too insensitive and distressing.

'We don't even know who they are, anyway,' Emelia adds.
She's still visibly upset, but I notice the relief sweeping her
features. She clearly doesn't want to pursue that avenue any
more than I do.

'Do you have a surname?' Jack asks.

'No.' Emelia drops her gaze. 'I didn't know her that well.'

'Moore,' I supply.

'Might be worth searching online,' Jack ponders, glancing
back at the photo.

'I think it will just open old wounds for them,' Emelia says,
a hint of panic in her eyes as she glances at me. I guess she's
thinking along the same lines I am, that it must have been Tom
or Richie who'd developed that film. She and I need to talk,
honestly, without laying blame. I realise I've been doing that.
That my *going on* about it, to quote Richie, might have
prompted whoever it is doing this into trying to silence me. I so

wish I could remember whether the camera was taken by the police along with the other items in her tent. They'd dropped one of her flip-flops, I remember that distinctly, the way it had lain on the beach looking as lonely as Pippa had when we'd found her. Almost at the point of giving up, we'd been walking along the beach once the tide receded, heading to the next cove. The image of her lying there all alone will be ingrained indelibly on my mind for the rest of my days.

'You're probably right,' Jack concedes. 'You really should think about reporting it, though.'

Emelia glances warily at me again, and then away as her phone rings. 'I should get that,' she says, hurrying to the lounge where she's presumably left it.

As she disappears through the door, Jack looks at me, his expression perturbed. 'You're on your own in that house, Becky. You're pregnant,' he says, worried, clearly. 'I know in normal circumstances it wouldn't necessarily make you vulnerable, but I think in this instance it does.'

My hand goes involuntarily to my bump.

'I know you lost your mother, but do you have any other family you can stay with? A sister? Your father possibly?' he asks.

I shake my head. 'I was an only child. I never knew my father.'

'I'm sorry.' He looks a little awkward. 'Look, it's just an idea, but we have a small apartment adjoining the house. It's sitting empty at the moment. You're welcome to use it, if only until you know how the land lies with your husband.'

I'm taken aback.

Jack obviously notices my surprise. 'Think about it,' he says. 'The offer's there if you need it.'

'Thank you.' I smile, appreciating his generosity. 'I'm not going to let anyone scare me out of my house, though,' I say, sounding braver than I feel.

'I get that.' He gives me a small smile back. 'Is it possible you and Emelia would be able to house share for a while instead?' he asks. 'I realise it might be a bit awkward but at least you would both be able to look out for each other.'

I think about it. It's an idea. Emelia certainly needs someone to look out for her right now. I debate whether to mention it to her, but I'm not sure the two of us together under one roof is really possible given all that's happened. I can see that Jack is really concerned, though, and that frightens me.

'That was Tom,' Emelia says, returning from the lounge looking flustered. 'He's on his way home. I told him about the photograph and explained about the back door. He said he would be right over. He's leaving the children with his mother for a while. He thinks we need to talk. He didn't sound angry, though. Do you think that's a good sign?' She glances hopefully at me.

'Possibly.' I actually don't think his leaving the children is a good sign, but she's so emotionally fragile, I daren't say so.

'I should shower. Do something with myself.' She pivots around to the stairs.

'Do you want me to stay?' I ask behind her.

'Oh.' Emelia turns back, looks from me to Jack as if she's almost forgotten he was there. 'No. I'll be okay now I know Tom's coming. Thanks, Becky,' she smiles tremulously, 'for everything.'

'No problem.' I manage a smile back.

She hesitates and then moves to lock her arms around me. 'I'm sorry,' she blurts into my shoulder, 'for what happened. I didn't mean it to. I would never have...' she falters. 'If Richie hadn't...'

'Hadn't what?' I ask, my heart faltering as she loosens her hold and steps back.

'Nothing.' Emelia's gaze hits the floor – and I guess she meant *if Richie hadn't initiated things*. 'I should go. Tom will be here soon.' Clutching the neck of her dressing gown tightly to her, she spins around again and hurries up the stairs.

Jack's expression is a mixture of sympathetic and embarrassed as I look at him. 'I have some time if you fancy a chat over coffee,' he offers.

'No. Thanks.' Tears threatening, I drop my gaze. He'd gleaned Emelia's implication too. *Had* Richie made a move on her? I'm not sure I can believe that. But then, I would never have believed he would turn on me the way he had either. 'I still have my client to see,' I explain. 'I can't just not bother. He's vulnerable.'

Jack nods, understanding, and walks with me to the door. 'Just promise me that once you're home you'll lock up securely,' he says, pulling the door open. 'And keep your phone close. Call me if you need to.'

'Thank you.' I smile, grateful – for him coming here, for being a friend when I needed one.

'Oh. You might want to take this with you.' He hands me the photograph once we're outside. 'I'm not sure it will be any good for DNA purposes now we've all handled it, but should the police need it...'

Trepidation clenching my tummy, I look from the photograph to his face. 'You think Richie's responsible for what happened, don't you?'

'I can't know, Becky. I wasn't there, but...' Jack scans my eyes, his expression uneasy, then glances back to the house. 'After what you told me about suspecting someone from your group might have been involved with Pippa, I wonder, is it possible that Tom might have been fooling around back then?'

I avert my gaze. I know he's intuitive by nature of what he does, but it seems he can read my mind.

'I might be way off the mark,' he goes on, 'but I can't help wondering whether Emelia might have known and been jealous?'

I look uncomfortably back at him. 'Do you mean you think Emelia might have had something to do with what happened to Pippa?' I'm asking him to spell it out, but it's obvious that he does.

Jack pauses before answering. 'As I say, I can't know, but it would appear that jealousy is an emotion she struggles with, hence her, shall we say, encouraging your husband.'

'But if she were trying to make Tom jealous, why choose Richie?' I ask, still unable to believe it, though I'd had those very same thoughts myself.

'Because there's some resentment of what you appear to have with Richie perhaps?' He studies me carefully. 'I'm speculating and I shouldn't be, but jealousy is one of the prime motives for murder, Becky. I can't help but be concerned for you. Extremely.'

TWENTY-EIGHT

EMELIA

Emelia almost jumped out of her skin as Tom came quietly into the kitchen from the hall. She hadn't heard him come in. 'What the bloody hell's been going on?' he asked, looking from the damage to the back door to her in shocked disbelief.

'Someone's been in the house,' Emelia answered warily. 'I told you.'

Tom glanced at the door again and then back to her. 'Are you all right?' he asked, his expression concerned. Emelia felt a rush of relief. When he noticed the glass she was holding though, his look soon changed to one of weary despair.

'It's orange juice,' she blurted as he dragged his gaze away. 'Just orange juice.'

'If you say so.' A scowl crossed his face. He clearly thought she was lying.

'Do you want a coffee?' Emelia moved across the kitchen to switch the kettle on, taking the opportunity to tip her 'orange juice' down the sink and swill the glass while she did. She'd needed a drink, badly. She'd told herself it was medicinal, and it was. She knew she would have had one anyway, though, even if it were a perfectly normal day. So did Tom. She had to stop.

With or without him, what kind of future would she have if she didn't? What kind of future would her children have? Reminded that that was probably precisely Tom's thinking, why he'd taken them away, she realised she needed to do something about it now, not sometime never.

'No. Thanks,' Tom declined. 'I've not long had one at my mother's. So are you going to enlighten me as to why the back door has been kicked in and, more specifically, who by?'

'Becky,' Emelia said quickly, not wanting him to think some madman had broken in and call the police, though, in actual fact, there had been a madman in the house. 'I called her. She was concerned about me. She rang me back and then she came over with that man from the funeral, the psychologist Jodie was seeing.'

'Right.' Tom sighed. 'Was she hinting you need his services? Or is she seeing him? She certainly needs to, harping on about the past as if we're all guilty of some big bloody conspiracy.'

'No.' Emelia could hear the agitation in his tone and, whilst she could understand he might be annoyed, she didn't much like it, particularly as he hadn't asked why they would have felt the need to break into the house. 'That's not why she came. She's my friend. She was worried about me,' she informed him, feeling defensive of Becky after all she had done for her. Also wondering whether Tom cared enough to be worried about her. Whether he ever had.

'Right.' Tom looked dubious. 'This would be the same friend who was majorly pissed off with you for hitting on her husband?'

Tears sprang to Emelia's eyes. 'Tom, don't,' she murmured, dropping her gaze. 'I was drunk. I didn't know what I was doing.'

He dragged in a sharp breath. 'No, but Richie wasn't drunk, was he? He knew *exactly* what he was doing.'

Emelia jerked her head up. Was he blaming Richie instead

of her? Did that mean there was hope for them? 'I don't know,' she murmured. 'I don't really remember very much.'

She felt bad immediately, as the words left her mouth. What she'd done had obviously caused massive problems between Becky and Richie – and Emelia was desperately sorry for that. That Becky had been there for her when she'd needed her had put her to shame – but she and Richie were a strong couple. Richie obviously cared for Becky a great deal. He would soon convince her she had no competition. She didn't. He'd always been dependable, attentive to Becky's every need. Feeling a pang of jealousy as she considered the sorry state of her own marriage, Emelia quickly quashed it. Could she not just stop being a completely self-centred bitch? 'Are you not even curious as to why she came over? Why she would have felt the need to ask Jack to come with her and break the door down?'

Tom gave her *that* look, and her heart sank. He obviously thought it was something to do with her drinking. 'Fine,' she said, heading for the hall before the tears that were dangerously close to the surface spilled over. She didn't want his sympathy, not that she supposed she would get it. She wanted his love.

'Emelia, wait.' Tom stopped her, catching her arm. 'Of course I want to know.' Kneading his forehead, he sighed wearily. 'So? What happened?'

'I said, someone came into the house.'

She noted the concern was back in his eyes and was grateful for that much. 'What? Actually in the house?'

She nodded. 'I saw him looking through the hall window and I ran upstairs. I thought my phone was up there. But then I remembered I'd left it in the lounge. I was coming back down and—' She stopped, a sob catching in her throat as she recalled reaching the top of the stairs to see the man standing halfway up them. She'd frozen. He hadn't moved a muscle. He'd simply stared at her, his hands in his hoodie pockets, his eyes over his mask ice-cold and unflinching. Her chest had banged so hard she'd felt she might have a heart attack. She was sure he would spring into action if she so much as breathed. That he would bound up after her if she tried to flee, hurt her, possibly kill her.

Panic and nausea clawing at her windpipe, she stayed frozen to the spot as he silently watched her in some nightmarish standoff. When he moved, causing her heart to stop beating, it wasn't to proceed up the stairs, but to turn and go back the way he came. Treading quietly down the stairs, he'd let himself out through the front door without uttering a word. That, in a way, had been the most petrifying thing of all, his complete calmness, until she saw the photograph.

'Christ.' Tom's face drained of colour. 'Did he hurt you?'

Wrapping her arms around herself, Emelia shook her head. For a second, thinking it might jolt him into realising he might have lost her, she'd been tempted to say he had, but she couldn't lie about that.

'Are you sure?' He moved towards her.

Emelia answered with a small nod.

Tom hesitated, scanning her eyes carefully as she looked tearfully at him, and then circled his arms around her. Emelia stiffened for a second, and then relief crashing through her, she melted into him. She couldn't lose him. She *wouldn't*. She loved him. She could forgive him his womanising, whatever he'd done, if only he could learn to love her again, as he once had, when they'd first met.

'I'm sorry, Em,' he said throatily. 'I must have left the back door unlocked when I went out to the bins this morning. *Idiot*,' cursing himself, he held her closer.

Emelia nodded. She'd locked it after the intruder had gone, but she couldn't blame Tom. She left the door open when she was home. It had never occurred to her not to.

'Did he take anything?' he asked.

She shook her head, wishing she could stay like this forever, safe in his embrace. Had she ever felt that, though? Truly?

Hadn't she always wondered who else had been in his arms? 'He left something,' she answered, her throat dry from too much alcohol and too many tears cried.

Tom eased away a little. 'Left something?' He searched her face in confusion. She wished he wouldn't study her so closely. She was a mess. She knew it. No amount of tweaking or elixirs promising younger, firmer skin could disguise it.

'Unless you left it?' she asked him, because she had to. She had so many doubts clouding her view of him. More lately, because of Becky's insistence on digging up ghosts that would be far better left buried.

'Me?' Furrowing his brow quizzically, Tom pulled away from her. 'I haven't been back since you threatened to ruin me. What are you talking about exactly?'

Emelia took a breath. 'A photograph,' she said carefully. 'A group photograph.'

Tom's frown deepened, and then he shook his head, smiling scornfully. 'Don't tell me. The beach party. This is bloody Becky's doing,' he grated angrily.

'No,' Emelia said forcefully. 'It's nothing to do with Becky. It was there before she arrived. And, anyway, she wouldn't have done the awful thing that truly terrified me.'

Tom's look was wary. 'What awful thing?'

Emelia faltered. 'My face was scratched out. Viciously. Jodie's too.'

Tom stared at her in disbelief. 'And you thought I would do something like that?'

'No,' Emelia backtracked. 'I don't know.' She looked away.

'Why would I?' Tom's tone was incredulous.

'To scare me,' Emelia murmured. 'Punish me maybe?' She looked cautiously back at him.

'Punish you?' Tom frowned, confounded. 'For what?'

Emelia hesitated. 'Because you don't like me.'

'What?' Tom's look was now one of complete astonishment.

'I feel like you hate me,' Emelia added, her voice small. She wasn't lying. She could see it in his eyes sometimes, nothing but disdain, and it hurt. So much.

'I don't *hate* you. Why on earth would you...' Trailing off, Tom dragged a hand over the back of his neck. 'I don't believe this. I really don't. That you would automatically think that I... Christ, we really are fucked up, aren't we?'

'Tom...' Seeing his hurt and bewilderment, Emelia wanted to reel the words back in. 'I didn't automatically think it was you. It's just that it has to be one of our group and—'

'It's that prick Richie who needs punishing, taking advantage of you when you were clearly drunk,' Tom growled over her. 'And he will be, trust me.'

TWENTY-NINE

Emelia stayed where she was as Tom strode off. *Well done.* She congratulated herself on driving another wedge between them, probably the fatal wedge, then wiped the tears from her face and went after him.

She found him in the bedroom, his hands shoved in his pockets, his back to her as he stared out of the window.

Hearing her go in, he glanced towards her, then fixed his gaze back on the window. 'Where is it?' he asked. 'This photograph I'm supposed to have defaced, because I'm obviously such a nasty bastard I would do something like that?'

Emelia tentatively approached him. 'I don't think you're that, Tom,' she said quietly.

Tom shrugged. 'No, you just think I hate you.'

Emelia had no idea what to say. There was nothing she could say that could fix anything. Why did she never think before opening her mouth?

Tom drew in a breath, blew it out slowly. Then turned to face her. 'I don't hate you, Em. I despair of you, but I don't hate you. I don't understand why you would think that.'

Perhaps it would help if you didn't cheat on me, Emelia

wanted to say, but didn't. She'd had plenty of evidence he flirted but no actual evidence he'd cheated, apart from the once. Finding those condoms years back had crushed her. Watching him flirting, simpering women being flattered by the attention, hurt. So badly. She didn't see how he could do it unless he wanted to hurt her. 'Because of the way you look at me,' she said instead. 'It's certainly not how you look at other women.'

Tom closed his eyes. 'I'm sorry,' he said quietly. 'I don't mean to. It's just... I get angry, Em. What you see is frustration, not hatred or anything like. If I hate anybody, it's myself for making you so miserable, which you clearly are, or you wouldn't drink so much.'

Emelia was taken aback. He'd never said anything that hinted remotely that he cared about the impact his behaviour had on her before, walking away if she raised the subject.

'You have to stop, Em.' He looked at her beseechingly. 'It's affecting everything. Our life together. The kids' lives. To say little of what it will do to your health.'

'I know,' she conceded, contrite. She'd wondered for a moment if he was shifting blame, but the tortured look in his eyes told her he wasn't. 'I will. I've decided to get some help.'

'Promise?' he asked, his look cautious.

'Promise.' She nodded. 'Will you come home?' she asked hopefully. She missed him, his presence if not his attention, which she hadn't had much of. She missed Josh and Charlotte with every part of herself. She would do better. She would be a better mother to her children than hers were. She made that promise to herself.

Tom glanced down and back. Noting his hesitant expression, Emelia felt her heart miss a beat. 'Would you have gone through with it?' he asked, after a second. 'With Richie, if Becky hadn't walked in on you, which I'm assuming is what happened?'

Emelia probably would have in a pathetic attempt to claw

back some of her self-esteem, but she thought better of telling him that. 'I don't know. I was drunk, upset. Honestly, though,' she took a breath, 'I did think that if you knew other men fancied me then you might.'

Tom's look was back to one of astonishment. 'I do fancy you. Of course I bloody well do.'

'And other women?' she asked. 'Do you fancy them, Tom?'

He sighed heavily. 'Okay, yes, I look. I might fancy some of them. It doesn't mean I do anything about it.'

She looked him over, surprised at his apparent honesty, but also suspicious. He must see she would struggle to believe that. 'And Pippa?' she asked him. 'Did you fancy her?'

'Jesus, not you as well?' Tom was back to irate in a flash. 'What is this obsession with Pippa? She's dead, for pity's sake. Will no one let her rest?' He eyed her with a mixture of incredulity and fury. '*No*. I did not fancy her. That was Richie. In fact, this is all on can-do-no-wrong Richie. It's an act! He's not Mr Perfect. Far from it. If anyone was with Pippa that night, it was *him*.'

THIRTY

BECKY

When I learned that my client had been contemplating suicide, I'd felt a jolt of shock right through me. 'I thought about ending my life this morning,' he'd said, quite calmly, stopping me in my tracks as I'd chatted away while setting up the video equipment. When I'd gently pointed out that he'd just spoken clearly and concisely, for the first time since his accident, he'd looked at me surprised, and then so relieved I could have cried for him.

As I leave him looking more optimistic about his future and climb into my car, I make my decision. I can't go back, put right what I did wrong, but I believe I can make amends and do some good with my life. I also believe, though, that I have to face the past to have any kind of future. Pippa's family deserve the truth, however uncomfortable it will be for me. For Emelia. However catastrophic it might be for Richie or for Tom. I have to go to the police.

I decide I should contact Richie first. I have to prepare him for the fact the police will want to speak to him. I'm about to call him when I realise he's called me. As I listen to his message, my heart lurches. '*I came by the house earlier but you weren't there,*' he says, his voice dejected. '*I noted you'd taken your work stuff so I'm assuming you're okay. I'm struggling, to be honest, after all you've accused me of. I was thinking, maybe we should give ourselves some space while we decide where we go from here. Call me if you get this, will you? Assuming you want to.'*

I can't believe it. He's really doing it, isn't he? Making this my fault. Is he trying to guilt me into apologising and asking him to come back, or is he conjuring all this up because he doesn't want to come back? I stare stunned at my phone for a second, and then, feeling jaded to my bones, I swipe the tears from my face and head home.

Once I've changed out of my work clothes, I drop wearily onto the bed and brace myself to do what I have to. The others might have tried to ignore the aftermath of Pippa's death, but I can't. And there had been an aftermath. Jodie is proof of that. Should I phone, or go to the station in person? In person, I decide. Face to face I'll be better able to judge their reaction. Fetching my phone from my bag, I hesitate, then decide I will call Richie back since he's put the ball in my court. I'll let him know what I'm going to do and tell him if he wants space, then he has it. I won't argue with him. I simply don't have the energy. His phone goes straight to voicemail. I try again five minutes later. Again, it goes to voicemail and I glean he actually doesn't want to speak to me, which speaks volumes.

My heart sinking, I swallow back the stone in my throat and try his office number. There's no answer. So where is he? A mixture of hurt and anger twists painfully inside me. I can't believe that in such a short space of time my life is unravelling. That the man I've loved and who I thought was dependable and caring is apparently ready to abandon our marriage while I'm carrying his child. I feel numb, so devastated and lonely. I have no idea how I will find the strength to get through this. My hand goes instinctively to reassure my baby. *I will, sweet pea. I will find the strength I need for both of us.* Squeezing back the tears I don't want to cry, because if I do, I feel I will crumble, I drop my phone back in my bag, then start as the front door bell rings. Curiously I go to the window, wondering who it can be. It can't be Richie. He would have his key. My heart almost stops beating when I look out to realise the police appear to have come to me.

Trepidation travels the length of my spine. Why are they here? And why a plain clothes officer, which the woman appears to be? I hurry to the landing and head quickly down the stairs. My hands are shaking as I reach to open the front door. 'Can I help you?' I ask, dread pooling in the pit of my stomach as my mind races through all sorts of terrifying scenarios.

The plain-clothed officer produces her identification. 'I'm Detective Inspector Megan Simons,' she says, 'and this is PC Dev Nayyar. Could we confirm that you are Rebecca Shaw and that your husband is Richard Shaw?'

'Yes. Why?' An icy dagger of foreboding piercing my chest, I scan the officers' faces for some indication of why they're here.

'Do you mind if we come inside?' Detective Simons nods past me to the hall.

I move back, every sinew in my body tensing as they step in and turn to face me.

'Is your husband at home, Mrs Shaw?' Simons asks.

'No.' I shake my head. 'No, he's not. He hasn't been back since... Could you please just tell me what on earth is going on?'

The two officers exchange wary glances. 'There's been a fire,' she answers. 'At your husband's business premises. Sadly, there's also been a fatality.'

THIRTY-ONE

I stare at her, frozen with incomprehension. And then it hits me, and I feel as if the air has been sucked from my lungs. 'Richie?' I squeeze the word out.

'We don't have a formal identification yet,' Detective Simons addresses me kindly.

It's not him. I place a hand over my tummy, as if to somehow shield my baby. *Please don't let it be him.*

'Would you like to sit down, Mrs Shaw?' she asks as I feel the floor tilt dangerously beneath me, the walls in the small confines of the hall close in on me. 'Go and grab some water, Dev.' Nodding towards the kitchen, she moves quickly as I grope for the hall table.

Helping me down onto the sofa a minute later, she takes the glass of water the male officer has returned with and offers it to me. 'Slow sips,' she says, her brow creased in concern.

I take it, press it shakily to my lips, but I can't drink from it.

'We wondered if you might have a recent photograph of your husband, Mrs Shaw?' she asks, as PC Nayyar retrieves the glass from me.

My heart beating wildly, I search her face. I'm hearing the words but they're not making sense to me.

'For preliminary identification purposes,' she adds, her expression somewhere between apologetic and sympathetic.

Understanding, I nod. 'My phone. It's upstairs,' I whisper, trying desperately to oust the graphic images playing through my mind, Richie trapped, terrified and choking.

'Do you mind if PC Nayyar fetches it?' the woman asks, placing a hand on my arm as I attempt to make my limbs function and stand. 'You're obviously in shock. It might be better to stay seated.'

I want to say I'm fine, but I'm not. I feel as if my world is crumbling. Everything Richie and I had together turning to dust. How can this be happening? My heart folds up inside me. My baby needs his daddy. *I* need him. I search the woman's face in bewildered disbelief, to see her looking at me questioningly.

'The phone,' she reminds me gently.

I close my eyes, swallowing back the nausea rising hotly inside me. 'In my bag.' I murmur. 'On my bed. First room on the right.'

'How far along are you?' Simons asks, as PC Nayyar heads out.

She's making conversation. An almost hysterical laugh bubbles up inside me. A tear escapes me. 'Almost thirty weeks,' I answer, my voice a dry croak. I can't do this. I don't think I can bear it.

'Would you like us to call anyone?' she asks softly. 'Someone who could be with you?'

To help me through this, she means. I shake my head. 'I don't have anyone.'

My thoughts swing to Emelia, the impossibility of turning to her, then to Jodie and, though I will it not to, my mind pictures her, her body lying bruised and broken at the foot of the cliff, her head smashed like an egg shell. Someone had done that to her. She hadn't jumped of her own volition. Someone had pursued her, possibly even have pushed her. I *know* it. Nausea swells so suddenly inside me, I struggle to hold it back.

As Nayyar hurries back in and offers me my phone, I take it tremblingly from him, press my thumb to the lock screen and go to my photos. The first one that pops up is of Richie and me together. He's standing behind me, a proud grin on his face and his hands crossed over my tummy. I'd been going to post it on Instagram, but Richie's such a private person, not big into social media. *Was?* My heart stalls. *Please God, don't let it be him.*

Cautiously, I hand the phone to Detective Simons, attempt to draw air into my lungs as she studies it, a deep furrow forming in her brow. 'It's not him,' she confirms after an agonising eternity, and my chest almost explodes with relief.

'I'm sorry we had to put you through this.' Looking uncomfortably back to me, she hands me the phone. 'The landlord informed us your husband was renting the property, so... I'm really sorry, Mrs Shaw. The deceased fits the description and we weren't aware of anyone else working from the premises.'

'Paul,' I whisper, guessing it must be Richie's assistant working late with the financial year end looming. Like Richie, he's dark and tall. 'Paul Holmes. He's married, has three children,' I murmur, then swallow hard, my heart splintering as I feel the unbearable pain his wife will have to go through, his innocent children. The oldest is only six. 'What happened? How did the fire start?' I ask, but I know.

This was no accident either. Fear pierces my heart like an icicle as I think of all that's happened recently, Jodie's supposed suicide, the seashells with sharp, jagged edges strewn across my floor, old photographs with scratched out faces, left deliberately and terrifyingly, as a reminder of Pippa's death. They'd been a warning. One we should have heeded.

'We can't be sure until the fire investigation officer and forensics specialists have been in,' Detective Simons answers.

'But you don't think it was an accident?' My gaze swivels between them. I note the cautious glance they exchange and a mixture of terror and anger unfurls inside me.

'As I said, we can't be sure until the scene has been thoroughly examined and any evidence gathered,' Detective Simons repeats. Looking me over guardedly, she draws a breath. 'Are you able to tell us whether your husband had any financial problems, Mrs Shaw. Business or personal?'

It takes me a moment to gather her implication. When I do, I stare at her, staggered. She thinks Richie started the fire. For *insurance* purposes? *No*. She's wrong. We struggle to stretch the monthly budget sometimes, as a lot of people do nowadays with the soaring cost of living, but we have no real financial problems. None that I'm aware of anyway. Unless he hasn't been being honest with me? That thought lands heavily, because he hasn't been honest with me, has he? About the way he feels, the fact that he clearly wants out of our marriage. Why else would he not answer my calls? If he hadn't deliberately started the fire, though, then this was a warning aimed at him. Unless, it's more than that this time, and the person responsible for all of this had actually been aiming to kill him. But *why*? Because he knew something and my digging it all up had made whoever it was take drastic action to silence him? A turmoil of emotions churn inside me – shock, confusion, bewilderment. Might it be a ploy? If Richie is seen to be a target, then he can't be guilty of anything, can he? No. It's unfeasible. I'd seen a side to him I didn't know, but he could never be capable of all of this.

I should tell them. Everything. Should I talk to Emelia first? My head whirls. Ask her more about the intruder? Richie's hoodie had the Adidas insignia on the front of it. It's possible she might recall it. Where was Tom? My mind races, my heart racing faster as my thoughts swing to him. He and Emelia had argued. About Richie. Tom had always been vexed by Emelia constantly comparing him to Richie, hence his comment at the funeral about his having a lot to live up to. If he'd been convinced there was something going on between Richie and Emelia... I remember what Jack had said about jealousy being one of the prime motives for murder and my blood runs cold. Where had Tom been when the fire started? Where was he now?

THIRTY-TWO

Once the officers have gone, leaving me reeling, I call Richie's number. I keep calling, send him several texts. He doesn't call me back, doesn't reply to my texts, and I feel as if a part of me has died inside. Where is he? Does he know about the fire? If he does, he'll be devastated. He can't be responsible. He's just not capable. I can't make myself believe he would do something so blatantly criminal as part of some insurance scam. He would have known Paul was there, working late. I'm growing sure it was Tom in a fit of jealous rage. I've always thought he must have a massive ego to flirt so openly with women, as if he never considered the possibility he might be resistible. It would have been badly dented, thinking Richie was having an affair with Emelia. She'd said Tom was on his way home before Jack and I left. Had he arrived there? Might he have gone out again? I have no way of knowing unless I speak to Emelia, and I have to know. If he's there now, if he's been with her all evening then it discounts him. I still don't know whether she and Richie are having an affair. I'd been so angry that night, so distraught after Jodie's funeral. My reaction to finding them the way I had was

extreme, I know it was. I'd jumped to the first obvious conclusion. Now, I'm filled with confusion. Is it really possible that
everything I know Richie to be is a lie? *Had* he been involved
with Pippa? A cold chill ripples through me as I recall the group
photograph, the way he'd been staring at her and she at him. It
might just be that the camera caught him looking across to her,
but still this gut feeling that gnaws away inside me won't let go.

My head swims, thoughts rushing pell-mell through my
mind and I can't make sense of anything. Part of me doubts him,
but still I'm clinging to the hope that he will walk through the
front door and somehow make everything all right.

I have to call Emelia. I have to find out what Tom's movements were this evening. I'm still furious with her for what she's
done, but I'm also frightened for her. Drinking so much, she's
clearly emotionally vulnerable, psychologically manipulable, as
Jodie was when Kelly and she split. As I was when Richie
stormed out. Might Emelia be the next target?

Squeezing back the tears I daren't cry for fear they won't
stop, I call her number. I'm about to hang up when she picks up.
'Becky?' She sounds wary. I guess why when I glance at the
clock and realise how late it is. 'Are you all right?'

No. I want to scream. *I don't think I'll ever be all right
again. And would you have to wonder why?* 'Reasonable,' I lie.

'Is everything okay with you and Richie?' she asks guiltily.
She's not slurring her words, I realise, and wonder whether all
that's happened might have been a wake-up call for her to stop
drinking so much before she ruins not just her own life but
other people's.

'As well as can be expected,' I reply, not wanting to go there.
'How about you? Did Tom come back?' I don't tell her about the
fire. If I do, I can hardly ask her where Tom was without
alerting her.

'He did,' she confirms, her voice tinged with relief – and I want to be pleased for her, but I just can't be. 'Things are precarious,' she goes on. 'We have a lot of talking to do. I'm not entirely sure things will work out, but he fetched Josh and Charlotte from his mother's this evening so there's hope, at least.'

Which means he *had* been out. How long had he been gone? I'm wondering how to ask when Emelia goes on, 'He had to help his mum move some furniture around in the bedroom, she struggles a bit since his dad had his heart attack, so they've not long got back. The children are fast asleep now and they seem okay. I've decided to get some counselling organised, though, so—'

'Emelia,' I talk over her. 'The man who was in your house, are you sure you didn't recognise him?'

Emelia goes quiet – and apprehension tightens like a slip knot inside me. 'I'd been drinking,' she admits eventually. 'But there wasn't that much of him to recognise in any case. He had a hoodie on and a mask over his face.'

'Right, of course. You didn't see any logo on the hoodie?' I ask. 'It's the sort of thing the police would find helpful.' I hold my breath and wait.

'Tom didn't think it was a good idea to report it,' she says, at length. 'He's getting a security camera and an alarm installed, but as there was no actual break in before you arrived... Plus, he thinks it will just dig up the past, which means dragging us all into it, Sophie and Dylan, too, most likely.'

There was an intruder in the house while his wife was alone and Tom doesn't want to report it? I can't believe that. I was right. Emelia is manipulable, certainly by Tom, whose attention she craves.

'As long as you're okay,' I say, my throat tight. 'I should go. I think I need my bed. I'm exhausted.'

'You must be,' she replies quietly.

'Bye,' I say simply, unable to bring myself to say *I'll call you* or *Speak soon.*

'Becky,' she says urgently as I go to end the call. 'I am sorry. Truly.'

I hesitate. 'I can't talk about that right now, Emelia. It's too raw,' I tell her honestly.

Once Emelia has gone with a plaintive goodbye, I make sure the house is locked up tight, then sit at the kitchen table and go to Jodie's Facebook page. I'm not sure why. I'm only going to be torturing myself, but I feel a need to connect with her, to remember her as she was. Emelia had been right about her to a degree, she was always fighting for some cause, strident in her campaigns to fight injustice. She wasn't the kind of person to give up easily. It struck me that that's what she'd done, and, no matter how hard I tried to accept it, it didn't feel right. It just wasn't her.

She hadn't posted much in the weeks leading up to her death. I notice she hadn't changed her profile and header photo. It's still one of Kelly and her together, Kelly's children between them, all beaming at the camera. They were a family. There was no doubt of that in my mind. They'd been going to get back together. Get married. Why would Jodie have ended her life when she'd been looking forward to the future? It didn't make sense.

My heart heavy, I scroll a little further down. When I come across her last post, my blood freezes. It's an old photograph, taken outside the university campus, and I immediately recognise the fresh face of the woman Jodie was with back then. *You were my friend, my inspiration, a beautiful chapter in my life, Zoe.* Jodie had commented below it. *I can't believe your shining light has been so cruelly snubbed out. RIP, my darling.*

I stop breathing, unable to comprehend for a second. When I do, I feel as if someone has punched me. Zoe is *dead? How? When?* My head a whirl of sick confusion, I scroll further down and find a previous post with a photograph of Zoe clearly taken a short while ago. She looks healthy, happy, cheek to cheek with a gorgeous little pug dog she clearly adored. I read Jodie's comment underneath and my heart stops dead: *Taken from life by a hit-and-run driver too cowardly to come forward. Whoever you are, I hope you spend eternity in purgatory.*

THIRTY-THREE

Nausea roils like acid inside me as the thought crashes into my head that Zoe's death might not have been an accident but deliberate. But who would do something like this? In God's name, *why*? What could it achieve? My hands trembling, I go to Richie's number, desperate to talk to him, the man I thought I would spend the rest of my life with. My thumb hovers, but I don't call him. What's the point? He suggested we *give ourselves some space.* He asked me to call him but he's not answering my calls, not calling me back, which sends me a clear message: He doesn't want to spend the rest of his life with me. What did his innocent child do to deserve this, though? How could he be so cold and uncaring, so different to the man I thought I'd married? Might he have been involved in this? That thought creeps into my mind too, and I try hard to oust it. It's simply not possible. Richie isn't capable. He's just not. But why not? Plenty of women thought they knew the man they were with only to realise they never did.

Pulling myself from my chair, I go to the sink for water, the glass clinking against my teeth as I try to drink. Unsure what to do, I go back to my phone, dearly wishing it was earlier so I could call Jack. He said to call him anytime. As desperate as I am to talk to him, though, someone I feel I can trust and who might convince me I'm not going out of my mind, I can't call him now.

An avalanche of emotions crashes through me, deep, visceral fury and fear. Fear for Emelia. For myself. I should have spoken to the police. Why the *hell* hadn't I? Blinded by impotent tears, I blink hard and, uncertain what to do, where to go, head for the lounge. There's little point in going upstairs. I'm so exhausted, I feel I could sleep for a week, but I daren't close my eyes for fear of what I might see. Shutting the lounge door behind me to conserve heat, I turn the gas fire on low, collect up the throw I keep on the armchair and curl up under it. I'm so cold. I don't feel as if I'll ever be warm again.

I'll go to the police station first thing tomorrow. I have to. Once my mind is made up, I send Jack a short text.

Sorry to bother you so late. No need to reply. Could you call me back in the morning? Thanks. Becks.

He's unlikely to see it until morning anyway, but my hope is he will ring as soon as he does. I really need his calm perspective. Guilt over all that's happened, the part I might have played in Jodie's death, in Zoe's and Paul's by not speaking the truth years ago weighs so heavily in my chest I feel it will burst. Richie had been in despair of my dredging up the past, accusing me of being paranoid. Emelia and he both had told me to let it go, but I couldn't. *Was* this all my fault? Was someone so desperate for the investigation into Pippa's death not to be reopened they would kill to stop that happening?

Would the police even take anything I said seriously? Recalling the apathy of the original investigating officer, I wonder. Tired now to my bones, I lean my head back and allow the tears to come. How terrified must Paul have been as the fire closed in on him? How desperate must his last thoughts have been? I squeeze my eyes closed, but still I can't banish the images that scorch themselves on my mind. I can almost hear it, fire crackling, flames curling like hungry tongues around the balustrades of the stairs that lead up to the office.

I hadn't realised I'd fallen asleep until I wake with a sharp cough. I snap my eyes open, fear gripping my chest like a vice as I realise the crackling is here, right outside the lounge door. *No!* It can't be. I jump to my feet. I'm dreaming. Imagining it. I have to be. Stumbling towards the door, I stop dead. Something *is* burning. I can smell it. Pungent. Choking. Unmistakable. My heart banging, I back away from the door, where the air is suddenly too thick to breathe and fly to the window. I have to get out. My *baby*. Feeling his small limbs flailing, as frantic as my heartbeat, I reach for the window latch. It won't open.

THIRTY-FOUR

'Help!' I slap my hand against the glass, panic spiralling inside me as I realise I'm trapped here. 'Dear God, *please*, someone *help* me!' I scream it. Acrid smoke sears the back of my throat and, desperation ripping through me, I press both of my hands against the window frame and shove hard. Finally, with a protesting creak, it gives, and I scramble up onto the shelf, swinging my legs out; then freezing in fear as a dark figure appears, looming in front of me. Instinctively, I recoil. 'It's okay,' the man says quickly. 'You're okay. I've got you. Lean towards me.'

Relief surges through me as I realise it's my neighbour from across the road. Never more grateful to see him in my life, I do as he asks, allowing him to slide an arm around me and help me, half-lift me, down. 'Is there anyone else inside?' he asks urgently.

'No,' I squeeze the word past the terror constricting my throat.

'Is Richie not here?' he checks.

I shake my head hard.

'Okay, Becky. It's all right. The emergency services are on their way,' he says, attempting to reassure me as he leads me towards the pavement where his wife rushes towards me.

'Oh, Becky. Come here, my lovely.' Amy wraps me in a firm embrace as he feeds me into her arms. 'Don't get too close, John,' she warns her husband as she steers me away from my house. My forever home. Not my forever home. It's broken. Everything in it, my baby's polka-dot giraffe, his pretty little rocking horse, turning to ashes behind me.

Minutes later, I'm installed in her kitchen – I suspect because she doesn't want me to witness the horror through her lounge window – while she rushes upstairs. Coming back into the kitchen, she wraps a dressing gown around me, doubles a sheet and wraps that around me too. 'You're shaking like a leaf,' she says, crouching in front of me to take hold of my hands. 'I'm so sorry, Becky. I only saw the flames by chance when I went to the bathroom. Is there anyone I can call for you? Richie? Is he away somewhere?'

I open my mouth but no words come out, a sob that seems to wrench itself from my soul emerging instead.

Amy quickly drags a chair across to sit next to me. 'Come here,' she says, urging me to her and hugging me hard.

'Jack,' I manage, after several minutes sobbing like a baby into her shoulder. 'Jack Evans. Could you...?' I gulp back another ragged sob and hand her the phone I'm still clutching but had been too petrified with shock to use. The irony of having a mobile, being easily contactable at all times, strikes me as I realise I have no one else in the world I can trust enough to call.

Amy nods and, finding the number, gets to her feet. 'Hello, Jack?' she says when he picks up almost immediately. 'It's Becky's neighbour here. I'm afraid there's been a fire at her house and... No, she's all right. Extremely shocked obviously.

She's here with... Great. It's the house opposite. There are fire engines in the road, but I'll keep an eye out for you.'

Ending the call, she turns to me with a small smile. 'He's on his way. I'll make you a hot drink while we wait.'

She's talking to me as she flits around the kitchen, but I barely hear her. I feel numb, inside and out. Quickly, I press a hand to my tummy. My baby moves, as if he, too, wants to reassure me, and another bout of hot tears escape me.

'And John will be more than happy to help you with any renovations,' Amy is saying. I recall that her husband has his own building company and I marvel at the basic human kindness of people who hardly know me. Another part of me breaks as I consider the cruelty people are also capable of. None of this is accidental, coincidental. No one can convince me of that.

'I'll just go and check whether your friend has arrived,' she says, handing me a mug.

I try to make my face smile, wrap my hands around it, sip it, but don't taste it. *Where are you, Richie?* I ask silently, staring down into the mug. *What have you done? Why?*

I look up as I hear Jack in the hall, the man I feel I can rely on in the absence of the man I'd been so sure would always be there for me. 'You're sure she's okay?' he asks, sounding shocked.

'As well as she can be,' Amy answers sadly. 'She's in the kitchen. I'll give you a moment.'

As Jack appears in the doorway, blue lights rotating around the walls of the hall behind him, I feel tears rising all over again. His face is pale, his eyes flecked with palpable worry. As he looks me over, he musters up a smile, and then moves quickly towards me as I get shakily to my feet. His hug is instinctive, so comforting, so needed. As he tightens his hold around me, I lean into him, somehow feeling safe to.

'It will be okay. We'll sort this out,' he says, as if I'm

suddenly his responsibility. I'm not, but I'm more grateful for him coming here, for clearly caring, than he can possibly know.

He gives me a moment, then. 'Do you know what caused it?' he asks gently.

I shake my head. 'I was in the lounge. I couldn't sleep,' I try to explain, my throat hoarse. 'I... Richie's office caught fire,' I blurt it out. 'It can't be a coincidence, Jack, can it?'

Jack eases away, examining my face incredulously. 'You're joking?'

Again, I shake my head. 'There was a fatality. His assistant, I think. He has children. A two-year-old daughter. Had.' I choke back a wretched sob. 'Then I found out that Jodie's girlfriend back at university was killed in a hit-and-run, and... I don't know what to do. I don't know what to *do*.'

Jack pulls me back to him. 'Richie wasn't home, I take it?' he asks, his voice tight.

'He hasn't been back,' I murmur into his shoulder.

Jack breathes in hard. 'You're coming home with me,' he says firmly.

I ease back to search his face. Do I trust him enough to do that? I do, I realise. Jodie trusted him and he's been nothing but kind and supportive. 'But what about your family?' The thought occurs. It's way past midnight. Even if he calls her, isn't his wife going to feel compromised? 'I can't just turn up out of the blue.'

'Becky, you can,' he insists. 'It's really not a problem, trust me. The apartment is quite detached from the house. It was supposed to be for my father's use after my mother died. As it turned out, it never did get used so it's just sitting there, vacant.'

I recall what he'd said about his mother's brain tumour, his father tragically taking his own life, and I feel for him. 'Are you sure your wife will be okay with my coming back with you now, though?' The last place I want to be is alone with my thoughts in a soulless hotel room, but I really don't want to impose.

'Katie's away with the kids visiting her mother, but she's not likely to mind, particularly under the circumstances. I'll call her and let her know. Quite frankly, Becky, I don't think you have a lot of choice. Aside from the fact that it's not habitable, you won't be able to go back into your house until the fire officer has established the cause of the fire. It's not safe.' He hesitates. '*You're* not safe.' His deep hazel eyes grow a shade darker as he searches mine.

THIRTY-FIVE

JACK

'Welcome to The Granary,' Jack said as he pushed his key into the front door. 'So called because it was converted from an original corn store. You'll be relieved to know the works are almost complete and it now has all mod cons.'

'It's a beautiful property.' She swept her gaze over the front of the house.

Jack glanced at her. She looked shattered, unsurprisingly. After all she'd been through, he wondered how she was still standing. 'Thank you.' He smiled. 'It needed some loving renovation and a fair amount of money investing in it. It's still a work in progress, but it's worth it, I think.'

'Definitely.' She nodded approvingly.

'Watch out for Jester,' he warned her, leading the way in. 'He's as soft as a brush but a bit full—'

The dog was on them before he got the words out, bounding from his favourite position in front of the radiator to launch himself at them.

'Full on,' I was going to say, he finished, catching the dog's collar before he bowled their guest over. 'He's also a work in progress. Hasn't quite grabbed the basics of obedience yet, unfortunately. He's a rubbish guard dog, as well, aren't you, Jester, hey? You're supposed to bark when people arrive, mate.'

'Aw.' A smile brightening her face, Becky bent to give the dog a fuss as Jester duly barked, plonked his hindquarters down and offered her a paw. 'That will be because you're a Labrador, won't it, Jester? I had a Lab when I was young. They take an age to grow up.'

'Tell me about it.' Jack sighed good-naturedly. 'Come on, reprobate.' He smiled and ruffled the dog's head. 'Let's get you out into the garden, and then, depending on how many suspiciously chewed objects I find, I might even feed you.'

Becky laughed as he led the dog to the kitchen. Jack was pleased to hear her do that. He felt bad about all that had happened to her. She seemed to be the odd one out in what appeared to be a basically selfish group of people. He knew only too well that sometimes you ended up hanging with the wrong people during your student days, but he really couldn't work out why she'd continued to have anything to do with them afterwards. Because she'd been in love with the man she'd married, he supposed. Experience told Jack love really was blind sometimes, leading people to believe that the object of their affection could do no wrong. Until they got a rude wake up call, that was. It infuriated him how many people, women largely, were gaslighted into thinking that somehow they were responsible for the abuse they endured at their partner's hands, be it psychological or physical, or both, believing that the monster they were with loved them. That they would change. Jack didn't think people did. In his mind, their actions were who they fundamentally were at the core. Yet, still too many abusers got away with it. If he had his way, they wouldn't. They would have the same pain inflicted on them as they dished out.

Coming into the lounge once Jester had scampered into the garden to see what chaos he could create there, he went across to the fire to turn it on. She looked frozen to the bone and deathly pale. 'You're sure you're okay with the spare room for tonight?' he asked. 'I would have put the heating on in the apartment had I known it was going to be used. It's likely to be a bit cold being unoccupied. It shouldn't take long to air out, though.'

'Not at all,' she assured him with a smile. It didn't do much to mask her obvious devastation and clear exhaustion. 'I love what you've done with the place,' she said, gazing around the lounge area. He'd kept the original oak beams, stone walls and the décor was faithful to the period, apart from the cream leather chaise and reclining sofas. Jack thought it was a perfect meeting of old and new, modern offering essential comfort where seating was concerned. He was pleased she liked it.

'I take it you approve?' He smiled.

'I most certainly do,' she enthused. 'It really is amazing. I think I might be a little bit jealous.'

Jack eyed her thoughtfully as she gazed around. There was no envy in her tone, which definitely made her an enigma since she'd just left her own house still smouldering to walk into the worst kind of uncertain future, her husband seemingly having deserted her while she was carrying the man's child. 'I'll give you the guided tour tomorrow,' he promised. 'The apartment is yours for as long as you need it, and before you get a guilt complex – which I suspect, knowing you as I've come to, you will – no, you don't have to pay anything to stay there. Unless you love it so much you can't bear to leave, of course. In which case, we'll review it at a later date.'

'Thank you,' she murmured.

Jack noticed the tears welling in her eyes as she glanced down and felt for her. 'Are you okay?' he asked softly.

She gave him a small smile. 'I'm okay,' she assured him. 'A bit emotional, that's all.'

'As you're bound to be.' Jack sighed inwardly. 'Tears are good. They're therapeutic,' he assured her. 'Why don't you grab a seat and get comfortable while I go and put the kettle on and feed the dog before he's writing to the RSPCA accusing me of dog abuse. Once that's done, I'll show you where everything is.'

He was five minutes feeding Jester and making them both a hot chocolate, but when he got back to the lounge he found her on the sofa fast asleep. Shock probably. It would be catching up with her, hitting her hard. Deciding to leave her be, he collected the bag her neighbour had put some essential clothes and toiletries in for her and took it up to the spare room, grabbed the duvet from the bed and took it back down with him.

She was still holding her phone, he noticed, as if holding on to hope. He wished she wouldn't. She was a beautiful woman, open-faced and pretty without seeming to be aware of it. She was also obviously a kind person, far too considerate of a man who clearly cared little for her. Jack found her intriguing. Her eyes, the colour of forest fern, were quite captivating. As was her mouth, which curved so easily into a smile, behind which she hid her vulnerability. She brought out his protective instinct, but it was more than that. He was attracted to her. He'd tried to deny it but he couldn't. He needed to curtail his feelings, though, if he was going to convince her to stay. He wanted her to feel safe. She wouldn't if she thought he might have ulterior motives.

Suppressing an urge to reach out and brush a stray tendril of hair from her cheek, he beckoned the dog to stay down, who miraculously obeyed him, eased the phone from her hand and placed the duvet over her. She stirred slightly as he adjusted the sofa to a more comfortable position, but didn't wake. He should probably encourage her upstairs, but it would do her no harm to rest there for a while.

Going back to the kitchen, he pulled open the fridge and checked the contents. He doubted she'd eaten but guessed she wouldn't have much of an appetite. Deciding to give her half an hour, he got the ingredients together to make her some light toast and an omelette, then sat down at the kitchen island with her phone. He was setting it on silent, when he noticed an incoming call. *Richie.*

'What do you think, Jester. Yes or no?'

The dog cocked his head to one side, his look quizzical.

Jack smiled. My sentiments entirely, he thought. *I have no idea why he would imagine she would want to speak to him either.*

Letting the call go to voicemail, he waited a minute and then went to her messages and played it back. '*Becky, where are you?*' The man's voice was frantic. '*I'm going out of my mind here. I've just driven past our house, what's left of it. What the bloody hell happened, Becks? The police have just been to my parents' house. My father called me to say they'd found signs of an accelerant?*' Jack noted his puzzled enunciation of the word accelerant, as if he couldn't believe it. Was Becky likely to believe him? Jack doubted it.

'*They said they were still looking into the fire at the office, but... Christ.*' Richard paused, his voice cracking. '*I need to know you're all right, Becks. I'm sorry for all the stupid things I said. I was angry and upset that you would think... Please call me back, will you?*'

Jack debated for a second, and then hit delete. He would call back. He had no doubt about that. He would need Becky on his side if he was going to convince the police he had nothing to do with what would appear to be two cases of arson. By his side, supporting him, where she'd clearly always been. Before Jack had spoken with her at any length, he'd assumed she was of a similar ilk to her friends, self-centred, oblivious to the hurt they caused other people to serve their own ends. He knew now that he'd been wrong. He wasn't wrong about Richard Shaw. He was pretty certain of that. Becky would take his calls. In Jack's opinion, though, she would be safer if she had nothing to do with him.

THIRTY-SIX

EMELIA

Emelia couldn't understand it. Becky had been the one who'd called her last night. She was sure she hadn't said anything to her that might upset her more than she obviously already had. She'd apologised for her selfish, drunken behaviour, meaning it with her whole heart. Becky had been a bit cool, which was only to be expected, but she had still been speaking to her. So why did she appear to not be taking her calls this morning?

After sending her a text, she tried one last time to call her. Her phone wasn't even ringing out now before going to voice-mail, which must mean it was either dead or switched off. An uneasy feeling creeping through her, Emelia decided she had no choice but to go over there. Becky had been there for her when she needed her. Emelia hadn't been much of a friend to her – she was probably the last person she would want to see, particularly if there was a crisis with Richie – but she had to try to be there for Becky if she needed her to be.

'Come on, guys, eat up. We'll be late otherwise,' she chivvied Josh and Charlotte on with their breakfast, then went to the stairs. She was about to call up to Tom that she was going over to Becky's after dropping the children at school, when he appeared on the landing. 'I thought you were going to have an extra hour in bed?' She looked him over, puzzled.

'Can't sleep,' he said. 'I might as well go into the office.'

Emelia frowned. He look possibly worse than he did last night. She'd been concerned when he'd come back from his mother's, looking horribly pale. He'd been quiet, subdued, and she'd worried that he'd been mulling over what they'd talked about and decided he didn't want to be with her despite all he'd said. He'd told her he was fine when she asked him. Nursing a bug, he suspected. He didn't look fine. He'd tossed and turned all night. He couldn't have slept much. 'Are you sure you should be driving?' she asked. 'You really don't look well.'

'I'll be fine.' He gave her a distracted smile. 'I'll probably come home early and try to grab some sleep later.'

Emelia was surprised. That would be the first time in a long time he'd come home early. She took it as a good sign, though. At least he wanted to come home, which was also probably a first in a long time. Maybe they could work things out, after all, if they both tried a little harder. 'I'm going to drop by Becky's on the way back,' she said, catching hold of Charlotte as she attempted to whizz past from the kitchen to the lounge, no doubt hoping to install herself in front of the TV. 'Coat on, madam,' she instructed her. 'It's school time, not television time.'

'But, *Mummy*, I've got a poorly tummy.' Charlotte looked beseechingly up at her.

'Oh dear.' Emelia emitted an elongated sigh. 'You'll be too poorly for McDonald's straight after school then? That's a shame.'

Knitting her brow, Charlotte considered. 'It feels a little bit better now,' she said with a brave nod.

'Good.' Emelia glanced up at Tom, expecting to exchange amused eye contact with him.

Tom, though, was still looking distracted. 'Why do you

suddenly feel the need to see Becky every five minutes?' he asked her.

Emelia was taken aback. Becky was her friend, at least she hoped she still was. They weren't in each other's pockets but they checked up on each other. Supposing he was still annoyed because of this whole thing with Richie, she sighed inwardly. She shouldn't have to offer explanations, but she didn't want to risk another argument.

'She's not answering her phone. With her being pregnant I'm a bit concerned about her, so I thought I would check she's okay.'

'That's nice of you, considering she was ready to accuse you of sleeping with her husband,' Tom commented, coming down the stairs.

'Tom.' Emelia gave him a look, her eyes flicking to their daughter who was now looking curiously between them. 'She was there for me,' she pointed out.

'I guess.' Tom crouched to help Charlotte on with her coat then grabbed his jacket from the clothes hooks. 'Just as long as she's not going to start banging on about the past again, trying to convince you we should all be living our lives consumed with guilt. She's enough to drive anyone to drink.'

That was a sideways dig at her, Emelia had no doubt. 'So what time will you be back?' she asked, ignoring it.

'Not sure. Not too late,' Tom replied, already backsliding on the *coming home early* as he headed for the door. 'Catch you later, Josh,' he called to his son and then sailed out, leaving Emelia deflated. She knew things were far from being fixed between them, but he could have said goodbye to her. Given her a peck on the cheek, at least. Had he ever considered that it was his indifference to her, unless it suited him to be otherwise, that drove her to drink?

Why was he so down on Becky lately anyway? She couldn't help but wonder. Yes, he would be wary of having much to do with either Richie or Becky after recent events, but before then he'd seemed agitated with Becky, particularly at Jodie's funeral. What was it he'd asked her to forgive him for? He'd said he'd been out of order. Far from his usual confident self, he'd looked contrite. Emelia wasn't proud of her own behaviour, but what had Tom done that he'd felt the need to corner Becky at the funeral? Whatever it was, he clearly hadn't wanted to share it with her.

THIRTY-SEVEN

Driving into Becky's road, Emelia pulled over and stared out of her window in shocked disbelief. Fear for her friend gripping her, she shoved her door open and flew across the road, getting blasted by an oncoming car she hadn't seen as she did.

'Excuse me.' Swallowing back her racing heart, she called to a police officer who was liaising with a woman outside Becky's house. Becky's burnt-out house. Where was she? Panic unfurled inside her.

'Excuse me,' she shouted again as, appearing not to have heard her, the officer turned around to walk towards the house.

The man stopped and turned back.

'What happened?' she asked, her fear mounting as unbearable scenarios flashed through her mind.

'There was a fire,' the man answered, arching his eyebrows.

Was he being facetious? Really? She could bloody well see that. 'My friend, Rebecca Shaw, she lives here,' she said, curbing her urge to snap at him. 'Is she all right?'

'And you are?' he asked.

Her friend. 'Emelia Connor. I need to know whether Becky's all right. She's pregnant. Please could you just tell me?'

She waited, her stomach churning as the officer seemed to take his own sweet time answering.

'Everyone got out of the property safely, yes,' he replied eventually.

'Thank God,' Emelia murmured, closing her eyes. 'Do you know where she is?'

'I don't have that information.' The officer looked apologetic, probably because Emelia had no hope of stopping the tears that were cascading down her cheeks. Tears of relief and confusion. When had this happened? She'd only spoken to Becky last night. *How* had it happened? Richie and she had been renovating the property. Financial constraints meant they'd been doing it slowly, but they hadn't taken any shortcuts, particularly with electrical and gas works. In fact, Emelia herself had given them details of a plumber and gas fitter she'd found on the Checkatrade site. As far as she was aware, they'd used him.

'She did provide her mobile number should we need to contact her while the forensic investigation is underway,' the officer provided.

Forensic? Cold trepidation pooled in the pit of Emelia's stomach. 'Do you think someone did this deliberately?'

The officer frowned. 'I'm afraid I'm not at liberty to discuss details. Sorry. You might do better to contact Mrs Shaw directly. I'm sure she would appreciate her friends being there for her.'

Breathing out a sigh of frustration, Emelia nodded. She'd never felt more selfish in her life than she did in that moment. She hadn't been there for her, had she? That Becky hadn't felt able to contact her when she'd clearly needed help was proof of just how much of a friend Emelia had been to her. She must have been so terrified, feel so utterly traumatised now. What kind of a monster would do something like this? More, *why*? To Becky, who hadn't got a selfish bone in her body. She was a kind person. Far kinder than Emelia was or could ever be. Becky dedicated herself to helping other people. She cared about people. She'd cared about Jodie, about Pippa too, whereas Emelia... She really wasn't a very nice person, was she? Becky had been so worried, so certain that Jodie's death was somehow linked to what happened to Pippa. Yet Emelia had shut her down, told her to let it go, as if she were irritated by her insistence on bringing it up. She was irritated, but more because she was scared, because though she and Becky never spoke about it, she felt they both shared the same doubts about the men they were with.

'Do you want to give me your contact number?' the officer said, cutting through her thoughts. 'It's possible we may need to contact friends and family as well as people in the vicinity,' he clarified with a smile that was meant to be reassuring, but wasn't at all. He'd just as good as confirmed this was arson.

Her stomach twisting, she reeled off her number. 'Do you know how long the investigation's likely to take?' she asked, her mind whirling now with thoughts about how she could be of any practical help. She and Tom had a spare room. She could always give over the room she used as a beauty parlour to make some extra space. It would be a squeeze with the children, but it was the least she could do. Assuming Becky would want to be anywhere near her. That she would trust her to be anywhere near Richie. Emelia hoped she could, that she knew she could.

'I'm afraid that's the fire officer's department,' the officer said with another apologetic smile. 'Mrs Shaw will be kept up to date...' He stopped as someone called from across the road.

Emelia glanced in that direction to see a woman hurrying towards them. 'Hi,' the woman said, smiling. 'Sorry to interrupt. I live opposite, as you've probably gathered. I assumed you were asking about Becky and I just wanted to let you know she's okay. Well, as much as she can be.'

Seeing the warmth in the woman's eyes, Emelia felt reassured. 'Do you know where she is?' she asked.

'Why don't you come over to mine,' the woman suggested. 'Sweet tea's not likely to numb the shock, but you look as if you could use a hot drink.'

Emelia could definitely use a drink, but tea wasn't it. 'Thanks,' she said, glad of the opportunity to talk to someone who might impart more information than the officer was inclined to.

Once through her front door, the woman turned to her. 'I didn't want to mention it outside. I'm guessing the police are looking for any links, but I wasn't sure whether you knew.'

'Knew what?' Seeing the cautious expression now on her face, Emelia felt the knot in her stomach tighten.

The woman hesitated, then, 'There was a fire at her husband's office last night too. A fatality,' she said. 'Not Richie,' she added hastily. 'His assistant, I gather.'

Emelia felt her blood turn to ice. It was linked. It had to be. Jodie's apparent suicide, all of it was linked back to Pippa. Becky's intuition had been right. She'd been begging her, Tom and Richie to listen to her. Emelia wished to god that she had. 'And Richie?' she asked past the tight lump in her throat. 'Is he all right? Is he with her?'

The woman shook her head, her look guarded. 'He hasn't been much in evidence. Becky had me call someone called Jack. Jack Evans. She went home with him. She could have stayed here. I told her she could. I hope I did the right thing.'

It wasn't Tom, was all Emelia could think. Tom was home. It couldn't have been him.

THIRTY-EIGHT

Once back in her car, Emelia called Becky and was relieved on some level when the phone rang out. Please pick up, she willed her, to no avail. Frustrated and wretched with worry, she left a message, then went online to search for information about Jack Evans. Finding his LinkedIn profile checked out, another surge of relief swept through her. Drawing on her vape stick – another habit she had to kick but definitely not now – she was looking for a contact number when her phone rang and Becky's name flashed up. *Thank God.* Emelia quickly accepted the call? 'Becks?'

'No, it's Jack,' the man himself answered.

Emelia felt a prickle of apprehension. She had no reason to doubt him – he'd counselled Jodie and hadn't hesitated to come to her rescue when Becky had called him, but still she was wary. To have gone home with him, Becky must trust him, possibly on the basis of what Jodie had told her, but surely she couldn't know that much about him? 'Where's Becky? Why isn't she answering her phone?' she asked, not much caring that he could probably hear the suspicion in her voice.

'I switched it to silent late last night in case it woke her. It was dead this morning. Once I'd charged it I thought I should check it for calls. Sorry about that. I should have thought earlier.'

Emelia nodded. That made sense, she supposed. 'She's all right, though?' she asked, worry still gnawing away at her – about the baby, whether Becky might have been injured, her state of mind. She would be in pieces.

'She's in shock, obviously, as she's bound to be, but uninjured,' he provided. 'I just looked in on her. She's still sleeping. I thought it best to leave her. It will do her good.' He paused. 'I gather you know what happened?'

'I've just come from her house,' Emelia confirmed, a shudder running through her.

'You're aware her husband's office mysteriously caught fire too?' he asked cautiously.

'Her neighbour told me.' Emelia's stomach tightened afresh as she recalled what the woman had said about Richie not being much in evidence. Where was he? Had they argued because of what Becky imagined had gone on between Richie and her? As much as Emelia didn't want it to be that, she also hoped it might be, that Richie might have gone off to his parents, possibly, as Tom had when they'd argued. The alternative scenario, that Richie might have had something to do with the fires, didn't bear thinking about. 'The police think it was arson, don't they?' she asked.

He hesitated.

'Do you?' she added, wondering whether Becky might have given him any hint about who she thought it might be.

'Honestly?' He drew in a breath. 'I think it would be too much of a coincidence not to be.'

'But who would do something like this? *Why?*' Emelia's voice caught. 'Sorry,' she mumbled, struggling to hold her tears back.

He gave her a moment, then. 'Are you okay?' he asked, concerned, obviously.

Emelia wiped a hand across her face. 'I'm okay. Thanks. Just worried about Becky.'

'She's okay, I promise,' he reassured her. 'I'll make sure to look after her, and I'll get her to call you as soon as she's awake. I know she's been worried about you, too.'

'About me?' Emelia was surprised. The last thing Becky should be doing now is worrying about other people, especially her.

Again, he hesitated before answering. 'About your health,' he went on diplomatically. Emelia guessed Becky had confided her concerns to him about her drinking too much. But then, he'd seen the evidence of that with his own eyes. She'd been reeling on her feet at Jodie's funeral. Probably reeked of alcohol when he'd come with Becky to her house. Emelia didn't like herself very much right then. The fact was, she never really had.

'She's a good friend,' she murmured. 'I wish I'd been a better friend to her.'

'Now might be a good time to reach out and try to mend your friendship,' Jack suggested.

Hearing the kindness in his tone, Emelia could understand why Becky would trust him. He was obviously caring of other people, as Becky was. He'd clearly cared about Jodie enough to have made the effort to come to her funeral. She supposed he might feel guilty that she'd done what she had despite seeing him professionally. He shouldn't. The only way he could have helped her was to undo history. Emelia so wished that were possible.

'Regarding your question about who would do something like this,' he went on, after a moment, 'I can't know, obviously, but I wonder whether it might be someone with a grudge of some sort. Or someone with something to hide, perhaps?'

'Why do you say that?' Emelia's heart rate kicked up.

'Something Becky said. Another friend died recently apparently. She'd only just learned of it.'

Emelia felt herself reel even without the assistance of alcohol. 'Who?' she whispered. 'How?'

'Someone from university. Jodie's previous girlfriend, I gather, which I imagine wouldn't have helped her state of mind. Becky said something about a hit-and-run.'

Oh no. Emelia's hand shot to her mouth.

'She's worried that people are being targeted because of something that happened in the past, I suspect.'

'Pippa.' Emelia breathed out her name.

Jack was quiet for a moment. Then, 'Someone Becky also mentioned,' he said. 'Look, Emelia, you might not want to, but if you think it would help to talk, I'm an integrative therapist, meaning I offer most therapies. I can't fix your problems, but I can help you explore what's at the root of them. Perhaps teach you coping mechanisms to help you deal with them.'

She did need to talk. She needed to talk to Becky, whose concerns she'd dismissed because she was scared of lifting the lid on the past and the worms that might squirm out. Now, she was petrified. Zoe dying in such a way might well have precipitated Jodie's downward spiral into depression – they'd been inseparable at university – but it couldn't explain all this. The madman who'd broken into her house and stood silently watching her, the photograph with her face scratched out. The fires. Who was doing this?

Nausea rose inside her as her mind veered to Tom. He was home last night. But not all night. He'd gone to collect the children. He'd been gone ages. Just as he'd been gone ages on that long ago godforsaken night on the beach. *It wasn't him.* She told herself over, as she had a million times before. She *knew* it wasn't. Had to believe it wasn't. He was flawed. She'd accepted he was. But he wasn't a murderer. He was the father of her children. She *knew* him. Her heart twisted painfully as she acknowledged the fact that she didn't really know him. That there were aspects of his life she was certain he'd lied about.

THIRTY-NINE

JACK

Hoping he'd convinced Emelia, who'd sounded wary about his sudden involvement in Becky's life, that he had no agenda other than to help, Jack texted her his details, then checked Becky's messages. His assumption that Richard would have tried again to contact her was right. Seeing he'd left several messages, he selected the first and played it back.

'*Becky, if you get this, please call me, will you?*' the man asked, sounding both agitated and fearful. '*I need to know you're okay.*'

Jack shook his head in despair. How okay did he imagine she would be exactly? Sighing at the man's inability to grasp the enormity of all she'd been through, that the very last person she would probably want to talk to would be him, he listened to his next message. '*Look, Becky, I know you're going to be in shock right now, and I'm guessing after all the idiotic things I said to you that you might be wary about talking to me, but if you don't feel able to, could you at least text me? Just let me know you're all right. Please.*'

He had some conscience then. Still, Jack couldn't help but be cynical. What kind of man cheated on his pregnant wife?

Then, while she's reeling from the impact of finding him as good as in the act, tries to convince her she's paranoid? A man who'd been role-playing for years, in his estimation, trying to convince her he was caring and dependable when in reality he had nil respect for her or women in general. Becky wasn't paranoid. Jack wished it were possible to convince her of that. Sadly, he didn't have a way to. Not yet, at least. She would realise it in time.

Steeling himself because, frankly, the man's self-indulgent bleating irritated him, he played the next message. *'Becky, I know I've been a complete bastard saying the things I did, but I'm worried to death about you. I've even rung round the hospitals. I need to know you're all right, Becks. That everything's okay with the baby. Please call me or text me.'*

Jack's thumb hovered over the delete button. Should he get rid of them? Or leave them? The latter, he decided, though he would have to confess he'd listened to them. From the fact that the man hadn't approached the police or the neighbours to ask about her welfare or whereabouts, he guessed Becky would conclude that Richard had something to do with starting the fires, one of which had robbed her of her home and might have robbed her of her child or her life. That was enough, Jack considered, to convince her that he didn't give a damn about her. Or it should be.

'In a minute, Jester.' He smiled at the dog, who was sitting by the back door, his tail thumping expectantly on the floor in anticipation of his morning walk. 'Stay,' he instructed him, knowing the dog would launch himself from the landing straight through the spare bedroom door and onto the bed in one second flat if he followed him upstairs. Then, turning the phone's sound back on, he went up to have another check on Becky, who'd finally given in to her exhaustion and slept in the spare room like a log.

Tapping lightly on the bedroom door, he waited. Hearing

nothing from inside, he pressed the handle down, peered around the door, then went quietly in. She stirred as he approached her. 'Hey,' he said, as she opened her eyes and blinked blearily up at him. 'How are you feeling?'

'Wiped out,' she murmured with a small smile. 'What time is it?'

Jack checked his watch. 'Ten thirty,' he said, placing the phone on the bedside table and collecting up the mug of half-drunk drinking chocolate he'd made her.

'You're joking.' She baulked. 'I must have been uncon-scious.' Throwing the duvet back, she scrambled to sit up, then pressed a hand to her forehead, woozy, clearly.

'Steady,' Jack advised, moving to help her lean back against the headboard. 'You'll still be suffering from shock, which is undoubtedly why you slept so heavily. It's the body's way of recovering. I would take it slowly if I were you.'

She nodded and managed another weak smile. Then, obvi-ously realising where she was and that there was a man she didn't know that well standing over her, she reached to tug the duvet back up.

Jack smiled quietly. With her auburn hair tumbling over her shoulders and wearing one of his shirts, she definitely look enticing. The shirt was buttoned just high enough to preserve her modesty, but he understood she might feel uncomfortable. 'I'll give you some privacy,' he said. 'Be careful how you stand. You might be a bit wobbly on your feet.'

'I will,' Becky promised. 'Thanks, Jack,' she said, as he headed for the door. 'For everything.'

'No problem,' he assured her. 'We'll get you moved into the apartment later. Meanwhile, I'll be downstairs. Just yell if you need anything. Oh—' he stopped and glanced back '—there are several messages on your phone from your husband. I did listen to them in case they were urgent enough for me to wake you. I'll leave it to you to decide whether to call him back. You might want to drop him a text if you don't feel up to talking to him.'

Leaving her to it, he closed the door behind him, then gave the dog a mock scowl, who'd snuck up after him regardless of his instruction and was now eyeing him beseechingly. 'I lied. It will be about another half an hour, Jester. Sorry, mate.' He felt bad making the dog wait but he would rather make sure she was okay before going out.

Bending, he ruffled the dog's ears, who seemed content enough with that, his tail going like a windmill as he bounded after him back down the stairs and followed him to his study. 'So what do you think?' Jack asked him as Jester plonked his hindquarters on the floor and looked up at him.

The dog answered with a deep 'woof' and offered him a paw.

Jack laughed and dutifully shook it. 'You're right,' he said, straightening up and retrieving the packet of sedatives from his pocket. Opening the bottom drawer of his desk, he pushed the pills, Amitriptyline, a mild sedating antidepressant, into it. He didn't use them often, but they were there, if he needed them. 'She is nice.'

Definitely not like the others in her circle of so-called friends, he mused, whose focus was all on themselves.

FORTY

BECKY

Still yawning and feeling as if I could sleep for a week, I wander into the kitchen to find Jack on his phone. Noticing me, he beckons me in as I hesitate inside the door. 'He's fine,' he says, giving me a smile and going back to his call. 'He's just about to take me out for a walk.'

He pauses. 'No, I'm not overfeeding him.' Glancing at the dog, who's sitting by the back door with a ball stuffed in his mouth, he gives him a wink and presses a finger to his lips.

I smile. I can't help myself despite the fact that a minute ago I'd been disorientated with a combination of exhaustion and shock, and perilously close to bawling my eyes out.

Jack's gaze travels to me. 'Katie,' he mouths, another reassuring smile curving his mouth. 'She's doing okay,' he says into his phone. 'Tired, but okay.'

I gather he's mentioned I'm here and I'm hugely relieved. I can't imagine what his wife would have thought if she came home unexpectedly to find a woman standing in her kitchen wearing one of her husband's shirts, albeit with leggings under. But I can imagine. My chest constricts, tears rising dangerously again as I recall walking in on Richie. She would feel as if someone was slowly ripping her heart out.

'I'd better go,' Jack says, as I swallow the tears back. 'I will. Give my love to the kids.'

Ending his call he comes across to me and offers me some kitchen roll, intuitive, as ever. 'Grief has a habit of doing that,' he says softly. 'Creeping unexpectedly up on you.'

I see a flash of deep sadness in his eyes and I guess he's thinking of his parents, as I often think of Angel. I'd learned to cope with the routine everyday grief. Sometimes, though, when I'm reminded of her, perhaps seeing a new mum pushing a pram in the street, the raw emotion that rushes to the surface no matter how hard I try to keep it at bay, almost knocks me sideways. What I feel now, isn't the same. Yet, it is. The grief I feel at the loss of Richie, of everything, my home and all the things that are dear to me, is like a physical thing inside me, and it hurts. So badly.

'Coffee?' he asks. 'Or would you prefer tea?'

'Tea. But I'll make it,' I offer, needing to do something. Also not wanting to be a complete miserable burden to him. 'I think Jester might be trying to tell you something.'

He follows my gaze towards the dog, who, with his ball still wedged firmly in his mouth, is staring at the back door as if willing it to open.

'I'd better take him,' Jack says with an eye roll. 'The exercise might settle him down, but I wouldn't hold your breath. I'll only be half an hour or so. I'll be going into the office later. I'm thinking you'll be needing some things from the shops. You'll find a pen and paper in the bureau in the lounge if you want to make a list. You can use my laptop to shop online when you feel up to it.'

'Thanks,' I say again, inadequately, given all he's done for me.

Jack smiles and grabs the dog's lead from the hooks by the door. 'Help yourself to anything you need. Back later,' he says, reaching to open it.

I watch him go, the dog bounding joyfully alongside him. He really is a thoughtful person. I wish I'd met him sooner. Perhaps if I'd spoken to someone like him I wouldn't have been so obsessed with *digging things up* and none of this would have happened.

Going across to the kettle, I switch it on. After pausing for a second as another bout of giddiness washes worryingly over me, I head back to the stairs, supposing I should retrieve my phone and listen to Richie's messages. I haven't been able to bring myself to yet, because I know that whether I'll want to speak to him ever again will depend on what he says, whether he has any feasible explanation at all as to how our home and his office caught fire at the same time. But there is no feasible explanation, is there, but the one I don't want to consider?

I'm about to climb the stairs when a loud knock on the front door jars me. Attempting to still my palpitating heart, I turn around, debating whether to answer it. It's not my house, after all. As I reach it, I notice the blue uniform through the opaque glass in the door and my stomach lurches. Bracing myself, I reach to open it.

'Mrs Shaw.' DI Simons smiles, but I note the wariness in her eyes. 'Do you mind if we come in?'

My gaze swivels between her and the officer who'd been with her last time. The look in his eyes is one of sympathy almost, and trepidation tightens inside me. 'What is it?' I ask, clutching Jack's shirt closer to my chest as I move back to allow them in. 'Have you discovered how the fire started?'

Once inside, DI Simons draws in a breath. 'Do you know the whereabouts of your husband, Mrs Shaw?' she asks, avoiding the question. 'We're having trouble locating him.'

'I... no.' I shake my head in confusion. 'Staying with his parents, I think.'

'He's not been in touch then?' She glances quickly around, as if Richie might be here, hiding in the kitchen or under the stairs, then back to me, searching my face carefully.

'Yes,' I answer, searching her face in turn, looking for some clue as to where this is leading. 'I mean, he's called. I haven't actually spoken to him yet, though.'

She arches her eyebrows in surprise.

'I was asleep. I slept heavily. The shock, I think. Look, what is this about?' I glance between them again, my heart rate escalating as I imagine something terrible might have happened to him.

'We've tried his parents' house,' she answers evasively again. 'He's not there. We've located the signal on his phone a couple times, but it would appear it's now switched off.'

I stare at her, trying to comprehend. 'Do you mean he's *missing*?'

'Possibly intentionally,' PC Nayyar confirms almost apologetically, and nausea swills inside me.

'Would you like to sit down, Mrs Shaw?' Simons asks, as my hand goes instinctively to my tummy.

'No.' It comes out sharply. 'No, I'm fine,' I lie. I feel as if my legs are incapable of supporting me. 'Please, can you just tell me why you need to speak to him?'

The two exchange cautious glances, and apprehension crawls over me.

'Further forensic testing needs to be carried out,' Detective Simons picks up, 'but we have found traces of an accelerant.'

My stomach twists violently, terror permeating every pore in my body as realisation crashes through me. They think it was him. They really do.

'Mr Shaw's father confirmed that Richard had been having some financial problems, something about losing a key client,' she goes on. 'His father seemed to think that it was just a cash flow problem, but you can see why we would need to—'

Her words are lost on me, her features swimming in and out of my vision as the floor tilts, and then rips itself from beneath me.

FORTY-ONE

Jack's face is ashen as he watches the hospital consultant checking my blood pressure. 'It's a little high but nothing I would be unduly concerned about,' she says with a confident smile. 'And baby's heartbeat is nice and strong, so I don't think we need to worry. I suspect it was just baby turning, which can be a bit of a shock to the system. Have you had dizzy spells before, generally or during your pregnancy?'

'Not really.' I frown and try to think back. 'A little in the first trimester, but mostly just today.'

'It's probably due to hormonal changes, but it might be an idea to book a follow-up appointment with your GP.'

'I will.' I nod and close my eyes in relief. I'd imagined all sorts of scenarios. That they might even have to deliver him early. I desperately don't want that. I want my baby to be as strong as he can be.

'Have you decided on a name yet?' she asks conversationally.

'No.' I shake my head. 'Not yet. We...' I stop and swallow, sudden acrid grief overwhelming me. Richie's not dead, but the Richie I knew is gone, metamorphosed into a monster that would kill his wife and his *child*? It doesn't seem possible. The phone messages I'd listened to on the way to the hospital, Jack trying to persuade me not to because they would only upset me, sounded frantic. Was it all a front to convince me he cared? Had everything between us over the years been fake? I *can't* believe he could have pretended it all, yet I'm terrified. What if he had? Why hadn't he asked the police about me? They would have told him I was safe. Why hadn't he asked the neighbours? Is my reality that I am married to a pathological liar? I think back to what Jack said: *narcissistic personalities will often go to terrifying extremes to avoid having their lies exposed and the truth coming out.* He said they find it difficult to truly connect with people on an emotional level. That they may appear calm in a crisis. The latter described Richie, but he hadn't been calm on the phone. The fact was, he was running. Running scared. Because he had started the fires? Or because he knew he was going to be accused of starting them? Might he be as terrified as I am? My head whirls, endless questions firing scattergun through my mind, and I have no answers.

I do know, though, that Richie's not here for me, where he swore he would be. That it's Jack who's been there through all of this. Who's here now, when I desperately need someone to be. 'The truth is, I've been a bit scared of naming him after losing my first baby.' My gaze meet Jack's as I answer the doctor's question.

He closes his eyes, and then nods and smiles sadly, and I guess he will understand where some might not, that, just as I'd put off decorating the nursery, I'd put off naming my baby until I knew my pregnancy was viable.

'Right. I think you're good to go,' the doctor assures me, after checking my file. As she heads for the cubicle exit, she places a hand on Jack's arm. 'Congratulations.' She smiles.

Jack looks awkward, but he doesn't say anything, possibly because he realises I will feel Richie's absence more sharply.

'Sorry.' I murmur as the doctor disappears through the curtain.

'Don't be,' he says. 'I obviously look like the fatherly sort.'

'You do.' I smile, betting he's a good father, patient and understanding. 'Thanks for all you've done for me, Jack, being there, being a friend when I needed one. I hope we can stay friends after the birth. It would be lovely if my little one could meet your children. And your wife, of course.'

He doesn't say anything for a moment and I worry he might not have envisaged my becoming quite so embroiled in his life. And then, to my immense relief, he smiles. 'I'm sure my children would love that,' he says. 'Meanwhile, we need to get you back. Settle you into the apartment and make sure you have plenty of rest. What you're going through now is a nightmare, but it will be over at some point. It won't be easy building from the ashes, but I think you're strong enough to do it. You have to be for your child.' He nods down at my bump. 'You need to look after yourself, Becky. You'll be feeling desolate right now, but just know you do have someone there for you, okay?'

I feel my throat close. 'Thank you,' I murmur.

'That wasn't supposed to make you cry.' He wipes a tear from my cheek with his thumb. 'Speech over,' he says softly. 'I told DI Simons to call you and arrange to meet at my house at some point, by the way. I hope that was okay. She's clearly keen to discuss some issues with you.'

I nod, but dearly wish I didn't feel so confused and emotionally depleted. I'm assuming she wants more information about our financial situation. I should also talk to her about the event years ago, which I believe shaped our lives. We'd made a vow of silence. I'd broken it. Now, it appears – to me anyway – that someone is prepared to go to any lengths to make sure that past secrets stay buried.

I will have to speak to her. I have no choice. For all that points to Richie having started those fires, though, and however naïve it makes me, I'm struggling to accept it. What I feel in my bones is that this isn't some scam to obtain insurance monies. Two fires? It's too obvious. The petrifying fact is, there have also been three deaths. Four, counting Pippa. If Richie hadn't started the fires, then he was probably supposed to have been next. As was I.

FORTY-TWO

BECKY

'We were toying with the idea of putting it on Airbnb. To be honest though, the hassle of actually running it as a holiday let didn't appeal,' Jack says, as we walk the short distance from the house across to the apartment, a beautiful single-storey, glass-fronted building, built in the same local pinkish-grey sandstone as the house. 'Then we thought we might advertise it for rent,' he goes on, 'but we haven't got around to it yet.'

I feel a stab of guilt. They won't be able to if I'm installed in it. The rental income they will lose will be substantial.

Jack clearly notices my worried expression. 'Are you okay?' he asks, concern sweeping his features. 'We can always do this later if you don't feel up to it.'

'I'm fine, honestly.' I smile, touched by his concern. 'I'm sure my dizziness was due to the baby turning so suddenly, as the doctor said. Plus I hadn't eaten. He's fine, that's the important thing. Obviously a little fighter.'

'He'll definitely be that if he takes after his mum,' Jack says, opening the front door to the apartment then moving back to allow me to go in before him.

As I step inside, it almost takes my breath away. The lounge area is furnished with the same impeccable taste Jack and his wife obviously have, a perfect blend of antique and sumptuous new leather. My gaze travels to the patio doors and the stunning views of The Granary's vast gardens and meadowland beyond the courtyard, and now I'm overcome with guilt. My life is in tatters. I have very little in the way of savings and I'll have nothing but my statutory maternity pay soon, but I have to offer to pay him.

'Jack,' I turn to him, 'I need to pay you something. I don't have much,' I admit, hating the sudden helplessness I feel, 'but I can't live here rent-free when you could be getting an income from it.'

Jack raises an eyebrow. 'I understand you would want to pay your way, and why.' He nods. 'I think we can manage without the income, though. Also, forgive me if I'm wrong, but I don't think you have anywhere else?'

'No,' I concede, as he eyes me questioningly.

'It's yours for as long as you need it,' he assures me. 'And if you decide you love it so much you want to stay, as I said, we'll talk about the details at a later date.'

I glance away, excruciating sadness sweeping through me as my mind goes to my house, the house I'd worked so hard to make into a home. I had an idea I would rise from the ashes and rebuild it. I can't imagine the insurance company will pay out when they find out it was a fraudulent claim, though. If it was. I don't know yet and I cling desperately to the hope that it's nothing of the sort. That Richie will somehow convince me of that.

'No strings, by the way,' Jack adds, clearly misinterpreting my silence.

I look up to see him studying me anxiously and I'm overwhelmed with gratitude to him. For him, the one shred of light that's come into my life. 'Thank you,' I whisper.

'You've already thanked me... once or twice,' Jack reminds me with an amused smile. 'So, are we good?'

'We're good,' I assure him, my voice choked.

'Good.' He smiles his ready smile. 'Fancy the guided tour?'

'Please.' I nod and compose myself. He'll think I'm a hormonal mess if I keep bursting into tears all over the place.

Jack leads the way along the short hall leading from the lounge area. 'Master bedroom,' he says, opening the first door. 'I'll need to order some new bed linen. There's only one set to fit that bed, but the sheets on it are clean. What do you think?'

'Wow,' I murmur, walking in to find a beautiful, exposed stone wall as the main feature. The rest of the walls are painted in a warm, light grey, complemented by a dusty pink duvet cover and curtains. It's gorgeous, homey looking and inviting.

'We turned a section of this room into a compact shower room so it's a bit small, but cosy, I think.'

'It's perfect.' I smile my approval.

'Glad you like it,' he says. 'My wife's the interior designer. She has great taste.'

'Definitely,' I agree, noting the combined sink and toilet unit as he opens the sliding doors leading to the bathroom, all in complementary grey with soft rounded edges. 'Is that what she does.'

'No, though I think she should. She's a special needs teacher. She took some time out after having the children. She's thinking of going back next year, depending on family circumstances.' Jack turns to the bedroom window. 'This is the fire escape window,' he says, demonstrating how to open it. 'The patio doors obviously offer an exit route too. Are you okay with that?'

Turning, he searches my face carefully, as if he realises escape routes will be important to me. Reminded again of how thoughtful he is, I count my blessings. Without his support, I would have been lost.

'I am,' I assure him. 'More than.' I hadn't envisaged being on my own, but I couldn't have found anywhere more perfect. And with Jack close at hand, at least I won't feel so isolated and lonely.

'There's a small second bedroom. Unfurnished, as yet.' He leads the way back to the hall. 'It's a work in progress,' he says, showing me in. 'Open to ideas.'

This room's decorated in neutral colours too. It would make a perfect nursery, I think, gleaning his meaning. Again, I'm so grateful, with no idea how to express it, but still another wave of crushing sadness crashes through me as I recall the plans I'd made, the polka-dot giraffe and the little rocking horse, which would be sitting blackened and burned and abandoned in my own house.

'The kitchen is well-equipped,' Jack says as we head back that way, 'microwave, kettle, cutlery, plates and so on. Hopefully, there's everything you need, but just let me know if there's anything crucial I've forgotten. Oh, and obviously feel free to personalise the place and make it your own.'

'It's perfect, Jack,' I say, looking out through the large kitchen window, which offers a similar view over open country-side as the front. It's like a tiny piece of paradise. 'I really can't thank you enough.'

'There's no need, you know.' Jack smiles. 'Oh, I almost forgot. The security light switch is next to the patio doors. Might be an idea to keep it on at night.'

Worry flecks his eyes and I nod. He thinks I might be in danger. The police no doubt think the same. But still I struggle to believe it's my husband who means me danger.

'I think that's pretty much it? What do you think?'

'That you might possibly be a saint.' I swallow back a huge lump of emotion.

He laughs self-effacingly. 'I don't think my wife would

agree with you. I have no doubt she'll fill you in on my flaws when she gets back.'

I'm sure he has some, but I can't imagine what they might be. 'Will she be back soon?' I ask as we head back to the front door.

'Not sure,' he answers with a sigh. 'Her parents live in Suffolk. Her mother's just had a cancer diagnosis. She's not doing too well so Katie's staying on for a while. I'll probably drive over and fetch the kids, depending on what she decides to do.'

I see a flash of something else in his eyes. Grief? Probably. He's obviously reminded of his own parents and I feel for him. 'I'm sorry, Jack,' I offer sympathetically. 'That must be difficult for both of you.'

Jack smiles reflectively. 'Life can be, can't it? But we get through it.'

'Sometimes with a little help from our friends,' I add, reminded again of how grateful I am to have him as a friend.

He nods. 'True,' he says, his smile brightening a little.

'It really is a beautiful property,' I tell him. 'You've clearly done well for yourself.'

Jack looks pleased. 'I've worked hard,' he says, 'but I've been lucky in that respect. I haven't always been able to live like this.'

I eye him curiously as he turns after closing the front door.

'Things were tight when I was growing up,' he expands with a shrug. I note the clouds flitting across his eyes, his averted gaze, and guess he might be reluctant to say more.

Once in the courtyard, he hands me the keys. 'The key to the main house is on there. I have an appointment right now, but you're welcome to use my car to go shopping when I get back if you feel up to it, or else tomorrow. I'm guessing you might need to. Meanwhile, help yourself to anything you need. I was thinking of grabbing a takeaway later if you'd like to join me?'

'I'd love to.' I take the keys, hesitate, and then move to brush his cheek with a kiss. It's uncanny, I haven't known him for any length of time, yet I feel that I do know him. That I'm safe with him. 'I have no idea what I would have done without you.'

Jack's smile is now one of pleasant surprise. His expression changes, though, turning to concern as my phone rings. Quickly, I check it. 'Richie,' I murmur, my heart faltering.

'Are you sure you want to take it?' Jack asks, studying me carefully.

I note his cautious expression and I hesitate. 'I can't not. I have to hear what he has to say, Jack.'

'Just be careful,' he warns me. 'He's going to be desperate, Becky. He's obviously going to say what he thinks you want to hear.'

FORTY-THREE

Jack glances back at me as he climbs into his car. He looks worried, his forehead creased with obvious concern. He really does think Richie means me harm, doesn't he? Still, though, I can't make myself believe it. No matter how slim it seems, I'm clinging to the hope that it wasn't Richie who'd started those fires, killing a man in the process. That he will convince me my conviction that he could never do such a thing isn't horribly wrong.

Waiting until Jack drives off, I walk slowly back to the house. He hadn't said so, but I could see he didn't want me to speak to Richie. I think again about what he'd said about narcissistic people going to terrifying extremes to avoid having their lies exposed. Did Jack think he would try to manipulate me in some way? Clearly he thought he was going to lie to me. How can I not speak to him, though? Aside from the fact that Richie is the father of my child, I have to ask him outright whether he was involved. And if he does lie, will I know? I have no idea anymore, but I have to hear what he has to say before I walk away.

Once I'm inside the house, I go to the lounge and steel

myself. My hand trembles as I select the number Richie called me on. It's not his number. I wonder why he's changed it, but I know. He's trying to avoid being located by the police, isn't he? Sick trepidation grips me, but I call it anyway, wondering as I do whether this might be the last time I talk to him, whether I should change my own phone number to avoid his calls in future. I can't believe this is happening. I quash the tears that rush to the surface, fight back my anger as the phone rings.

He picks up almost immediately. 'Becky?' he asks warily.

'You called me,' I reply, my own tone flat.

'Thank Christ.' He draws in a sharp breath. 'Are you all right?'

I don't answer. Does he honestly think there's any way I could be?

'Where are you staying?' he asks. 'I've been worried to death about you. I thought... Why didn't you return my calls, Becks? You must know how desperate I was.'

He was desperate? 'Jack has an apartment that's vacant. I'm staying there for now. Where are *you*?' I ask past the hard stone in my throat I can't seem to swallow.

'In my car,' he says, after a moment. 'My father called me to tell me the police had been back to their house so I can't go there. I've been driving around. I stopped for a couple of hours in a car park. I didn't sleep, obviously. I—'

'*You* didn't sleep?' I gasp, incredulous, my mind shooting back to the night the house was broken into, stuff littered around, that photograph left to deliberately petrify me. The night of the fire. I don't think I will ever sleep soundly again. 'Do you have any idea what I'm going through? What I've been through? Do you *care*? In the slightest?'

'Of course I care. For pity's sake, Becky, that's why I've been trying to get hold of you. I've been going out of my mind wondering whether you were all right.'

Is that what he wants, I wonder cynically. Pity? For me to

feel sorry for him? 'The house was on fire! With me *inside it*!' I shout. 'And you ask me if I'm *all right*?'

'I know!' Richie's voice rises. 'I know,' he says, more quietly. 'I saw it. I saw your car still there and I thought... *Jesus*. I've been calling you ever since, Becky. Of course I need to know you're all right.'

My hand goes to my tummy. 'You thought I might be injured?' I ask.

'Yes.'

'Dead possibly?' My voice is calm, despite the turmoil of raw emotion roiling inside me.

'Don't, Becky.' Richie's voice is strained. 'I'm sorry for what happened. *So* fucking sorry. You shouldn't have been on your own. I should have been there. I should have—'

'Why didn't you ask the police about me?' I cut across him. 'They were there at the house. Everywhere.'

'I know. I...'

'Why didn't you, Richie? Why didn't you ask the neighbours? Amy could have told you where I was. Any one of them could have told you by now. The police certainly could.'

He goes quiet for a moment. 'The office burned down, too,' he says throatily, as if I wouldn't be aware of this. 'It's obvious it was arson, isn't it?'

'Yes,' I grate the word out.

He tugs in another tight breath, blows it out slowly. 'The police said they found evidence of an accelerant. I mentioned it in one of the messages I left you. They obviously think it was me and... I was scared, Becky. I'm still scared. I have no alibi. I was there at the office, going through some stuff with Paul shortly before... They'll have me on CCTV, don't you see?'

I don't see. I don't see anything but a graphic image of a man burning to death. 'Was it you?' I ask bluntly.

Richie emits a choked laugh. 'You have to be kidding.'

I say nothing.

'Becky, please tell me you don't believe I could do something like that? That I would *ever* put you or our baby in danger?'

Still I don't respond. I don't know how to.

'You *know* me, Becky,' he says, his tone desperate.

I swallow hard. 'Do I?' I ask, my throat tightening.

Richie falls silent. 'Is this something to do with what I'm supposed to have done with Emelia?' he says eventually. 'Why you've decided to move in with some bloke you hardly know? Is it some attempt to get back at me?'

'What?' Is he actually doing this? Twisting things around, *again*?

'Nothing *happened*!' he insists. 'Not then. Not now. Not *ever*. Becky, please don't do this.'

'I'm not doing *anything*, Richie,' I retort, seeing nothing now but deep, dark red. 'I'm not *accountable* for anything. You—'

'He's moving in on you,' Richie cuts agitatedly across me. 'Surely you can see that?'

'Stop, Richie. *Right* now.' Fury unfurls inside me. 'You don't get to do this, deflect blame, as if *I've* done something wrong. I haven't. Jack offered me his *vacant* apartment, because I have nowhere else to go. He's been nothing but kind and caring and there for me, where *you* weren't.'

'It's an *act*, for Christ's sake. You must see that. Does it not strike you as convenient that he's always there? At the funeral. Bringing you home. At the end of a phone. He's trying his luck. Of course he—'

'I'm pregnant!' I yell, since he's obviously unaware that having an affair is not top on my list of priorities. 'He has a *wife*. Children. Even if he was the slightest bit interested, which he isn't, because he's a man who happens to be in love with his wife, do you think *I* would be interested? That I would ever consider doing that to his family?'

'No, I didn't mean...' Richie wavers. 'It came out wrong. I—'

'You're clearly measuring me by your own standards,' I seethe. 'For the record, Richie, I took my wedding vows seriously.' I stop, breathing in hard.

Richie sighs wearily. 'I'm not involved with Emelia, Becky. Why won't you believe me?'

'I wonder?' I reply facetiously. 'Are you in debt?' I add quickly. I have no more emotion to waste on pointless argument.

'What?' Richard is obviously blindsided. As I expected he might be.

'It's a simple question, Richie. Do you have any financial problems you've kept hidden from me?'

'You really do think I did it, don't you?' he answers my question with another.

'Stop deflecting, Richie,' I warn him. 'Just tell me. I'll find out anyway.'

He's says nothing for an excruciatingly long moment. Then, 'Yes,' he admits wretchedly.

I don't respond. I can't. With my heart wedged in my throat I feel I might choke.

'I lost a key client,' he goes on falteringly. 'I couldn't keep up with the year-end accounts last year. I tried, you know I did. I worked all night, but... He took his business elsewhere, to a big accountancy firm, and... word got around.'

I try to take stock. 'You mean you lost other business?'

'I thought I could get it back,' he says quickly. 'Work harder, smarter. I took Paul on and we were making headway, but I'd overstretched myself buying the office property, and...'

I drop heavily onto the sofa, tighten my grip on the phone. My chest pounds.

'I took out a loan,' he admits. 'Against the house. I know I shouldn't have, that I should have talked to you, but you were pregnant, and... I didn't want to worry you, Becky. I messed up, spectacularly, and I didn't know how to make things right.' I hear him catch a sob in his throat. 'I'm so, *so* sorry.'

I wipe away the tears spilling down my cheeks. 'So it was an attempt to defraud the insurance company then?' I ask, feeling nothing now but hollow emptiness inside.

'No!' Richie denies vehemently. 'No *way*, Becky. Please listen to me. Please, *please* believe me. It wasn't. I would never have...' he falters. 'I didn't pay the insurance. I hadn't paid the premium. I've been juggling my outgoings, missing other payments. The policy lapsed ages ago. They wouldn't have paid out. I didn't do this. I swear on my life I didn't.'

FORTY-FOUR

JACK

Steepling his hands under his chin, Jack studied Emelia over them. 'Would you say you're an anxious person, Emelia?' he asked her quietly, after a moment. Even without knowing about her various addictions, and despite outward appearances, she was clearly lacking in self-esteem. He couldn't help thinking it might be because of the man she was married to, who was obviously a self-serving, egotistical prick with nil conscience. She was possibly financially dependent on him. Jack's guess was that she was also emotionally dependent on him, needing him to appreciate her in order to validate herself. She was undoubtedly beautiful. As observed by the Roman poet, Ovid, however, 'beauty is a fragile gift', vulnerable to the whims of time. Sadly, exacerbated by impossible social expectations and Tom's obvious predilection to gravitate towards younger women, Emelia would be becoming aware of the impermanence of her attraction, leaving her insecure and flailing to hold on to him, along with her sense of self.

'You see through my disguise.' Emelia smiled whimsically. It didn't reach her eyes. Skittering this way and that, they were filled with edgy nervousness. It was as if she were forcing herself to sit still.

Jack considered. He probably shouldn't lead the conversation, but, 'Would you like to elaborate?' he asked.

She hesitated. 'It's all a front.' She shrugged, her eyes flitting away again. 'People think I'm confident, but I'm not really, not underneath.'

'Do you find attracting attention bolsters your confidence?' he asked, making sure to sound curious rather than judgemental.

'Definitely. It would certainly bolster my confidence if I could attract my husband's attention once in a while.' Again she smiled, but now there was a deep sadness, bordering on longing, in her eyes.

'There are problems between you, I take it?' he probed gently.

'Other women do tend to be a bit problematical.' A wry laugh this time.

He gave her a moment. 'And do you think you use alcohol to boost your confidence in social situations?' he asked, getting to the nub of the reason she'd come to see him.

'It makes me less inhibited.' Her eyes flicked embarrassedly to his. 'More outgoing.'

Jack nodded. 'Reducing your anxiety, therefore helping you cope with stressful situations.'

She drew in a long breath. 'That's right. The trouble is I don't seem to know when to stop anymore and I end up making a fool of myself or upsetting people. I did after Jodie's funeral. I'm not sure Becky will ever forgive me. Sometimes I really hate myself. I think people would be better off without me.'

Jack paused for a moment. 'I don't think I'd be speaking out of turn to suggest that Becky is dealing with some big issues right now. She's more likely to be focused on those than anything else. I can't comment for her, but it might be an idea to reach out to her.'

'As in, stop being a selfish cow and be there for her, you mean?' Emelia emitted a despairing sigh. 'I'm not sure she really wants anything to do with me, but I'm trying to be. I rang her on the way here. She was on the phone though.'

To Richie? Jack felt himself tense. He'd hoped she might have realised that the man wasn't all he appeared to be. He couldn't stop her talking to him but, for her own sake, he really wished she wouldn't.

'Regarding your drinking,' he went on, getting back to the subject he wanted to explore more, 'there is data to suggest that, though alcohol can dampen responses to stress, it can also increase anxiety in some people.'

'I'm certainly more anxious the morning after.' She didn't quite joke.

'Often it's a way of avoiding rather than confronting life issues,' Jack went on. 'Unfortunately, that can lead to higher consumption if those issues remain unresolved. With your agreement, I'd like to look at cognitive-behavioural therapy to explore any historical issues or feelings that might impact on your drinking and recovery. CBT can also treat co-occurring disorders such as anxiety, so it would certainly be worth a try.'

'Would that involve hypnosis?' Emelia looked uncertain.

Jack guessed why. Because she was worried she might reveal something she would rather not. 'Possibly,' he answered. 'But contrary to popular belief, people usually remain fully awake during hypnotherapy and have full recollection of all that happens. It would be subject to you feeling comfortable with the idea, obviously.'

She didn't look very reassured. Again Jack was pretty sure he knew why – because there was an issue that would never be resolved. The same issue that gnawed away at Becky; that being the girl on the beach they *weren't very nice to* and who'd subsequently died. The girl whose death Becky was scared one or more of that clique had had a hand in.

'Are there any issues you'd like to explore now, Emelia?' he asked kindly. 'Issues in childhood possibly? Children who are exposed to alcoholism are often more at risk of falling into a dangerous drinking pattern.'

Shaking her head, she looked away.

'Something that happened later, perhaps, that might have led to your tendency to drink in excess?' He pushed it. 'I wonder whether the incident Becky believes is the reason members of your group are being targeted has heightened your anxiety? Do you feel able to talk about that?'

She snapped her gaze sharply back to him. 'I have to go,' she mumbled, grabbing her bag and shooting up.

Jack stood and followed her. 'I hope I haven't upset you,' he called after her, as she flew through the door and headed for the stairs. *Be careful*, he thought, as she almost stumbled, hurrying down them.

He hadn't been very diplomatic for a trained psychologist. That was unprofessional. He would have to be more aware of that. He didn't want Becky to think he was anything less than professional.

FORTY-FIVE

BECKY

Too stunned to move, I sit motionless on the sofa, trying to digest all that Richie had said. I'd asked him again about Pippa. *'Were you with her, Richie? You need to tell me. Did you meet Pippa on the beach that night?'* I'd hated the tremulous edge I could hear in my voice. I don't want to be that person, scared, weak and insecure, doubting my judgement, everything about myself for placing my trust in a man who'd abused that trust, who might have done something so unspeakable my mind recoils at even the thought of it.

He'd turned the tables, *again*. After a loaded silence, where I'd thought he actually had hung up, he'd eventually replied, his voice hollow, 'You really don't know me at all, do you, Becky? You know, I can't help but wonder whether you ever actually loved me,' he went on as I struggled to answer. 'You can't have done, can you, to imagine I'm capable of what you're implying I am?'

'But that's just it, I don't know whether the man I'm in love with exists,' I started, about to point out that it was finding him with his arms full of Emelia that had caused the seed of doubt already inside me to grow. That now it just wouldn't let go. His vehement denials, his twisting things around, as he was now. The fires. A man had *died*. Could he not see that I would be questioning everything about him? 'You can't blame me for having doubts, surely?' I asked, only to realise he'd ended the call.

Now, I have no idea what to do. Numb with shock and confusion and feeling so very exhausted, I don't feel capable of doing anything. I debated whether to ring him again or send him a message, but then wondered what the point was. I can't play this ridiculous blame game. I need to preserve my energy. I need to eat and sleep in order to be strong and healthy for my baby. I need to stay strong.

I should order some food for the apartment. Some basic clothing items for myself too. Up until my life unravelled, I'd enjoyed pottering around the shops, looking at maternity wear and impossibly tiny baby clothes. Now, such an excursion would be tinged with unbearable sadness as I consider that Richie might not be part of the most important event in my life, that he clearly doesn't consider it to be the most important event in his. I can rebuild the material things. Somehow, I will find a way to put the pieces of my life back together. My heart, though, I'm not sure that will ever mend.

I'm alive, I remind myself. My baby is alive. He needs me to be functioning, not sitting here wallowing. No matter how much I feel like curling up into a ball and hiding away from the world, I can't. Taking a deep breath, I hold it for a second, then breathe out slowly and pull myself to my feet. I'm on my way to the kitchen to make tea and toast, which is all I feel I can manage, when my phone rings. *Emelia.* My thumb hovers over the call-receive button, and then I reject it. I can't talk to her now. I still don't know what happened between her and Richie, if anything. She'd said she was sorry, that *'she would never have'*, which I'd taken to mean she would never have slept with him. Wasn't she bound to say that, though? She'd also implied that it was Richie who'd made a move on her. The fact is, though, I feel I can't trust either of them, that my world – what's left of it – has grown suddenly smaller, no one in it now I can trust, apart from Jack.

A minute later, she texts me: *Please can you just let me know you're okay, Becks. I'm really worried about you. Where are you staying? I know you probably wouldn't want to, but there's always room for you here for as long as you need it. Love, Em. X*

Guilt blooms inside me. She's obviously trying to reach out and make amends. As much as I might want to, I can't keep ignoring her. We have to talk at some point, long and hard, but not now. I feel too fragile. Too vulnerable.

I text back, *Thanks. I'm okay. Exhausted right now. I'm staying with Jack for a while. He's offered me the use of an apartment attached to his property. I'm grateful, to say the least. He's being really supportive.* I pause, unsure how to sign off. Then add, *I'll call you soon.* I can't do the love and kisses thing. I hope she understands.

I'm about to put my phone on silent to give my mind space to think when it rings again. My heart jolts as I realise it's Richie, calling on the same number he had previously. Apprehension ripples through me, and I wonder whether to ignore his calls too. He's said all he has to say, after all, each word like an icicle straight through my heart. Manipulative, all of them. Conscious or not, he's trying to lay the blame for the fact that he's blowing our marriage apart at my feet. My only crime has been silence. My sin: not to allow Pippa to rest in peace. Perhaps this is my punishment?

I deliberate a second longer, and then decide to take it. I don't want to listen to any more of his denials or excuses. I need him to know I simply won't.

'I have to tell you something,' he says immediately. 'I should have said something back then. I...'

Cold trepidation crawls through me. 'What?' I murmur, my heart palpitating.

'About what happened at the beach party. With Pippa,' he goes on stumblingly. 'I need to tell you something.'

He falters, and fear tightens like a hard fist inside me. 'Richie! *Talk* to me!' I implore him.

I hear him draw in a tight breath. He doesn't speak.

'It *was* you, wasn't it?' I whisper, icy coldness spreading through me. 'You were with her, weren't you? You had sex with her. You left her—'

'No!' Richie grates forcefully. 'I did *not*! For Christ's sake, Becky, you were carrying our *baby*. How could you think that? *Why* would—'

'Tell me!' I scream.

'It was Tom!' Richie yells. 'It was Tom,' he repeats raggedly. 'He was with her. He had sex with her.'

Staggered, reeling inside as I try to process, I'm incapable of speaking for a second. Then the enormity of it, Richie's complicity in all of it, hits me like a sledgehammer. 'And you lied for him?' I can barely get the words out.

'He *asked* me to,' Richie says, a beseeching edge to his voice, as if I'm supposed to *understand* why he would lie for a man who would hurt a woman – and he had hurt her, obviously. 'He swore she was all right when he left her. He said he left her on the road, that she was heading back into town. He said that all our futures would be ruined if the police got wind of it. It was bullshit. I knew it was,' he goes on, talking fast, panic breaking through his every word. 'I shouldn't have gone along with it. I know I shouldn't, but... He was in bits, Becky. I've never seen him like it before or since. He was crying. I...'

'So you buried it,' I finish, nausea roiling like rancid acid inside me. 'You allowed Pippa to be buried, and her fear and her pain and her humiliation along with her.'

FORTY-SIX

EMELIA

'Is Daddy coming home soon, Mummy?' Charlotte asked as she wriggled down under her duvet.

'Ooh, I should think so.' Emelia smiled reassuringly, placed her *Bedtime Stories* book down and leaned to tuck her in. 'He's having to work late tonight, sweetie, but he won't be long now.'

'Will he be here when I go to bed tomorrow?' Charlotte looked beguilingly up at her.

'Probably,' Emelia answered, though she had no idea whether he would be. Tom hadn't mentioned he was working late tonight, obviously assuming she would assume he was, just as he always had. He'd made a half-hearted effort to get back early when he'd said he might, seven o'clock being early for Tom, but it was obviously a one-off. She'd thought they'd made a little headway towards trying to fix their relationship. She was clearly wrong. Today was their anniversary. There'd been no flowers, no surprise dinner reservations, not even a phone call to say where he was. She wondered why he stayed with her at all if he didn't want to be with her. Because of the money she'd inherited, she supposed in her bleaker moments, the only legacy her parents had left her apart from abysmally low self-esteem.

Burying a sigh, she fixed a smile in place for her little girl, whose forehead was creased into a worried frown. Emelia prayed she wasn't picking up on her worry. 'Why do you want to know if he'll be here tomorrow, sweetheart?' she asked her.

'Because he was reading me a story from *The Very Hungry Caterpillar* pop-up book and he did all the voices and everything,' Charlotte informed her, her face brightening.

Emelia noted the excited sparkle in her eyes and couldn't help but smile, despite it being obvious she preferred her very absent father to read her bedtime story.

'He said he would finish it tonight,' Charlotte added, her gaze now downcast.

Emelia felt for her. She was used to being disappointed by Tom forgetting arrangements, but she so wished he wouldn't disappoint their daughter. 'I'll remind him to make sure he's home early tomorrow,' she promised, tucking her Hungry Caterpillar soft toy under the duvet with her.

'Okay.' Charlotte seemed placated by that, snuggling happily down in the bed.

Emelia stood and kissed her cheek, dutifully kissing the caterpillar, too, when Charlotte offered it up, and then went to check on Josh.

She found him still glued to his Kindle. 'Five more minutes, Josh,' she said.

'Okay.' Josh sighed, glancing up.

Emelia ventured in, hesitated and then bent to ruffle his hair. 'Night, sweetheart,' she said, smiling. She resisted giving him a hug, though she badly wanted to. She guessed that Josh wouldn't be very receptive if she did. He'd clearly been picking up on the vibes between her and Tom and had her down as the bad guy. Rightly, she supposed, since in her children's eyes, she was the emotionally unpredictable one.

Josh looked her over as if assessing her, and then, to her joyful surprise gave her a small smile back. Emelia's delight turned to a deep sense of shame as she realised it was probably because her son had realised she was sober. She steeled her resolve to remain so. She knew all too well the risks to children who were exposed to alcoholism, the uncertainty they lived with, the bewilderment and fear whenever their parents would have booze-fuelled arguments. She hadn't needed Jack to remind her. 'Sleep tight,' she whispered.

'You, too. Night, Mum,' Josh answered distractedly, his eyes back on his Kindle.

Swallowing back a lump of emotion, Emelia left him to it. Her children shouldn't be worrying like this. She *had* to stop drinking. It didn't numb the pain, only ever bringing the problems between Tom and her into sharper focus.

Closing Josh's door quietly, she headed down the stairs to find her phone and braced herself to call Tom, something she rarely did now. Instead, she would drink, growing more lonely and miserable and angry with each glass. Of course, his coming home to find her inebriated and slurring her words was a perfect excuse for to him to stay out. Well, he wouldn't have that one anymore.

She was fully expecting his phone to go to voicemail and was surprised when he picked up. 'Hey, what's up?' he asked, also sounding surprised.

As if he wouldn't be aware of what was *up*. That being him noticeable by his absence, both as a husband and a father. Emelia quashed her irritation. 'Charlotte was expecting you to finish her story,' she said, keeping her tone calm.

'Crap.' Tom sighed. 'I forgot.'

'I gathered,' Emelia replied. 'Charlotte didn't, unfortunately. Children tend not to. Where are you?' she tacked on before he could respond.

'With a client,' Tom reeled off his stock answer. 'It's going to be a late one, I'm afraid. There's some complicated stuff to get through. I wouldn't worry about waiting up for me.'

'Right.' Emelia felt her heart sink. 'Male or female?' she enquired.

'Here we go.' Tom emitted another heavy sigh. 'Have you been drinking?' he asked, his tone one of weary resignation.

'Actually, no,' Emelia informed him, still the epitome of calm. 'Despite the fact that it's our wedding anniversary, I decided I didn't want to celebrate on my own.'

'Oh *hell*,' Tom groaned. 'I'm sorry, Em. I got so bogged down with work, I—'

'Forgot,' she interrupted. 'Not to worry. Just so you know, though, you needn't rush home. You'll find the doors bolted.'

'Emelia...' Tom drew in a long breath. 'Look, don't start. I'm with a *client*. She's only yards away in the next room. I've already had to interrupt our meeting to answer your call.'

'Oh dear. Do tell her I'm sorry for the inconvenience, won't you?' Emelia drawled factiously.

Tom drew in a tight breath. 'I have to go. I can't do this right now, Em. You know I—'

'Bye, Tom. Enjoy the rest of your evening.' Emelia got little satisfaction from it, but ending the call she thought was best. If he wanted to be with her, with their children, then he was going to have to work a lot harder to prove it.

Placing her phone on the kitchen table, she stared at it. She stood there for a full minute, a tiny part of her hanging on to the hope that he might call back full of apologies. She even fantasised that he would suggest an exotic holiday, a mini getaway, anything to try and make amends. Another minute ticked by before her tears exploded with frustration and anger. He really didn't care, did he? She went on autopilot to the fridge, opening the door and staring at the open wine bottle, her water bottle still topped up with 'orange', then snatched both bottles out. Strangely, it didn't take quite as much willpower as she imagined it might to pour the contents down the sink, along with the contents of several unopened wine bottles, lest she be tempted.

In fact, she did get some satisfaction from that, though she suspected it wouldn't last long.

Going back to her phone, she checked her messages, thinking he might have at least made that small effort. There was nothing from Tom. She really wasn't that surprised. He probably thought she would hit the bottle now, and then crawl into bed, as she had so many times on her own. She so wished she had someone to talk to. In times past, she would call Becky, but Becky was apparently staying with Jack. Emelia had been taken aback when she'd texted her to say she was. Jack hadn't mentioned anything when she'd gone to his office. She wondered why he wouldn't have. Because he'd stepped beyond counsellor/client relationship, obviously. But then, she supposed Becky would need someone there for her. She would be feeling so lonely, so let down by the people who should have been there, namely her. She wasn't sure she trusted Jack completely, though. It seemed to Emelia that Jack was a little overly interested in Becky. Concerned for her welfare he might be, married he might be, but whenever did that stop men going after someone they fancied? She might be wrong. Her suspicion had been in overdrive for so long, her own view of men was probably jaded, but he had Becky installed in his house, as good as. Emelia was worried for her friend. Her whole world had fallen apart. She would be distraught, confused and vulnerable. She was about to text her to tell her she was here if she needed to talk, when the doorbell ringing, followed by a rap on the door, made her jump almost out of her skin.

Her nerves were shot. She was already having to work to quash the longing for a drink, she realised miserably, as she headed for the hall. She would quash it, though, for her children's sake more than her own.

Seconds later, she was face to face with the officer she recalled seeing outside Becky's house, the woman he'd been talking to standing next to him. 'Emelia Connor?' the woman asked.

Emelia nodded, her gaze travelling warily between them.

'I'm Detective Inspector Megan Simons—' the woman smiled tightly and held up her identification '—and this is PC Dev Nayyar. Do you mind if we have a word with you about your whereabouts and also the whereabouts of your husband, Tom Connor, on the night of fifth of April?'

The night of the fires? Emelia's heart faltered.

FORTY-SEVEN

With no choice but to, Emelia invited the officers inside, leading them to the kitchen which was well away from the front windows and the prying eyes of the neighbours. She had no doubt curtains would be twitching, people itching to find out why the police were at her front door. The arguments between her and Tom that had spilled out onto the drive as he strode off sprang to mind and she felt a burning sense of shame. In her more sober moments, she realised that their neighbours weren't jealous of all that she and Tom had. They would be more fascinated and appalled by the sideshow she provided screaming after him. If they knew why she did, perhaps they wouldn't judge her. The fact was, though, they didn't know. What they saw was poor, hard-done-by Tom making a quick getaway from his drunken, deranged wife. How could they not judge her?

Closing the kitchen door behind them in case the children should overhear, she turned to her unwelcome guests. 'Are you asking if we have alibis?' she asked, bracing herself for what they had to say.

'It's simply to eliminate people from our enquiries at this stage,' PC Nayyar informed her with a ghost of a smile.

A knot of apprehension tightened Emelia's stomach. 'But you do think the fires were started on purpose?'

Nayyar glanced at Simons.

'We have CCTV evidence of someone in the area at both locations,' the detective provided vaguely. 'We're trying to establish whether persons known both to Richard and Rebecca Shaw would have had reason to be in the vicinity of the business premises as well as their private address.'

Emelia's heart boomed a warning. 'I was here,' she said quickly. 'In fact, I had a long conversation with Becky on the phone.'

'And Mr Connor?' The woman waited.

Emelia's heart rate escalated. 'He was here too,' she answered, and faltered. But he hadn't been, had he? Not the whole time. He'd gone to collect the children. She recalled how Becky had asked her on the phone whether Tom had come back. She hadn't thought much of it then, but why would Becky have been interested in his movements? She tried to remember how long he'd been gone and cursed her hazy memory. His father was not long back from the hospital. He'd said he'd had to help his mother rearrange furniture in the bedroom. He'd been gone ages. Icy fear crawled over her skin. *It wasn't him.*

'And he was here all evening?' Nayyar asked inevitably.

'He popped out; just to collect the children from his parents' house. He wasn't gone long.' Emelia swallowed back a hard lump in her throat.

'And his parents can verify this, I take it?' Detective Simons enquired.

Emelia's gaze pivoted from Nayyar to her. 'Yes, absolutely.' She nodded. Her heart sank as she realised the detective's gaze was drifting around her kitchen, coming to rest on the worktop next to the sink, on top of which were lined up several empty wine bottles.

'Are you able to let us have the address?' the woman asked, her gaze settling back on her.

Emelia scanned the woman's face, trying to read what was behind her eyes. Suspicion, it was obvious. 'Yes. Right. Of course.' She pulled her gaze away. 'It's on my phone.' Turning around, she collected her phone from the kitchen table and selected her contact details. Finding the address, she handed the phone to her. She felt her cheeks burning as she realised her hands were shaking. She had no doubt the eagle-eyed detective would notice that too.

'Thanks for that.' Simons passed the phone to her sidekick for him to note the details. 'There was just one other thing, if that's okay?' She looked back at her with an inscrutable smile.

Emelia felt another cold shiver of apprehension crawl over her. 'It's fine.' She smiled stiffly back.

'I hope you don't mind my mentioning it, but we're a little concerned about some information about you that was passed on to us.'

'What information?' Emelia frowned, the panic that had taken root inside her rising steadily. 'Passed on by whom?'

'We can't reveal our source.' The woman smiled shortly again. 'The person was sufficiently worried, though, that we felt obliged to carry out a welfare check since we were due to call on you anyway.'

'I don't need my *welfare* checking.' Emelia laughed in bewilderment. 'I'm perfectly fine. Who the hell told you I wasn't?'

'I'm afraid we're not at liberty to share that information,' Detective Simons repeated, at least having the good grace to look apologetic. 'As I say, the person in question was quite worried about you. They thought you might be depressed, possibly enough to harm yourself.'

What? Emelia's mouth dropped open. She stared at her in stunned disbelief for a second, and then, tears dangerously close to the surface, she wrapped her arms around herself and looked away.

'They thought the basis of your depression might be guilt,' the detective went on, her tone curious.

'Guilt?' Emelia's gaze shot back to her. 'About what happened to Becky?'

Simons paused before answering. '*Are* you feeling guilty, Emelia?' she asked pointedly.

'Of course I am,' Emelia snapped. 'But only because I wasn't there for her when she needed me to be.'

The detective conceded that with a small incline of her head. 'And why was that, if you don't mind my asking? Did you have a falling out of some sort?'

'*No*,' Emelia denied. 'Yes.' She backtracked, as the woman eyed her steadily. 'But not so badly I would burn her house down, if that's what you're getting at.'

Simons said nothing for a long moment. Emelia could almost feel the accusation oozing from her. 'And are you able to tell us what the argument was about?' she asked.

Emelia tightened her arms around herself. 'It was a personal matter,' she answered, her throat feeling parched. She needed a drink. She hadn't even got her vape stick to calm her nerves and had no idea where she'd left it. She needed for this woman to leave. *Hell*. Her panic rose so fast it almost choked her. Did she need a solicitor?

'The person who spoke to us thought that guilt might be the root cause of your dependence on alcohol,' Simons went on bluntly, as if reading her mind. 'They thought it might be related to something that happened in the past? Something to do with a student you were all at university with, Pippa Moore?' She stopped and let it hang.

Emelia felt that like a punch to her stomach. Someone had told. Someone had shared the secret they'd all sworn to keep. Because they were scared. Because two of the people who were on the beach that night had recently died under terrible circumstances. Reflecting on how Jodie had died, apparently having taken her own life despite having everything to live for, how Zoe had died, in a hit-and-run accident, Emelia was more than scared. She was petrified.

Who would have broken their promise? Becky had been adamant they should bring it all out and re-examine what happened that night. She wouldn't stop going on about it. Emelia recalled what Jack had said when he looked at the photograph that had been left by her silent intruder. *You need to involve the police, Becky. I don't think you have any choice but to now. This is clearly a threat.* He'd been right. Emelia's face had been cruelly scratched out. Her blood turned to ice as she considered that whoever had left it had been hinting she was next.

Becky must have heeded Jack's warning and gone to the police. But however angry she was with her and Richie, surely she wouldn't have for fear of what they might discover if the case were reopened. Becky loved Richie. Like her, she'd kept silent all these years precisely because she'd been concerned about what the police might uncover.

Detective Simons was studying her carefully, she realised, her sharp grey eyes narrowed as she waited for her to answer. Emelia had no idea how to. She'd never envisaged having to answer questions about Pippa while standing in front of the police on her own. *Why* was she on her own? Again. Where was Tom when she needed him? Missing. Just as he had been on that long ago night. Nausea curdled Emelia's stomach. She had no idea what to say. She needed help. She *did* need a solicitor, urgently. She needed Tom. Here. Now.

'Are you able to recall the event, Mrs Connor?' PC Nayyar asked.

Emelia's heart lurched. 'No, not really. I'd drunk a lot,' she answered shakily. 'I have to go. I need to see to my children. I think you should leave now.'

'Certainly,' Simons answered with a brusque smile. 'Just one more question, if you wouldn't mind?'

'I do.' Her legs like putty beneath her, Emelia headed towards the door, holding it open for them as the officers made no move towards it.

Following her in her own good time, Simons faced her. 'I wonder if you could tell us whether your husband owns a black hoodie?' she asked. 'We have CCTV evidence of someone in the vicinity of both fires wearing one.'

Emelia's mind swung to the man on the stairs and fear pierced her chest like a knife. But it couldn't have been Tom. That was preposterous. She would have recognised him. Would she have though? He'd been wearing a mask. The hood covered his hair, and she'd been in shock. But he didn't own a black hoodie. Did he? She had no idea, she realised. Tom went to the gym straight from work. He kept his sportswear in his office.

FORTY-EIGHT

BECKY

'What did you tell them?' Emelia demands as soon as I answer her call.

'Who?' I reply apprehensively. After what Richie had said about Tom, I'd debated whether to take the call. I wish I hadn't now.

'You know damn well who. The police,' Emelia spat. 'Why did you do it, Becky?' she goes on furiously while I'm trying to make sense of what she's saying. 'Is this some attempt to get back at me because of what you imagined happened between Richie and me? Nothing *happened*. I told you. Why can't you just bloody well let things go?'

'Emelia,' I shake my head in confusion, 'I have absolutely no idea what you're talking about.'

'Two of the people who came away from that beach party are dead!' she goes on, as if she hasn't heard me. As if I don't know this. 'You're stirring up a hornet's nest, don't you see? Jodie was obviously riddled with guilt because you had to keep going over it and over it. Can you not see what you're doing?'

That hits me like a body blow. I take a sharp breath.

'Emelia, you need to stop,' I warn her. Does she not realise how guilty *I* feel because of Jodie? Does she not think it eats away at me every second of every day? That it doesn't haunt my every waking night, just as Pippa's death does? And now there's Zoe. Also Paul Holmes. His death might have been accidental, but it was clearly linked. A shiver of fear prickles the length of my spine as I realise the implication. Emelia and I need to be together on this, there for each other, not pulling away from each other.

'Do you want *me* dead, is that it?' she growls, stopping my thoughts short. 'Do you think if you pile guilt onto my shoulders, you'll get rid of me too?'

My heart almost stops beating. 'This is insane,' I murmur, my throat catching. 'I'm going to end the call, Emelia. You've obviously been drinking.'

'Unlike you, Miss Goody-two-shoes, never touches a drop,' Emelia retorts.

No, I think angrily. Because I know the devastation it can wreak, the things a person might do or say that can never be undone or unsaid. Things a person might never regret because they couldn't remember. 'You need to stop this, Emelia. We'll speak when you're sober.'

'That was a nice touch, by the way,' she ignores me, 'making them think I'm a depressive, suicidal drunk. You really hate me, don't you? What were you going to do? Push *me* off the edge of a cliff? Mow me down in your car, possibly? Although that would be a bit obvious and wouldn't pass as suicide, would it? You could always invite me over and drop some pills in my drink. You'd have to make sure I'd had a few drinks beforehand but—'

'Emelia, for God's sake, stop!' I shout. 'I don't *hate* you. Why on earth would you think that? I care very much about you.'

Emelia falls silent for a second. 'But more about Tom,' she says.

'Tom?' I wipe away the tears spilling down my face, lock eyes with Jack, who's appeared from the kitchen, his expression perturbed as he no doubt wonders what's going on.

'You were quick enough to get Richie out of the house, weren't you? Strange how that happened after your cosy little conversation with Tom at the funeral reception,' she goes on, her tone scathing.

Is she saying what I think she is? I frown in confusion. Does she actually think that Tom and I... 'You're being ridiculous, Em.' I soften my tone, try hard to quash the anger writhing inside me. It's not her fault. She's ill, obviously frightened and confused after the police calling, which I assume they have, and is no doubt why she's drinking so hard. She needs help. She needs to get Tom out of her life before she *does* kill herself. 'And you're wrong,' I add firmly. 'Completely. I would never do something like that to you. You know I wouldn't.'

She doesn't answer. I hear glass clinking against glass in the background. Liquid being poured. How much *has* she drunk?

I glance at Jack as he comes towards me, wiping his hands on a tea towel and a deep furrow creasing his brow. 'Okay?' he mouths.

I nod and shake my head all at the same time.

'What was it Tom didn't want me to find out about, Becky?' Emelia asks.

I hesitate. What do I say? I can't tell her the truth, that Tom had been doing what he does and had decided to try his luck with me. Not when she's in this state. 'Nothing. It was nothing. Something that happened years ago. A misunderstanding. It was my fault. I misread something he said, that was all.'

More silence from Emelia. 'Yes, and what happened to Pippa happened years ago, didn't it?' she goes on coldly after a moment. 'But you couldn't leave that alone either, could you?' I hear her topping up her glass again and now I'm growing scared for her. 'Is it because you knew Richie had been with her?' she asks bluntly, astounding me.

Is that what she thinks? All these years, has she been thinking that Richie...? I cast my mind back to what she'd blurted out about Pippa not being the little Miss Innocence she pretended to be, clearly implying that Richie had been involved with her, or at least that Pippa had had designs on him, and I feel sick to my soul. 'Don't do this, Em,' I beg her. 'You've been drinking. You don't know what you're saying. We'll talk when you're not so upset. Please just go to bed now and—'

'Oh, but I do,' she interrupts. 'Is the baby you're carrying Tom's, Becky?' she asks, staggering me. 'You and Richie couldn't get pregnant, after all, could you?'

I feel as if she's just punched a knife straight through my chest. How could she? Knowing all she knows of my history, how could she be so cruel?

'Did you use Tom to make it happen?' she goes on as I reel from the impact of her words. 'And then use what *supposedly* happened between Richie and me as the perfect opportunity to get rid of him and take Tom away from me? Is that it?'

'That's *enough*, Emelia.' I grip my phone hard. 'Where's Tom now?' I ask, struggling hard not to tell her some home truths of my own, starting with Tom's behaviour back at university.

'Don't know. Don't care,' she retorts immaturely.

'Are the children there with you?' I ask. I'm hoping they're not, or else safely in bed while she's doing *this*: drunkenly ranting and ripping what's left of my heart from my chest. She's clearly out of control.

'Yes, but why would you care?' is her next juvenile response.

'I'm going,' I respond tightly. 'You need to go to bed, Emelia.

Sleep this off and get a bloody grip before you lose everyone who gives a damn about you.'

'That's fine. I was about to end the call anyway,' she counters. 'And just for clarification, you said that I'd stop at nothing to get my man. That Pippa would attest to it, if she'd lived. You know what though, Becks? If she had been able to, I reckon her finger would be pointing right at you and Richie.'

FORTY-NINE

'You're shaking.' His forehead creased with concern, Jack places a hand on my shoulder.

Glancing down to see Jester has plonked himself next to me and is gazing up at me in that empathetic way only dogs can, I inhale sharply, trying to hold the tears back.

'She's been drinking, I take it?' Jack asks warily.

Nodding, I stroke the dog's head, at which Jester emits a relieved little pant and gets to his feet, tail wagging. Wiping a hand over my face, I give Jack a tremulous smile and attempt to compose myself. 'I'm worried about her,' I manage.

'Do you want to go over there? I don't mind driving you,' he offers, aware that my house is still cordoned off, for safety as well as investigative reasons, meaning I still don't have my car keys. I don't even know where they are. Inside the house some-where, in amongst the debris of my life.

His expression is cautious, I note, and I guess he doesn't think it's a good idea, given the fraught tone of the conversation. I take another deep breath. It does nothing to quell the nausea swirling inside me. What if she does something unthinkable? She's clearly emotionally unstable. Josh and Charlotte should be in bed now, but even so... 'I need to call Tom,' I say. 'If I can't get hold of him, I think I do have to go over there, although I can't see her answering the door to me.'

'I'll leave you to make your call,' Jack says, smiling supportively. Beckoning Jester, he heads back to the kitchen, where he's preparing a meal for us, insisting I join him at the house rather than spend too much time on my own in the apartment 'dwelling on things'. Feeling as lonely and bereft as I do just now, I do wonder how I would have managed without him. I would have – somehow, I would have found a way to – but I'm so grateful for his support.

Tom's phone rings out for what seems like an eternity. When it finally goes to voicemail, my heart plummets. I hate myself for thinking it, but I can see why he wouldn't want to be at home very much. Why can't he see, though, that his *not* being there for Emelia isn't helping her? She needs to confront her problem to try to tackle it. She's not going to do that with him crushing her self-esteem. I know I'm judging him badly based on my own experience – also what Richie told me, though I only have his word for it. I can't know everything about their relationship: How he feels about Emelia, whether his flirting is just that, or whether he actually cheats on her. If he doesn't want to be with her at all, though, why doesn't he leave and be done with it? Emelia would be crushed – of course she would, but isn't she that now?

With no choice but to, I leave him a message: 'Tom, I've just spoken with Emelia. The police have been at your house and she's in a dreadful state. You need to go home, for the children's sakes, if no one else's.'

Ending the call, I head to the kitchen, wondering what to do.

'No answer?' Jack straightens up after placing Jester's food bowl down.

I shake my head. 'I left a message.' I sigh in despair. 'Why were the police there, do you think?'

Jack looks at me curiously, and I realise he wasn't privy to all of the conversation between Emelia and me.

'She wasn't talking much sense but I gathered the police had been to see her,' I explain. 'She seemed to think that they'd called because I'd spoken to them. I haven't, other than about anything to do with the fires, but she started bringing up the past, as if they might have asked her about that.'

'The incident you spoke about from your university days?' Jack enquires.

I nod, glancing briefly at him, and then away as an image of Pippa lying on that beach, so cold and lonely, flashes into my mind. I can almost feel her fear and her pain in those last few moments of her life, and it breaks my heart.

'If she's been drinking then she probably wouldn't be making sense,' Jack points out, dragging me back to the present, the cosy interior of his beautiful house. Despite all that's happened in my life recently, I count my blessings, which have come in the guise of this man. 'She was probably being defensive of her husband,' he goes on. 'Didn't you say that you thought it was one of your group with whom the unfortunate girl who died had had relationships?'

My heart jars as he repeats what I'd told him. I'd almost forgotten I had. 'I suppose,' I murmur an answer.

'As for why the police called, I imagine they would be making enquiries about the fire, collecting witness statements, eliminating anyone known to the victims, talking to people of interest. That sort of thing.'

'Richie's of interest.' I wrap my arms around myself as a cold chill prickles my skin. 'They think it was him. I'm sure they do.'

I look back to Jack, useless tears welling again in my eyes. Do I think it was Richie? The truth is, I don't know. He's in a mess financially. He's admitted that much. When I'd asked him whether he'd been involved with Pippa, he'd been shocked. He'd said I didn't know him, that I can't ever have loved him, imagining him capable of such a thing. He'd said it was Tom. That Tom had asked him to lie for him. Had he? Was any of Richie's emotion real? Or had it all been deflection, something he must be adept at? I think again about what Jack had said about narcissists using the pretence of emotion to control others, about how such people will try to deflect blame if they feel caught out. I want to ask him about it, but how can I, without admitting to so much more?

'They don't know that, Becky,' Jack says kindly, more to reassure me than because he believes it wasn't Richie, I suspect.

'I think I should go over there.' I check my phone. There's nothing back from Tom and Emelia hasn't called back or texted as I'd half-hoped she might. At least then I would know she was all right. 'I'm sure Emelia won't want to see me but I can't just leave it.'

'Look, the food's keeping warm in the oven. Why don't you let me take a drive over there while you eat something? She might not want to talk to me either but, without wishing to inflate my own importance, I am a psychologist. I might just be able to persuade her. It's worth a try.'

He's right, I realise. If anyone can get through to her, I think he might be able to. If she'll listen. If she's capable of listening. If he can even get a response from her, it will put my mind at rest. 'Do you mind very much if we take it out of the oven?' I ask, feeling awful now about him having gone to the trouble of preparing it, especially as he's spent the whole day away at a conference on psychology in London, meaning he'd set off at the crack of dawn this morning. I'd just about managed to summon up the energy to call the surgery to make my doctor's appointment. Then I'd lain on the bed in the apartment and fallen fast asleep. I felt hopelessly exhausted, yet I was doing hardly anything. It would be the shock of all that had happened, Jack said. 'Feeling fatigued or sleepy is sometimes part of the body's natural healing process.' I guessed he was right, but I wish I felt stronger.

'You prefer to come with me,' he says astutely now. 'I get it. It might be for the best as she doesn't know me that well. I'll order that takeaway we never got around to once we get back.'

'Can't we just warm the food up again?' I ask, feeling worse as I follow him to the hall.

'I'm not sure ham and cheese omelette will survive two rounds in the oven and still be edible. Just don't let me be persuaded by Jester's beguiling eyes to feed it to him. I think I'll be joining him in the dog house if I keep feeding him leftovers. Katie will not be amused.'

How does he do that? Manage to make me smile? 'In which case, I'll keep a careful eye on you,' I promise.

'Later, Jester,' he tells the dog, who's joined us in the hall in hopes of a walk. 'We won't be long.' I can't help but smile again as I note the way he talks to him, as one would a child, the way he looks at him, with obvious love in his eyes. The feeling's plainly mutual. Jester adores him.

Grabbing two jackets from the clothes pegs, he offers me one. 'It's threatening rain,' he says. 'It might be a little on the large side, but it will save you going back to the apartment.'

Marvelling again at how thoughtful this man is, I place my phone on the hall cupboard and accept the jacket. I'm about to pull it on when the phone beeps an incoming text. Thinking it must be Tom, I retrieve it and check it. Not Tom, I realise, both relief and trepidation sweeping through me. Emelia. Quickly, I read the text and a new wave of panic unfurls inside me.

Does Richie have a black hoodie?

I hesitate and then reply, *I'm not sure. Are you all right?*

'Emelia?' Jack asks as I glance at him while waiting for her to text back.

I answer with a nod, my mind racing as I wonder what she's thinking. What she's doing. Had she told the police about her intruder? My heart lurches as I wonder whether they might have mentioned someone being seen in a black hoodie outside Richie's office building. Might it have been Richie? He'd hardly set fire to it in his business suit. *He hadn't!* I squeeze my eyes closed.

'Okay?' Jack places a hand on my arm.

I look at him, attempt a smile, then go back to my phone and send another text.

Jack and I are on our way over. I'm worried about you.

Emelia texts back in a flash.

I'm fine. I don't want you bringing that man here. I don't trust him. I don't think you should either.

FIFTY

'I'm sorry,' I say, looking up to see Jack watching me worriedly as I push my food around my plate. Jester is glued to the spot by my side, also watching me, though I suspect rather more hope-fully, than worriedly. 'It's lovely, but I'm afraid I'm not very hungry.'

A frown flits across Jack's face. 'I'm not bothered about the food, Becky. I'm just concerned you're not eating enough. That said, I'm not surprised you don't have much of an appetite.'

'I'm still upset about Emelia,' I admit.

'As she knows you would be.' I note a flash of anger in his eyes as he reaches to collect my plate. I don't blame him for being angry after what she said about him, which has no substance whatsoever. She's barely spoken to him, except for that once when he was at her house trying to help her.

'I'm sorry about her silly comment.' I sigh, wondering what on earth had got into Emelia that she thought the very people who cared about her were out to get her. I'd hesitated to share her text with him, but as he'd been standing right in front of me when she'd sent it and it was such a ridiculous thing to say, I decided I should, possibly in the hope he could shed some light on it. He'd looked as perplexed and shocked as I felt.

'Don't be,' Jack says, his mouth curving into its more familiar smile. 'You shouldn't be apologising for her. She's obviously drunk and, to be honest, I understand why she would say something like that.'

I look at him in surprise.

'With the way her husband treats her she probably has little trust in men. Also, excessive alcohol consumption tends to bring your emotions to the fore, particularly negative emotion, anger, hurt, humiliation, grief. I imagine Emelia is going through the whole gamut right now. Try not to judge her too harshly.'

Now I'm definitely surprised, and quite humbled by this man's capacity to be so understanding and forgiving. I'm not sure I'm able to be.

'How about I fix us some sticky toffee pudding and ice cream?' he suggests, a mischievous twinkle in his eye as he tries to tempt me. 'You can't turn that down, surely, particularly as I've worked my fingers to the bone extracting it from the freezer and defrosting it?'

'I wondered why you were looking so flustered when you came back from the kitchen.' I can't help but smile, despite that I actually feel like crying, part with gratitude, part with fear for Emelia.

'Microwaves,' he says with a theatrical roll of his eyes. 'I swear you need a degree to operate them in defrost mode.'

'You should have consulted me,' I tell him. 'I passed my defrosting degree with honours.'

'I'll bear that in mind. You get the job next time.' Plates in hand, he heads for the kitchen, Jester trotting after him in hopes of titbits. 'Oh.' He pauses at the dining room door. 'Did Tom get back to you?'

Sighing again, I shake my head, wondering now at Tom's capacity to be so dismissive of Emelia. Clearly, he's not bothered about her, or the fact that the police had called, the reason they might have called. Does that mean he feels he isn't guilty of anything and is therefore quite happy to let Emelia deal with it? Or is he running scared too?

'I expect he's busy with a client,' Jack suggests. His expression is rather cynical as he turns back to the kitchen, from which I glean he's not very impressed with Tom either. Emelia might do well to realise that Jack is not the enemy and talk to him about all that she's dealing with. He's certainly helped me and, contrary to Emelia's thoughts about him, I feel I can trust him implicitly.

Burying another sigh, I reach to stroke Jester's head, who, clearly getting no joy in the kitchen, has bounded back and plonked himself down next to me. 'Sorry, boy, I don't have anything.' I splay my empty hands, at which Jester cocks his head to one side and then, obviously getting the message, shoots across the room to bring me his prized rubber ball.

'Who could resist?' I note his manically wagging tail and throw it for him. He's retrieved it in a second flat and is on his way back when a whistle from Jack stops him in his tracks.

'Are we walking, mate, or what?' Jack calls, at which the dog promptly about-faces, the ball and I abandoned in favour of his master and walkies.

As I ease myself from my seat, trying not to feel incredibly lazy, Jack glances around the dining room door. 'The pudding's in the oven. I'm pretty competent with the oven timer, you'll be pleased to know. I'll give him a quick run, but just in case...'

'I think I can manage to take it out,' I assure him.

'Teamwork,' Jack says with a wink. 'Right, come on reprobate,' he addresses the dog. 'Let's go and see what you can find to bark at.'

As he heads off through the front door, I go to the lounge, marvelling now at how at ease I feel with him. It's pouring with rain outside. I notice the raindrops pitter-pattering against the lounge window as I watch him go, the dog bounding happily alongside him. If ever there was a silver lining, though, it's Jack Evans. I will forever be thankful to him for being there for me during this, one of the bleakest times of my life, and always friends with him, assuming he would want that. My mind goes to his wife, who I've yet to meet. I hope I can do that soon. I feel like an interloper in her house while she's not here.

The pudding smells delicious. I feel a rumble of hunger in my tummy as tempting toffee aromas drift from the kitchen. I haven't been able to face food very much since finding out about Jodie, but Jack is right, I do have to eat. *We need the nutriments, don't we, little one?* I press my hand to my tummy, at which my baby kicks vigorously, as if tempted by the pudding too.

As I head back across the lounge, my eye snags on a photograph on the mantelshelf over the log burner. I go across and pick it up to examine it more closely. It's the same framed photograph Jack has in his office, I notice, one of his family. His wife is very pretty, I can't help but notice that too, naturally so with her long spiralled hair and sun-kissed complexion. Relaxed in jeans and an oversized shirt, she's sitting in a field, her daughter sitting crossed legged in front of her. The little boy is standing to their side, blowing a swarm of dandelion seeds into the air. It's a photograph that captures a perfect moment in time. Even a casual observer can see the warmth in the woman's smile, the love that radiates from her startling blue eyes. Did Jack take this? I'm thinking he probably did.

I place the photo back and glance around, hoping there might be more. I don't see any. No wedding photograph. That's a shame. I suspect they would have made a striking couple. She certainly would have been a beautiful bride.

Strangely, she seems familiar, and I can't help thinking I might have met her. Something tugs at the periphery of my memory as I head back to the kitchen to grab a glass of water, but it's gone before I can grasp it. The house is immaculately tidy, I can't help but notice the absence of children's toys too. Jack's clearly a natural tidier-upper.

Walking past his office door, I pause and backstep, wondering if he might have a wedding photograph in there. He keeps the door closed, as he does all the doors upstairs – to stop his overgrown puppy from leaving muddy paw prints on the duvets and causing general mayhem, he said. Jester, it seems, is particularly partial to manilla folders, chewing them up and spitting them out all over the house, which throws his client records into complete disarray. 'I shouldn't have hard copies lying around, but I'm not that great at typing up my hand-written notes,' he admitted. I'd offered to help out, since I'm cutting down my own client meetings ready for my maternity leave. Jack said he would appreciate it. 'But maybe in a couple of weeks,' he suggested, after I'd had time to process all that was happening in my life and taken some time out to rest.

It's comforting, I think now, to have someone around who genuinely seems to care for me. My heart twists as my mind goes to Richie and where he might be. He hasn't contacted me since his revelation about Tom, which I don't know whether to believe. The fact that he hasn't been in touch makes me think that he was lying in some desperate attempt to throw me off the scent. How many lies has he told me? Might the fires have been designed to detract suspicion from himself? A 'terrifying extreme' to avoid having his lies exposed?

Pushing thoughts of Richie and all the hurt and confusion that comes with them aside, I hesitate outside the study door, and then, with curiosity about the man I'm now almost sharing my life with getting the better of me, I push the handle down. I'm surprised when I go in. Far from files and paperwork every-where, as I'd expected there might be, Jack having hinted he was disorganised, the office is meticulously tidy. Also empty, apart from an antique desk in the middle of the room, on top of which sits a laptop. I walk across to it. There's no photograph on the desk, as I'd also thought there might be, particularly of his children; there's nothing but a small, neat pile of files, the top one of which bears a familiar name.

I step closer. *Emelia Connor?* Even reading it upside down, there's no mistaking it. Why would Jack have a file about Emelia? *Had* she consulted him? But he'd never said. My head a whirl of confusion, I go around the desk and open the file. As I register the long ago date at the top of the first page, the heading scrawled beneath it, capitalised and underlined twice: *THE BEACH PARTY,* my heart stalls. Then freezes, my blood running cold in my veins as I hear a key in the front door.

I hold my breath as the front door closes. There's nothing for an agonisingly long second, then, 'Come on, trouble,' Jack says, 'kitchen, before you tread mud all over the place.'

Listening, my chest palpitating, I hear Jester's claws scratting on the flagstones in the hall as he scrambles that way. I wait another second then, assuming Jack's followed him, head tentatively towards the partially open study door. My heart almost leaps right out of my mouth as I pull it open to find Jack standing right in front of me.

'Looking for something?' he asks, his eyes narrowed curiously.

'Um, computer.' I wave a hand vaguely behind me. 'I was thinking I should order some things online but I realised I don't have your password.'

Jack eyes me quietly for a second, and then nods. 'You should have said. I'll write them down for you.' He waits until I've joined him in the hall, then closes the door behind me.

FIFTY-ONE

EMELIA

Feeling a tug on her sleeve, Emelia woke with a jolt to find Josh standing over her. 'Where's Dad?' he asked, his eyes – cool grey eyes that mirrored his father's – flinty and dispassionate.

It took her a second to comprehend where she was, what day it was. On the sofa, she gathered, taking in her surroundings. And it was the morning after the dreadful night before, when she'd finally drunk herself into true oblivion. What had she done? Recalling the havoc she'd wreaked in the bedroom before half-stumbling down the stairs to make her way to the lounge, only just reaching the sofa before collapsing, she wanted to curl up and die.

Realising what she must look like – it was reflected in her son's unflinching, unimpressed gaze, she pulled herself up and the room tilted dangerously. How much had she drunk? Her gaze going to the coffee table, she noted the empty vodka bottle standing there, and deep remorse crashed through her.

She looked back to Josh who looked mutely back at her. He was waiting for an answer, and Emelia had no clue what to say to him. 'Is he not upstairs?' she managed, her throat like coarse sandpaper.

In that moment, Josh looked every inch his father's son, shaking his head in despair before tearing his gaze away and going to slump down in an armchair.

'He's not there, Mummy,' came a small voice from the lounge doorway. Emelia swung her gaze that way to see her little girl looking nervously at her over the Hungry Caterpillar soft toy she had tucked up to her chin, and her heart fractured. Not for herself, but for her children, who she was subjecting to the exact same trauma she'd suffered as a girl. A trauma she'd carried into adulthood, as would they. They would have no memories of her that weren't tainted by alcohol. What in God's name was *wrong* with her?

'Come here.' Thinking better of standing up and inevitably reeling, she extended an arm, beckoning Charlotte to her.

Charlotte hesitated for a moment, then, clearly in need of physical reassurance, flew across to her. Emelia drew her tight, breathing in the innocent smell of her. 'He had a long work meeting last night, sweetheart.' With no idea where Tom was, she lied for him, again. 'He probably decided to have a little sleep in his office so he could drive home safely.'

Easing back, she scanned her little girl's eyes. 'I expect he'll be home very soon,' she added when Charlotte looked as if she didn't quite believe her. 'All right, sweetheart?'

Charlotte hesitated. 'Uh-huh.' She nodded eventually, still not looking very convinced. Then, 'Did we have a burglar, Mummy?' she asked, a worried little v creasing her forehead.

Oh no. The bedroom. They'd obviously been in there, looking for their daddy. Emelia squeezed her eyes closed, images of a woman possessed pulling clothes from wardrobes and drawers, frenziedly searching through pockets – as if Tom would be careless enough to leave evidence of his infidelity for her to find – before tossing them arbitrarily around the room. She'd been going to stuff them all in black bin bags and leave the bags on the drive. She'd been too drunk to finish the job.

She'd told him she was bolting the door – she recalled as her brain cells kicked in. That's why he hadn't come back. It was nothing to do with the ridiculous insinuations that Simons woman made, implying that they thought Tom was responsible for starting those fires, dropping hints about Pippa. Tom was a lot of things, but he wasn't a monster. He might not love her, but he loved his children. He would never do anything that might hurt them.

It was her who was doing that. Emelia's heart plummeted to the pit of her stomach as another recollection of her pathetic behaviour last night came starkly back, the awful accusations she'd hurled at Becky of all people, the person who'd always been there for her. *Oh God.* She winced inwardly as she remembered accusing her friend of using Tom to get pregnant. She needed help. She really did.

And her babies didn't need this, a mother who prioritised drinking over their welfare.

'Come on, sweetheart.' Getting shakily to her feet, she took Charlotte's hand and led her over to her brother, who was still in the armchair, swiping moodily through his iPad. 'You two settle down in front of the television for a while, will you? Mummy has some things she has to do.'

'But, Mummy, it's a school day.' Charlotte looked up at her in wide-eyed surprise.

'I know, darling, but it won't hurt you to have one day off. We'll go out later to the park and then maybe go to McDonald's. Do you fancy that, Josh?' She looked hopefully at her son, as Charlotte settled happily down on the rug in anticipation of CBBC.

Josh shrugged. He didn't look up.

Emelia crouched down in front of him. 'I'm sorry, Josh,' she said.

His gaze flicked briefly to hers, and then he slumped further down in his chair. He gave her the impression he wanted to disappear inside himself, just as she had so many times as a child, and she hated herself for doing that to him. 'One of the things I have to do is make a doctor's appointment,' she added, and waited.

Josh glanced warily up, and Emelia felt a piece of herself die inside. He didn't trust her. How could he when she just kept letting him down, letting herself down? It had to stop. Now. 'I'm going to change, Josh,' she said determinedly. 'I'm not sure I can do it on my own, though. I might need some help from the doctor, but I'm going to try.' She told him honestly.

Josh looked at her full on, finally.

'Do you believe me?' she asked, hoping she wasn't putting too much on his small shoulders. But then, she'd already done that, hadn't she?

Josh searched her face, there was still a flicker of doubt in his eyes, there was bound to be that, but he nodded after a moment.

'Thank you.' Swallowing emotionally, Emelia straightened up. 'Do you think you could do me a huge favour and select something suitable for your sister to watch while I go and make that call and get showered?' she asked him.

'Yay! *Lu and the Bally Bunch*.' Charlotte clapped excitedly.

'Boring.' Josh sighed but slid dutifully from his seat anyway.

'Thanks, Josh.' Emelia smiled and turned to the door. She badly wanted to hug him but guessed that might be pushing it. She wouldn't blame him, but she didn't think she could bear it if he pulled away from her. 'We'll settle down together and watch a film this afternoon. Your choice.'

'Cool,' Josh answered with a trace of a smile.

'Subject to parental approval,' Emelia added as she headed for the hall. She managed a smile herself despite her pounding head when Josh rolled his eyes. He was more like Tom than Tom was sometimes. Her buoyed up mood deflated immediately as her thoughts went back to him, where he might be and who with.

Jack Evans had been right when he'd guessed she used alcohol to boost her confidence. He was shrewd, had a way of getting people to confide in him. Becky obviously had regarding the *incident* at university. Emelia had no way of knowing how much she'd told him without talking to her. The chances of Becky wanting to talk to her ever again, though, she imagined were nil, particularly now she was installed with Jack.

He'd wangled that well. Emelia just knew his interest in Becky went beyond professional. Did Becky realise it? Was it reciprocal? He was a good-looking guy, well off, charming, apparently caring, which Richie seemed to be anything but right now.

Where was Richie? she wondered. She'd said some awful things about him, too. Some of it was true. It was obvious that Pippa had fancied him from the doe eyes she'd made at him, particularly that day on the beach. Wherever he was he would be in a terrible state. Did Becky know where he was? She and Becky needed to talk, properly, not over the phone. And not when other people were around, namely Jack Evans, who, in Emelia's mind, appeared to be isolating Becky from everyone but himself.

FIFTY-TWO

BECKY

'Hey? How are you?' Jack smiles his usual smile as I open the front door of the apartment. If he was perturbed at finding I'd been in his office, he hadn't shown it. He'd simply written down the password to his PC on a slip of paper and handed it to me, which must mean he's unconcerned about anything I might see on there.

'Fine.' I give him a smile back. 'Sorry I couldn't manage to eat much last night. I think I must have been exhausted. I slept like a log,' I lie, rather than worry him. I'd hardly slept at all, my mind going over all that had happened until I felt I was going insane. When I had dozed off, I'd had the most bizarre nightmare, finding myself running through never-ending corridors of a house with no doors, where the walls turned to flames and arms with blackened, blistered flesh reached out, clawed fingers clutching at my clothes.

Then she'd been there, standing in front of me, her limbs and torso pale and naked, apart from the algae. *Becky. Becky, come with me.* Her voice was an urgent whisper. *You'll be safe with me. The flames won't reach you.* She stretched out a hand, her flesh touching mine, ice cold. *No one will find you. You'll be safe in the sea. With me.* A shudder runs through me as I recall her eyes, wide, opaque, looking into mine right down to my soul.

'That will be your body telling you you need to slow down,' he says, concern in his eyes as he looks me over. 'You're cold. Go back inside. I just came across to let you know I have a couple of appointments this morning. I should be back around three. Jester will be fine until then.'

'Right.' I nod and smile. 'Are you sure you don't want me to walk him?'

'Only if you fancy some air,' he says. 'He's obviously taken a shine to you and he's always up for it, but don't feel obliged. He's been out this morning and he's getting used to being on his own, which is a good thing with Katie thinking about going back to work. I'd better get off. See you later.'

'How is she?' I ask quickly, as he turns to go.

Jack turns back. 'Good,' he says. 'I chatted to her first thing. She's tired, obviously, but doing okay.'

'And her mother?' I enquire after her. 'Do they have a prognosis yet?'

'Not yet, no.' Jack sighs. 'She's having a scan later today to check the lymph nodes. Obviously her treatment plan will depend on the outcome of that.'

I note his troubled expression and guess he must be worried. I can't help wondering why he's not more in touch with Katie, though. I haven't seen him talk to her, other than that once. But then, I suppose they might have an agreed time to talk, given how full her hands must be caring for her mother. 'Give her my best, won't you?'

Jack looks me over for a second, then nods. 'I will.'

'How are the children?' I stop him again as he steps away. 'It must be difficult for them being away from home,' I venture.

Jack's forehead creases into a thoughtful frown. 'I think they're a little bit bewildered by all that's happening, but Katie's great with them. She's explained everything to them in terms they'll understand, and they enjoy being with their nana and gramps so... She'll call me if she thinks they need to be at home.'

I nod. 'Are they not missing school, though?' I ask, pressing it a little. 'I assume the school's okay with them taking time off?'

Jack's scans my eyes, his own curious. 'They're on their Easter break right now. If they do have to stay for a while, though, Katie's a teacher,' he reminds me. 'So I imagine the school would be okay with her home-schooling for a while.'

'Ah, yes. You did say.' I roll my eyes, as if in despair of myself. 'Sorry. My head's like a sieve lately. And I've been so preoccupied with my own problems, I forgot to ask you about yours. I was just a bit concerned.'

'No need to apologise. I understand why you would be.' Jack smiles. An inscrutable smile this time, and perhaps a little less effusive. Looking away, he checks his watch. 'I should go. My first appointment's due.'

'Yes, of course. Sorry,' I apologise, again.

Jack studies me for a second longer, then attempts again to head for his car.

'What are their names?' I call after him. 'The children? You never told me.'

Jack turns, studies me pensively. 'Mia,' he says. 'Mia and Ryan. I think that's your phone.' He nods past me to where my phone's ringing behind me.

As he walks away, I close the door and lean against it, my heart palpitating. I was cross questioning him. He knew I was. I have no idea why I was, except... While I understand his wife wouldn't want to be barraged with calls, and he had said he'd spoken with her this morning, I haven't actually seen him speak to his children at all. No phone calls. No FaceTime. Surely he would want to talk to them, ask them about their day, wish them goodnight before bed? I wonder again why I haven't seen any children's toys about the house.

FIFTY-THREE

After closing the front door, I grab up my phone, my stomach knotting as I note it's Detective Simons calling. Bracing myself, I tentatively answer it.

'Mrs Shaw,' she says, 'Detective Simons. How are you?'

'Coping,' I reply, not sure how else to answer.

'Silly question really, wasn't it?' she says, clearly realising it was. 'Did everything go okay at the hospital?' she asks kindly.

She seems genuinely concerned. She's obviously leading up to something, though. 'Yes, thanks. They think it was just the baby turning early.'

'Plus the shock of having your life ripped apart.' The detective emits a despairing sigh. 'You must be in bits.'

Finding my eyes filling up in the face of her sympathy, I take a breath. 'I've definitely been better,' I reply. 'I'm struggling to know where to start putting things back together, to be honest.'

'I can imagine.' Another sigh. 'Look, I know it's not much comfort considering the state the house will be in, but the forensic investigators have finished their examination and the fire officer says it safe to go back inside.'

An image of my home and everything in it burnt or smoke damaged flashes into my mind and I wonder if I can bear to go into it ever again. If I even want to. Did my baby's polka dot giraffe survive? His little rocking horse? If they did, will I ever get the smell of smoke out of them? I doubt it. Out of the nursery either. It will have permeated the walls. 'So I can go back?' I ask, not quite able to believe I just turn up there and they hand me the keys.

'You'll need to contact the fire officer,' she advises. 'He'll let you have a handover sheet, formally agreeing that the property has been handed back to you. You'll find he will have listed details of any recommended advice and known safety issues. If you don't move back in immediately – which I assume you won't, you'll need to remove any valuables or important documents from the property and make sure all windows and doors are locked, or else contact a contractor should any require boarding up. Your insurer would normally pay out for that type of work.' She pauses. 'Do you know whether your home insurance was up to date?'

'It was paid out of my account,' I answer, gathering why she would be asking.

'Well, that's a relief,' she says, as if anything could be. 'You'll need to fill in a claim form. I'll text you a reference number. Also make sure to get appropriate advice regarding reconnection of gas, electricity and water supplies.' She pauses again. Then, 'Have you heard from your husband at all, Mrs Shaw? He hasn't been interviewed yet and we're keen to talk to him, obviously.'

'We spoke yesterday,' I answer guardedly. 'We haven't been in touch much since it happened, though. I'm actually not sure how things are between us,' I add, guessing she will find out that Richie and I are not together anyway.

'I'm sorry,' she says, again sounding genuine, which

surprises me. 'I wonder, if he calls again, could you tell him to get in touch with us as soon as possible?'

'I will.' I take another breath and steel myself to ask what I have to. 'So, do you think it was him who started the fires?'

She hesitates. 'He is a person of interest, yes,' she replies, honestly. 'He was caught on CCTV near to the business property around the time the fire started. I admit, though, that we can't find a conceivable motive. We've checked his financial situation, which is messy, and followed up his claim that his building and contents insurance wasn't paid. It checks out. Also, it seems the insurance premiums on your life insurance policies haven't been paid, so there's no motive there.'

My stomach twists as I try to take stock. He really was in a mess, wasn't he? Why couldn't he have told me? 'He wasn't trying to murder me then?' I ask. It was a feeble attempt at a joke, but even I can hear the underlying fear in my voice.

'Not unless you can think of any other reason for him wanting to do so.' Detective Simons' voice is both curious and cautious.

Because he wants to be with Emelia. Because they both want to keep me quiet. That thought goes again through my mind. But that just seems ludicrous. None of it makes sense. Why would he burn his own office down? How could he live a life with me that was nothing but a lie, hiding a part of himself so completely? I recall what Jack had said about narcissistic personalities using the pretence of emotion to control others. But it can't *all* have been pretence. Can it? I'm struggling to believe it.

'I wonder if you could throw some light on some information that was passed on to us,' Detective Simons cuts through my thoughts. 'I mentioned it to Emelia Connor. She might have spoken to you about it?'

Recalling the awful conversation I'd had with Emelia, her vitriol and her furious accusations, about me, about Richie, I feel the knot of tension tighten inside me. 'She didn't mention anything specifically,' I say vaguely. 'We did speak recently, but mostly about her relationship with Tom.'

'The person we spoke to seems to think she's carrying some guilt about an event in the past,' the detective goes on, 'around the death of one Pippa Moore. As I say, I did ask Mrs Connor about it, but she seemed rather distressed by the subject.'

I feel the hairs rise over my body at the mention of Pippa. 'She never said anything,' I lie, my mouth running dry. Who'd spoken to Simons? Emelia thought it was me. I understood more now why she would.

'We made some preliminary investigations,' Simons continues, as my mind reels. 'Unfortunately, due to the nature of the girl's death and some less than diligent police work at the time, we haven't got very far. As yet.' Again, she pauses, pointedly. 'We do know she was at a beach party that night, along with yourself and your husband. Also Emelia and Thomas Connor.'

'That's right,' I manage. I hear the tremor in my voice and pray that she can't.

'I just wondered, was Pippa dating?' the woman asks, as if mildly interested. 'There's mention of her possibly meeting someone in the report, but it's very vague.'

'I'm not sure,' I answer, my chest banging. 'I think we all thought she must have been.'

Simons falls silent for a moment. 'But she wasn't dating Thomas Connor or your husband?' she asks, getting to the point. The point being that it might have been Tom or Richie she was with that night.

'No,' I answer quickly. 'Richie and I were together then, so were Emelia and Tom.'

'I see,' Simons says, at length. 'Just one more thing, if I may?'

I wait, a combination of nausea and nerves churning inside me.

'I did ask the same question of Mrs Connor,' she goes on.

'We caught another image on CCTV cameras, both outside your husband's business premises and one from doorbell footage near to your home, a man similar in height and weight to both your husband and Mr Connor. He was wearing a black hoodie. Mrs Connor doesn't recall her husband owning such an item. Does Richard own one, Mrs Shaw?'

FIFTY-FOUR

Having said I can't recall whether Richie owns such an item, I end the call as calmly as I can. It's another lie, one I doubt Detective Simons believes. Might they have historical CCTV footage? I've no idea how long doorbell footage is retained for, but if they have access to it, they're bound to pick him up out running. Where is the hoodie? Are they looking to retrieve it in the hope of finding damning evidence on it, accelerant or something? Is it really possible it was Richie who set fire to our house with me inside it? He hasn't been in contact since we last spoke, and his silence is beginning to scream guilty.

But why all of this now? As far as I can reason, it all goes back to Pippa. Someone is trying to ensure that what happened in the past stays there. People are *dying*. Being deliberately targeted. But why Jodie? Why Zoe? It was only ever Emelia and I who'd suspected one of our group had been with Pippa that night, and then we'd barely admitted it to each other out loud – until now. Emelia had said it out loud, screamed it. Despite knowing what Tom is like, even imagining he and I were having an affair, incredibly, still she thought it was Richie. He'd said it was Tom, but I just don't know. Why is Richie not in touch with me? About the baby? About the house and what happens next? I try to tell myself it's because he can't face me, but is it? I'm carrying his *child*. The man I know wouldn't just abandon me. The man I thought I knew.

Who passed 'information' on to Detective Simons? Would someone who was bound to be implicated do *that*? My heart twists with confusion and fear. I'm desperate to talk to Emelia, to know she's all right. I also want to know what the hell she meant when she said she didn't trust Jack. Telling me that I shouldn't trust him either, the man who's there for me when no one else cares enough to be. It's Tom who can't be trusted. I should have told her the truth about Tom, which might have stopped her verbal assault in its tracks.

I can't call her now, not when I'm feeling so emotional. With questions ricocheting around in my head, I decide to go for a walk and get some fresh air instead. Sitting around here worrying isn't go to help me or my baby, who's practically gambolling inside me. Taking calming slow breaths, I grab my phone and the door key. As I head through the front door, I'm surprised to see Jack pulling up on the drive.

'Hey.' He smiles, as he climbs out of his car. 'Off somewhere?'

'Just for a walk.' I give him a smile back as I head towards him. 'You're soon back.'

'Cancelled appointment,' he explains. 'Client had an important family matter to attend to.'

'Ah.' I nod. Emelia? I wonder, my mind going to the file I'd seen in his study. Her family matter being no more than that she's hopelessly hungover? I want to ask him about the file, in particular the date of the beach party he'd headed his first page of notes with. He'd said it would be unethical to disclose anything that went on in the therapy room, though, and I guess that includes disclosing who might have consulted him.

'Fancy some company?' he asks. 'I'm pretty sure Jester would be up for it.'

'I'd love some,' I say, thinking I might find an opportunity to broach the subject, amongst other things.

'Great. I'll be two minutes.' Jack heads for the front door. He's no sooner opened it than Jester is through it, bounding towards me, his tail going like a propellor.

'Jester, down!' Jack yells, racing after him to grab hold of his collar. 'Christ, sorry,' he says, relief sweeping his features as he stops him before he launches himself at me. 'He's obviously besotted with you.'

'Aw, he's just a bit overenthusiastic.' I bend to give the dog a fuss. 'He wouldn't have hurt me, would you, Jester?'

'I wouldn't be too sure about that.' Jack still sounds concerned. 'He must be at least half your weight. He might have knocked you flying.'

I smile up at him. 'I'll make sure to practise my *Down* command. It worked, didn't it, hey, boy? Good dog.'

'I'll go and grab his lead and give you two a moment.' Jack rolls his eyes as Jester stares up at me, looking, I have to say, a little bit besotted, and then offers me a paw.

'At least somebody loves me, hey, Jester?' I whisper, and I crouch to give the dog a hug.

'Don't mind me,' Jack says, finding me still fussing Jester when he comes back with the lead. 'I'll just look the other way, shall I?'

'If you could.' I laugh, straightening up to allow him to attach it.

'Unfaithful mutt.' Jack strokes the dog's head, clearly not the least bit perturbed by his unfaithfulness.

Minutes later, we're strolling along the country lane that leads to the house, Jester prancing happily ahead of us. There's a lull in the perpetual April rain and with the sun breaking through the clouds and actual blue sky overhead, I begin to feel a little less stressed.

'It's nice to see you relaxing,' Jack says, glancing at me as we walk.

I breathe in the clean air. 'It's nice to feel relaxed.' I smile.

'How's the little one?' he asks, nodding towards my bump.

I place a hand on my tummy. 'Kicking less frenetically. I think he's feeling more relaxed too.'

'Good.' Jack smiles. 'Too much stress isn't beneficial during pregnancy, as you would know.'

I nod, my mind flying back to the baby I'd lost all those years ago, our perfect little Angel. I recall how visibly heartbroken Richie had been as we'd parted with the few precious things we'd bought for her, the tears he'd cried. Those weren't the reactions of a man who couldn't connect on an emotional level. It wasn't a pretence of emotion. His pain had been raw. Real. At least, I'd thought it was.

'How are your children?' I ask, wondering now how Jack can bear not to be with them.

'Good,' he says. 'I haven't spoken to them for a couple of days. I'm aiming to catch up with them later.'

'Don't you miss them?' I probe a little. 'I think I would.'

'All the time.' He smiles sadly.

I note his downward glance and feel for him. 'Do you have any photos of them?' I ask, hoping he won't think I'm prying too much. 'I didn't see any around the house and I'd love to look at some.'

Jack stops walking.

I grind to a halt beside him, wondering if there's a problem. There doesn't appear to be. Jester is only yards away.

'I need to tell you something,' he says, glancing briefly at me and then away. 'I haven't been quite straight with you.'

I look him over warily.

'I didn't mean not to be.' His gaze flicks cautiously to mine.

'I just didn't want you thinking I had ulterior motives. I don't,' he adds hastily. 'I...'

'Jack? What?' I urge him, my stomach lurching. 'You're scaring me.'

'Christ, no. Don't be scared.' He moves towards me.

I move instinctively back. I can't help myself.

He stops, his expression a combination of guilt and panic. 'I didn't mean to do that. I just...' Again, he falters. 'Katie and I, we... we're estranged.'

'You mean,' I shake my head, incredulous, 'you're separated?'

He nods awkwardly. 'Temporarily,' he says. 'At least I hoped it was. She doesn't appear to be in a hurry to come back, though. There's no one else,' he adds, meeting my gaze full on at last, if nervously. 'At least, there isn't now.'

'But there was?' I study him carefully, uncertain how I'll feel if he tells me he cheated on her. Yet, I know. I'll feel let down, incredibly. Had I really set him up on such a high pedestal I didn't think it was possible he would do such a thing?

'A while back,' he confirms. 'The thing is, he lives in the same village as her parents. An old flame. Obviously the spark's still there. I'm sorry,' he says, his voice strained. 'I shouldn't have been less than truthful with you.'

I stare at him, stunned, which obviously makes him feel worse. He looks away, kneads his eyes with his thumb and forefinger, as if trying to hold his tears back – and my heart goes out to him. Is that why he didn't feel able to tell me, because he was embarrassed, because he felt inadequate in some way? Might that explain the lack of photographs? But, even though they're estranged, they're still talking, reasonably amicably if the one conversation I overheard is anything to judge by, which means there's still hope, surely? He'd said he loved her *very much*, I remember it distinctly. Would he really have taken down photographs of his family, his children?

FIFTY-FIVE

When we reach the courtyard, I glance at Jack, unsure what to say. He looks as uncertain as I feel. 'I should probably go in.' I nod towards the apartment. 'Emelia called me. I have to call her back,' I add, lying a little. How big does a lie have to be to make it unforgivable? I wonder.

Jack nods. 'Becky,' he stops me as I turn to go, 'I am sorry. I really didn't mean to mislead you. With my offering you the apartment, I genuinely thought you might think I had an ulterior motive. And I guess I was still hoping things would blow over and that Katie would come back.'

'You don't think she will then?' I search his face. He looks tired, dark bruises under his eyes I hadn't noticed earlier. He obviously hasn't slept well either.

'Honestly,' he takes a breath, 'I don't know.'

'Is her mother really ill?' I ask. I guess it sounds like I'm accusing him of lying about that too, but I have to know.

'She is.' He sighs and kneads his forehead. 'The thing is, I don't know whether that's why she really feels the need to stay, or whether...' He trails off with a disconsolate shrug.

It's an excuse to see the other man? To give herself time to make up her mind? I note the tangible hurt in his eyes, and I can't help feeling devastated for him.

'Don't suppose you fancy a coffee, do you?' he asks hopefully.

I guess he's worried he might have lost my friendship. He hasn't. I'd had him down as perfect. He's not, but it doesn't mean he was there any less for me than he was. If anything, I respect that he didn't try to play the sympathy card, which he could easily have done. He's clearly heartbroken, yet he went out of his way to help me.

'I think I just might,' I accept, empathising with how lonely he must be feeling. 'And I think Jester could use a drink too.' I nod at the dog, who's looking between us, tongue lolling, tail wagging, and covered in mud.

'And a bath.' Jack smiles. It suits him better than his downcast look of a second ago.

Once in the kitchen, I offer to make the coffee while Jack takes Jester upstairs to hose him off with the shower. He's back minutes later, a wet Jester close on his heels, who shakes himself all over the kitchen. 'I guess that's a small plus to being on our own,' Jack says reflectively as he watches him. 'We don't get told off for making a mess, do we, Jester?'

He beckons the dog across, who proceeds to shake himself all over him. 'Cheers, mate.' Jacks sighs and goes cross-eyed.

I laugh even though I've been caught in the spray. 'Coffee,' I say, carrying it across to the table.

'Thanks.' Jack glances at me as he sits, his expression cautious, as if he's not quite sure how the land lies between us.

I smile as I join him, at which his relief is obvious. 'What happened?' I ask. It's none of my business, I know, but I can't help wondering why, when he's obviously so caring, his wife would have become involved with someone else. 'You don't have to tell me if you don't want to,' I add, aware he might find it difficult to talk about.

'I think I probably do given I've lied to you.' He looks apologetically at me. 'Honestly, though, I'm not entirely sure. We grew apart, I suppose. My fault. I was so steeped in grief after my mother's death and my father's suicide I became emotionally inaccessible, retreating inside myself rather than talking about it, drinking too much, which is why I understand why Emelia feels the need to. It doesn't make it any less frustrating viewed from the outside, but I get why she does.'

He pauses, takes a sip of his coffee, and I want to ask him more about Emelia, the file that's sitting on his desk, but I stop myself. I will ask, but not now. I need to hear what he has to say about the state of his marriage.

He places his mug down, twists it round, stares at it contemplatively.

'I wasn't there for her,' he goes on after a pause. 'Katie was struggling. With two small children and me being emotionally inaccessible, she was bound to be. She tried to talk to me. I listened, but I wasn't hearing her. I suppose she might understand more now why I was struggling. Grief can sometimes be all consuming. I did something about it eventually, sought help when I realised I was sinking into a pit I might not be able to climb out of. Too late, unfortunately.' He draws in a tight breath. 'The affair happened. We tried to move past it, but I was angry and guilty in turn. She was stuffed full of guilt. There was a distance between us there never was before. We couldn't fix it.'

'Did you forgive her?' I ask.

He draws in a breath, picks up his mug and places it down again. 'I tried to. I guess I didn't try hard enough. It was always there between us, you know?' He shrugs. 'And then her mother got sick. I understood why she had to go back, but that was difficult, her going back to the village the guy still lives and works in.'

I see a flash of hurt and humiliation in his expression and I feel for him. 'Is she seeing him, do you think?' I ask tentatively.

'I don't know.' He blows out a breath. 'My gut tells me yes, but my heart... I guess I don't want to believe it. I still love her. I *really* wish I didn't.'

'I'm sorry, Jack,' I offer, not sure what else to say.

Jack nods and smiles. 'Whoever said love hurts, was wrong. It's being in love with someone who doesn't love you back that hurts.'

He runs a hand tiredly over his neck. 'I should stop before someone gets the violins out.' Standing, he walks across the kitchen. 'I have some very indulgent milk chocolate cookies somewhere. Fancy one?'

He's trying to make light of things, I realise, but it's quite obvious he's crushed. My heart aches for him. 'Why not? We might as well indulge together,' I joke. 'Oh.' I feel my cheeks flush as he arches an amused eyebrow in my direction. 'That didn't come out quite right, did it?'

He laughs and shakes his head. 'About the family photographs you mentioned,' he says, fetching cookies from the cupboard and carrying them across, 'I took them all down. I think I was thinking out of sight out of mind. They're not. Out of mind, I mean, obviously.'

'No. I understand what you mean,' I empathise. 'I don't think I'd want to look at my wedding photographs right now.' I sigh inwardly as I imagine them curled up and scorched anyway, which might just be emblematic of the state of my marriage.

He offers me a cookie. 'Shall we indulge?'

I can't help but smile. He really does have a knack of making me do that. I help myself to a very large, decadent cookie, probably full of sugar, but I figure, since I've been generally good throughout my pregnancy a little overindulgence won't hurt.

He bites into his with a smile, then rolls his eyes as his phone rings. Half-swallowing, he picks it up from the table and answers it between chews. 'Right. I'm on my way. Delivery van,' he says, ending the call. 'It's stuck in the lane. It will be the bed linen and summer duvet I ordered for the apartment. Back shortly.'

Taking his cookie with him he heads for the front door. It's no sooner closed behind him than Jester makes a bolt for the hall.

Oh hell, he's going up the stairs, and he's still wet. 'Jester,' I call, heading to the hall and then up the stairs after him when he pays no heed to my beckoning him down.

Seeing the main bedroom door open and hearing suspicious snuffling noises from within that sound very much like he's jumped on the bed, I hurry in that direction. My heart sinks as my fears are confirmed and I find him ruffling up the duvet. 'Jester, down!' I walk across to him and attempt to shoo him off, which Jester thinks is great fun, and proceeds to scoot around in a circle. 'You are going to be in big trouble,' I warn him, finally managing to encourage him off. 'Huge.'

I start after him as, following my firmly pointed finger, the dog bounds towards the landing. Then stop. The bedroom seems bereft of anything female. No make-up, hair parapher-nalia or perfume on the dressing table. No dressing gown on the back of the door. But she'd probably taken that with her. How much had she taken? I can't help but wonder.

I shouldn't but... Curiosity gets the better of me and I check through the window for signs of Jack coming back, then go to the wardrobe. Tentatively, I open the wardrobe doors. Men's clothes, Jack's clothes, hang on one side of the wardrobe. There are no clothes on the other side, nothing but a few empty coat hangers. She'd taken everything? Surely that must mean she has no intention of coming back?

Closing the doors, I head quickly back towards the bedroom door. Then stop again, dead, as I spot something on top of the chest of drawers against the door wall. An asthma inhaler. But Jack doesn't have asthma.

FIFTY-SIX

DETECTIVE INSPECTOR SIMONS

Megan peered over the shoulder of the digital forensic investigator, hoping for something that might help identify the person captured on CCTV in the vicinity of Richard Shaw's business premises and also his home. They had a clear image of Shaw minus the hoodie entering the business property prior to the fire being reported. No evidence of him leaving, but as the DFI had pointed out, the entrance at the back of the premises could be accessed from both sides of the building. There were no cameras covering one side, meaning he could have taken that route. They had no other images of him until he'd been picked up in the town centre hours later. What they did have were images of someone in a black hoodie pausing outside his home address, and a similar image of someone wearing a hoodie going around the back of the business property. 'Are you sure it's a black hoodie?' Megan peered more closely at the second video. In the footage outside the house, the hoodie looked black, but the footage outside the business premises was grainy and blurred, the colour shades shifting depending on light and movement.

'It's certainly dark in colour.' Calvin clicked through the

individual frames. 'And see here,' he zoomed in on one, 'the light bouncing off the shoulder area?'

Megan squinted at the screen.

'It looks to me like three white stripes running from shoulder to elbow.' Calvin indicated with his pen.

'As in the same garment worn by the person outside the house?'

'It would appear to be,' Calvin confirmed. 'There's also this.' He scrolled the footage back to another image of the person approaching the building and zoomed right in. 'It's a logo,' he said. 'I'll try to enhance it further but it looks to me like the classic Adidas badge.'

Which the hoodie in the first video also bore. 'And you reckon it's definitely a man?'

'From the height, approximately six foot, and the gait,' he rolled the video to show the person walking, 'I'd say it was.'

Which meant it could be Richard Shaw or Thomas Connor – both were a similar height and size. Then again it could conceivably be any other man around that height. Straightening up, Megan blew out a sigh of frustration. She'd been positive Shaw had set the fires, but with nothing to gain financially he appeared to have no motive. She didn't think murder was it. He seemed devastated about the split with his wife, *because of a stupid argument about nothing*, he said when she had managed to speak to him at his parents' house before he disappeared off the radar. When she pressed him, he admitted his wife thought he was involved with Emelia Connor, which was apparently *all in her mind*. That comment didn't endear him to Megan, but not rating the guy was no reason to suspect him capable of murder.

It did lead her to consider Thomas Connor, however, jealousy being one of the prime motives for murder. He wouldn't have been happy discovering his 'friend' was sleeping with his wife. It was the historical connection of all parties involved that was bugging her, though. She felt sure there was something they were collectively hiding from their past around the death of fellow student, Pippa Moore, the original investigation into which was lacking, to say the least. The senior officer in charge had been distracted by his kid's leukaemia diagnosis and treatment, apparently. She'd learned the child had died months later and the SOC had left the force shortly afterwards. Megan felt for him, more than he would ever know. Since her daughter's death five short years ago, she'd learned to cope with the everyday grief of her absence. The unexpected episodes, though, a tsunami of grief crashing to the surface when you least expected it, those sucked the breath from her body. Megan wondered if the grieving would ever stop. In a way, she didn't want it to. It was when she allowed herself to feel the emotions that she found herself in a place where she reconnected with her, where she could almost taste, feel and smell her. The drunken bastard that had taken her away from her in a hit-and-run could never take that away from her. Her memories were what sustained her in her bleakest moments. She'd almost lost her while she'd been carrying her. She supposed that was why she felt an affinity with Rebecca Shaw after her recent pregnancy scare.

She'd approached the DCI about looking into the Pippa Moore case and made a few preliminary enquiries but, as yet, she'd come up blank. With the advancement in forensic biology and DNA profiling, she'd hoped the clothing they'd found, the bikini bottoms and denim shorts, might yield new evidence. They'd yielded nothing, which was a blow. She might be wrong, of course, but Megan's gut told her there was a connection between what happened to Pippa Moore and what was going down now.

'Right. Thanks, Calvin,' she said, and headed for the door. She would have to dig deeper if she was going to catch her arsonist. She also wanted to know more about Jack Evans. His known association with Jodie Gallagher, Emelia Connor and Rebecca Shaw meant he might just know more than he was letting on. More than he was willing to share, too, probably, without a warrant. She sighed inwardly.

'Not much help, is it?' Calvin said behind her.

'It narrows it down,' she assured him. If only they could find the hoodie, it would narrow it down a hell of a lot further. She needed more. The forensics collected from the fire scenes yielded nothing. Fingerprint and DNA evidence belonged to the people who worked in the business premises, or else any number of clients visiting the building, including those obtained from the entrance at the back of it. That door had been found unlocked and the assumption was that Paul Holmes, who was a smoker, had gone out for a ciggie break. The only real lead was the same person showing up at both properties prior to the fires and the owner of the properties, Richard Shaw, acting suspiciously. As with the business premises, there was clear evidence of an accelerant having been used at the house – confirmed by gas chromatography to be petroleum – and multiple sites of ignition, meaning someone was inside the house pouring petrol around. Rebecca was asleep, apparently, therefore heard no one entering. The doorbell camera belonging to a neighbour they'd hope might reveal something had also come up blank. It was clear to Megan, though, that the person who'd gained access must have had a key, probably accessing the property via the back gate, which was out of range of the camera, and that pointed right back to her husband.

What Megan needed was a concrete link that would tie the Pippa Moore case to the fires. There had to be one. The group of people being targeted were all at that beach party on the night she died, and therein would lie the motive, she felt sure.

FIFTY-SEVEN

I stop halfway down the stairs as Jack comes through the front door. He places the parcel he's collected from the delivery van on the hall floor and faces me. 'Everything okay?' he asks, his gaze gliding to the landing above me and then back to me.

His eyes are narrowed, I note, with a lurch of uncertainty. 'All good.' Continuing on down, I smile and try to dismiss it. Jack has never been anything but kind to me. Still, though, my stomach flutters with nerves. 'Jester followed you to the hall and shot up the stairs,' I explain quickly, feeling the need to. 'He was in your bedroom before I could stop him. I think you must have left the door open.'

'Don't tell me, he's been on the bed.' Jack shakes his head. There's a flash of irritation in his eyes, barely discernible, but it was definitely there – because I was upstairs, seeing things I shouldn't see? I wonder.

'Afraid so.' I shrug apologetically. 'He's not too wet now, though,' I assure him, trying to still the sudden rapid beat of my heart. *It's just me being oversensitive.* He's annoyed with Jester because he doesn't want dog's hairs all over the bedroom. That's perfectly understandable if he does have asthma. 'You might find a few dog's hairs on the duvet, but he hasn't done much damage.' I fish a little, hoping he'll pick up on it.

'Hence the reason I try to remember to keep the door closed,' he says, dropping his keys on the hall table. 'He's like greased lightning, I swear. Sees an opportunity and he's in there. Aren't you, reprobate?' He scowls at the dog as he comes in from the kitchen with his ball in his mouth. 'Sit,' he commands him, at which Jester wags his tail, drops the ball at Jack's feet and stares hopefully at it.

'Instant obedience, as per.' His annoyance seemingly forgotten, Jack rolls his eyes, picks the ball up and throws it along the hall into the kitchen. 'Thanks for fetching him down,' he says as Jester skids after it.

'No problem. I'm actually surprised he obeyed me.' I try to curtail my ridiculous suspicions. He got a little annoyed. It's a perfectly normal reaction. Still I feel wary, though. Unnerved. I've never felt that before around him.

'Switching affections, definitely.' Jack sighs in faux despair. 'It was the bed linen arriving,' he says, glancing back to the parcel. 'Good job it wasn't a bed I ordered. I might have struggled to carry that down the lane.'

I smile, but I find I'm having to force it a little. 'You shouldn't have gone to the trouble of buying it, Jack,' I tell him. 'It's really appreciated, but I could have got some bits and pieces when I go into town.'

It occurs to me now that he's perhaps being a little *over* helpful. Controlling even? As soon as I think it, I berate myself. I am being neurotic now. The man's showed me nothing but kindness, offering me a roof over my head when I had none. It can't be easy suddenly having a pregnant woman so enmeshed in his life. That thought lands with a jarring thud, because I feel I am enmeshed in his life – and he in mine. Is that what I want? More worryingly, is it what Jack wants?

'It was no trouble,' he assures me. 'I was thinking you might be a little strapped for cash until you get your affairs sorted out, so anything I can do to help.'

'Thank you. That's really kind.' I give him a grateful smile and try to quash the doubt that seems to have crept up on me out of nowhere. But I can't, quite.

'Uh, uh.' Jack stops me as I bend to lift the parcel. 'I know being pregnant doesn't mean you're incapacitated, but there's a summer duvet in there as well, so it's quite heavy. Probably better not to risk it after your dizzy spell. Do you want me to take it across to the apartment?'

I'm floored for a second, unsure what to say. It's not that heavy. 'Please,' I accept his offer, nevertheless. I don't want to offend him. I'm getting things out of proportion. Aren't I bound to be after realising Richie's not the man he pretended to be?

Jack opens the door for me and picks up the parcel, stepping back and waiting while I go out before him – and I can't help feeling I'm being almost shepherded out.

I hesitate as we walk across the courtyard, and then decide to just ask him about the inhaler. I would like to ask him about the clothes, or lack of, which make me wonder whether his wife has ever even lived here, but that would only alert him to the fact that I'd been going through his personal things. 'Can I ask you something?' I start tentatively.

'Feel free. I don't have any deep, dark secrets,' Jack replies good-naturedly. 'Well, not many,' he adds, looking a bit sheepish as he no doubt remembers what he omitted to tell me about his marital status.

'I just wondered—' I glance at him '—do you have asthma?'

He takes a second to answer. Then, 'I take it you noticed my inhaler?' he asks, a furrow forming in his brow.

'I did,' I admit, turning my attention to opening the door as we reach the apartment. 'I wasn't poking around,' I add, looking quickly back at him. 'It was lying on top of the chest of drawers. I couldn't help but notice it as I came out of the bedroom.'

'I didn't imagine you were,' Jacks says with a short smile. 'Shall we?' He nods past me to the inside of the apartment.

'Oh, yes. Sorry.' I step back and allow him in with the parcel.

Jack carries it through to the kitchen. 'I'll leave you to unpack it here,' he says, lowering it to the table. 'In answer to your question, I do have asthma, yes,' he says, frowning as he turns to face me. 'It runs in the family. My father had it. My mother used to worry because he was quite sporty and was constantly forgetting to take his medication. She was sure he would have an attack and that it would kill him. It didn't, as I think I mentioned.'

He's scanning my face thoughtfully, a question in his eyes, as if he realises I'm doubting him, and I swallow back a sudden creeping sense of panic. Is that the truth? I've never seen him use the spray, never heard him wheeze or seen him short of breath. 'I'm sorry, Jack. I didn't mean to pry,' I say, uncertain how else to respond. He's looking at me now almost disappointedly, as if I was accusing him of something. I don't think I was.

'There's really no need to apologise.' He smiles, but his eyes are still locked hard on mine. 'You were probably wondering why you hadn't seen any symptoms. The spray I use is preventative, rather than curative; steroid based, meaning you only have to take it once a day. The asthma got quite bad around the time I was struggling with my mental health. The medication keeps it in check now.'

'Ah.' I nod. 'You certainly look fit enough,' I assure him, again for the want of something to say.

'Thank you.' He dips his head – and I curse inwardly as I realise that could be taken in a different way. I'm probably wrong about all of this. God knows, I'm confused enough, but if the niggling voice in my head that tells me he actually might have ulterior motives is right, then I shouldn't be encouraging him. It troubles me greatly, though, imagining what those motives might be. Aside from the fact that I'm heavily pregnant, I haven't just stopped loving Richie. My heart is breaking, fracturing another inch with every new twist my life takes, but still part of me hopes. Jack clearly thinks I'm hoping in vain. He thinks Richie's manipulative, a narcissist. He's concerned about me even talking to him.

'Okay?' Jack asks in that kind way he has.

I scan his eyes, see nothing now but concern there, and I'm more confused than ever. 'All good, thanks.' I quickly look away. 'I should get on,' I murmur. Feeling disorientated and in need of some space, I head towards the front door, hoping he will take the hint. 'I have to call Detective Simons.'

'About?' Jack asks as he follows me.

'I'm not sure,' I answer guardedly, feeling reluctant now to share everything with him where I wasn't before. I'm not entirely sure why. It could well be me, looking for faults because I'd been so blind to Richie's, but still my instinct is warning me to be wary. 'It's probably something to do with the house,' I add. 'She called me earlier to say that their investigations are finished and that they're ready to hand it back.'

'I expect you'll need to go and assess the damage.' Jack nods. 'Let me know if you want me to come with you. Or if she has any other information that might be worrying. I'm always available, you know that.'

'I know. Thanks, Jack.' I smile and see him out.

Closing the door behind him, I lean against it and take a steadying breath. Try as I might to tell myself this is all me, mistrusting his intentions, panic still rises steadily inside me. *He's moving in on you.* Richie's furious comments spring into my mind. *It's an act, for Christ's sake. You must see that. Does it not strike you as convenient that he's always there? At the funeral. Bringing you home. At the end of a phone...*

Always available. Fear grips me, refusing stubbornly to let go of me as I consider that Richie might be right.

FIFTY-EIGHT

I don't feel I can trust anyone. I stay where I am for a moment, my chest banging, a whirlpool of emotion churning inside me. My heart aches excruciatingly as I think of Richie and all that I thought we had together. I try to stuff it down. I have to move forward – without him, it seems, since he appears to be making no effort to stay in touch. I can't grieve for a past that was built on a lie. I have no choice now but to concentrate on the future, for my baby's sake. And I have to do it alone. I can be all my baby needs, two parents combined into one. I have to be. To be frightened of Jack because he might want more than a friendship seems preposterous. Yet, that's how I feel: frightened. Trapped suddenly. Jack might be well intentioned, but whichever way I look at it, I can't escape the feeling I'm being manipulated, and that makes me feel powerless. I can't let myself be that.

Taking another slow breath, I pull myself from the door and go back to the kitchen for my phone. Detective Simons hadn't called me. She'd texted me. For the first time, I'd found myself lying to Jack, because I hadn't wanted him to read it. Because I hadn't wanted to arm him with more information about Richie.

For Richie's sake, I wonder, or my own? My own, I realise. I don't want Jack to have any more proof that I'm so utterly alone.

Finding the text, I reread it, and another layer of fear grips me.

Could we have a brief chat when you get a moment? I can't get hold of your husband. His phone's switched off. Some video footage has come to light showing him out running. He does appear to be wearing a similar item of clothing to the one we spoke about. I wondered whether you could shed some light on that. Thanks.

Going to the patio doors, I notice Jack hasn't gone back to the house. He's halfway across the courtyard, looking this way, his head tipped to one side, his expression clearly troubled. He's probably noticed my wariness. That makes me feel bad, because he has helped me considerably, whatever his motives. He moves on after a moment, his gaze fixed down as he goes, as if he's deep in thought. I'll go across to him later, I decide, try to talk to him honestly – as in, ask him to be honest with me. I have to make sure he knows that he's not obliged to me in any way, nor am I dependent on him. I'll probably have to look for somewhere else to live, I realise, and that breaks another piece of my heart, because, though it's small, I really do love the apartment. If needs must I will, though, somehow. I have to think straight. I can't do that with someone else influencing the decisions I make.

Once he goes through the front door, I brace myself to call Detective Simons. She seems friendly enough when she answers the call. 'Hi, Rebecca,' she says. 'How are you?'

'Okay-ish. You know,' I reply. 'Working up the courage to go back to the house.'

'Let me know if you want some company,' she says, surprising me.

'Thank you, but I think I'll be okay,' I assure her. I doubt I will be, going back there on my own, but I don't think Jack coming with me is a good idea.

'You have a lot on your plate.' She sighs sympathetically. 'I'm sorry to keep pestering you while you're trying to deal with all of this. I just wondered if you'd had any more thoughts about whether your husband owns a black hoodie? You couldn't recall when I asked you previously, but I realise you would have had other things on your mind.'

She doesn't believe me. Trepidation creeps through me. 'I honestly don't remember seeing one,' I answer cautiously. 'If he has, it must be a new purchase. I haven't noticed one in the wash.'

'And you've never noticed him wearing such an item when he leaves the house to go running?' she asks – with a degree of scepticism, I detect.

'He runs early.' Shame crawls over me as I add another lie to my lie. I have no idea why I'm covering for Richie when he's ghosting me, which must mean he's either guilty of something or doesn't care at all for me. I can't make myself believe that some- how. There's still a tiny part of me that is holding on to the hope that he will surface, be the man I thought he was and make everything all right. Do I not want to acknowledge the truth? I wonder. Accept that I'm guilty too? Complicit not only in what happened to Pippa, but in allowing someone to get away with what she went through before she died so that I could live my life, have my baby, my marriage, everything the way it was meant to be? I've never felt more disillusioned with myself than I do right now. My first child was snatched cruelly away from me. Now my marriage has been snatched away too. My house. Is this the punishment I deserve?

Detective Simons is quiet for a moment. Then, 'So you've never noticed him wearing it or seen the item of clothing in his wardrobe?' she checks.

'Sorry,' I mumble, wanting to backtrack but unable to push that nail into Richie's coffin, though I have no idea why. 'I've been a slow riser lately. He's usually showered by the time I'm up and he often plays squash during the day so tends to keep his sports gear in his sports bag.'

'I see,' she says crisply. 'And he hasn't been in touch?'

'No.' I don't lie about that. And now, despite all that's happened, my gut is thick with worry for him. Where is he? He can only be running scared. If he is, I pray it's because he's terrified of being accused of something he didn't do. The alternative, that he's guilty, is too unbearable to contemplate.

FIFTY-NINE

RICHIE

Richie climbed into the car he'd hired rather than risk his car being picked up by CCTV cameras, the cost of which had pretty much depleted the funds in his bank account. Aware that Detective Simons would be looking for him, he'd bought a pay-as-you-go phone but he'd been wary of keeping even that switched on. He debated and then turned it on briefly to check whether Becky might have tried to contact him. When his phone fired up and he realised there were a string of missed calls from her, he laughed ironically. He didn't feel like laughing. He felt like weeping his heart out. They'd been together since university, shared everything together, lost a child together, and now their lives were unravelling and he couldn't find a way to stop it; couldn't get his head around why she would imagine he'd been having an affair with Emelia of all people. Did Becky not realise how much he loved her? That he would do anything for her? He wasn't perfect. He could never hope to have half the panache Tom Connor had, the assets bloody Jack Evans had, but he'd strived to do his best, to be supportive, reassuring her whenever she worried that she might have the same genetic make-up as her mother. He'd sometimes wondered whether that was why they couldn't get pregnant, whether perhaps deep down Becky didn't want to get pregnant. She'd spent hours online researching her mother's illness, only to find there was no definitive data. He never complained. Even when her preoccupation with what happened at that fucking beach party had turned into an obsession that drove him insane, he'd tried. He'd never strayed, not once in all the years they'd been married. Before then, he'd made one mistake. Just one. He'd vowed on his baby's life he would never repeat that mistake and he'd stayed true to his vow. How cruel was it that their baby had died anyway?

And now, by some miracle they were expecting again. They'd been looking forward to the future and suddenly their lives had been blown apart. *His* life. This had all started with her association with that bastard Jack Evans. The man had been Jodie's counsellor apparently. How long had he been counselling her? How long had Becky known him? She'd obviously been seeing him before now. There was no way she would move in with some bloke who was a complete stranger. Richie's gut twisted, a toxic mixture of anger and hurt burning inside him as he considered whether Becky getting pregnant when they'd almost given up hope was really such a miracle?

Reminded that he'd accused her of sleeping with Tom on the godawful night Pippa had died, he cursed his stupidity. He hadn't meant to. It had just spilled out, thanks to Emelia planting the seed of doubt in his mind which had wormed away at him. He'd tried to dismiss it as another one of Emelia's drunken ramblings. Now, though, he was beginning to believe it was possible. Also that Angel might not even have been his. Tom was full of bullshit back at university, full of himself, winding him up about how hot Becky was in bed. Richie had never repeated the things he'd said, some of which had made him want to shut the bloke up, permanently. He hadn't believed Tom. Becky went out of her way now to avoid getting too close to the man whenever they were together. Because she didn't like the way he treated Emelia, she said. Was that the truth? Or was it that she kept her distance so no one would read the body language between them? Richie felt as if *he* was becoming neurotic, but he couldn't escape it. Becky had thrown him *out*. And no sooner had he gone than she's moved in with Jack Evans. Given their financial constraints, Richie had expected she would move into a Travelodge or some other cheap accommodation after the fire. That she would be lonely, regretting being so judgemental and suspicious of him. Instead, she'd shacked up with the psychologist. She certainly wouldn't be lonely, would she, he thought bitterly.

Tossing his phone on the passenger seat, he started the car and stepped hard on the accelerator. He didn't want to frighten her, but he was determined to see her, to talk to her face to face. In Richie's mind, she owed it to him to do that. She seemed happy enough talking to Jack Evans. After trailing the man from his office, he'd seen them out walking together, playing happy families together, the Labrador dog bouncing alongside them completing the picture. They looked like the perfect couple. One small problem: the woman Evans had clearly set his sights on was Richie's wife, and that seriously pissed him off.

SIXTY

BECKY

I try Richie's phone again in the hope he will have switched it on, that he'll answer. When he doesn't a surge of anger pumps through me, swiftly followed by gripping fear. Why is he doing this? He must know that, whatever's happened between us, I'm worried sick about him. Why can't he at least text me to let me know he's all right?

An icy shiver crawling over my skin, despite the warmth of the spring evening, I wrap my arms around myself, my thoughts going to Emelia. She hasn't called me, as she'd promised to. Concerned that she might be drinking, I try her number, apprehension churning inside me as I imagine what new vitriol she might spew at me if she has. She doesn't answer either, and now I wonder if she really believes the things she said and has decided to ghost me too. She accused me of hating her. That hurt when, even aware of how selfish and unpredictable she can be, I've been a friend to her. Tried to be. I recall her almost incoherent ramblings over the phone, the awful, insane accusations she'd made. Thanks to what she'd heard Tom and I talking about at the funeral, she really does think that he and I are having an affair. That the baby I'm carrying is Tom's. I've no doubt that's to do with Tom's proclivity to chase after other women, but what does that say about how she sees me?

The insinuating comment she made before she hung up shook me to the core. *You said that I'd stop at nothing to get my man. That Pippa would attest to it, if she'd lived. You know what though, Becks? If she had been able to, I reckon her finger would be pointing right at you and Richie.*

She also clearly thinks that Pippa and Richie were involved with each other and that I knew they were. Does she really believe that I was so consumed with jealousy I would have followed Pippa? That it was me who was responsible for her dying alone out on that beach? Why has she turned on me when I've always tried to be there for her? It's a mess. Our lives are a mess, each of us falling apart. Or else dead. My chest constricts as I realise that Richie was right about one thing: our past isn't coming back to haunt us. It's always been with us. What happened to Pippa is never going to go away.

Feeling desperately lonely even with Jack yards away, I go back to the patio doors and gaze distractedly across the darkening courtyard and gardens. Where will this all end? I wonder. My hands go protectively to my baby, who kicks softly, reminding me of my priorities. I can't let misplaced loyalty bring any harm to him, now or in the future. I have to be honest with Detective Simons about Richie. Megan Simons will keep digging until she uncovers the truth about the fires. She's not going to stop trying to find a link to the hoodie, to the past, to theorise about what happened back then. I have to talk to her before she does that.

Feeling more in need of a friend than ever, I'm wondering whether to go across to the house and talk to Jack, to try to establish how the land lies between us, when I catch a sudden movement directly opposite the apartment. My pulse quickens as I squint through the low sun that cuts through my vision. There's someone out there, lurking beyond the foliage and tall shrubbery that divides the garden from the meadowland. I'm sure there is. I can't make out much other than a dark silhouette. It's definitely a person. Fear freezes me to the spot as whoever it is appears to stand still, staring back at me. Shielding my eyes, I squint harder. The meadowland is still bogged down after being flooded by torrential rain so it can't be a random dog walker. In any case, why would they just be standing there, motionless, watching? Watching me. Terror strikes right through to the core of me as I recall the fire, the flames creeping insidiously closer, the acrid smell of smoke searing the back of my throat as I'd screamed desperately for help. One match is all it will take and the apartment with its wooden cross beams could go up like a tinderbox.

Stumbling away from the window, I spin around, indecisive for a moment. Then, a primal urge to protect my baby kicking ferociously in, I clutch my phone tight and fly to the hall. I'm halfway across the courtyard to the house when I realise I've left the apartment without my keys. Cursing, and feeling horrendously exposed, I hurry on to the front door and knock hard on it. *Please hurry, Jack,* I will him after waiting a few seconds which seem like an eternity. I'm about to call him when my phone pings in a text. Seeing it's from Emelia, I quickly check it – and my heart stops beating.

Becky, please call me. I need you. Tom's dead.

SIXTY-ONE

My hand flies to my mouth. But this can't be right. It *can't* be. A knot of terror tightens inside me and I bang on the front door. 'Jack!' I shout, glancing desperately over my shoulder. Another jolt of fear surges through me as I realise his car's not on the drive. Where is he? I can hear Jester barking and pawing at the inside of the door and panic escalates so fast inside me I'm sure it will choke me. Jack wouldn't have gone out leaving the dog with the run of the house. Fumblingly, I search for his phone number, try to still the dread churning inside me as I pray he will pick up. Relief permeates every cell in my body when he does. 'Where are you?' I blurt before he speaks.

'Just driving,' he answers curiously. 'I sensed you might need some space so—'

'There's someone here,' I cry, panic spiralling inside me. 'Someone in the grounds. They're watching me. I don't know what to do. I've locked myself out and—'

'Go around the back of the house,' Jack instructs me. 'The back door's open. Do it now, Becky,' he adds, his tone firm. 'I'm on my way.'

Realising he's ended the call, I step away from the front

door and, with my chest banging and my back pressed to the wall, make my way cautiously to the side gate. Finding it unlocked, I race to the back door, almost crying with relief when I find it open as Jack said it would be.

Hurrying inside, I close the door and turn the key in the lock, then lean against it, attempting to slow my frantic heartbeat. Jester, who's been bounding excitedly beside me, drops to his haunches, looking worried as he stares up at me and, fighting back my tears, I crouch to give him a firm hug. 'It's okay, boy. We're safe now,' I murmur, swallowing back my fear and pressing my forehead to his. I've never been more grateful for a dog's company in my life.

My thoughts shooting back to Emelia, I straighten up and find her number.

I pray for the first time that she *has* been drinking as I call her, that the message she sent somehow isn't true.

'Becky?' Emelia answers, her voice small and tremulous.

'Yes. Yes, it's me,' I answer quickly. 'What's going on, Emelia? What's happened?'

'It's Tom,' she sobs wretchedly. 'He's *dead*. Tom, he's...' A low moan escapes her, raw, primal, that of a wounded animal.

Oh dear God, no. I feel the blood drain from my body. 'How?'

She doesn't reply, nothing now but pitiful whimpering.

'Emelia, please talk to me,' I urge her. 'Em?'

'They don't know,' she replies after an excruciatingly long silence. 'He was with a woman. Naked.' She emits a short, bitter-edged laugh. Then chokes out another sob. Raw and raucous, it seems to come from her soul.

Swiping the tears from my face, I hold my breath and wait.

'They said he might have had a heart attack,' she continues falteringly. 'But it wasn't that. I know it wasn't. There's nothing *wrong* with his heart. It was made of stone, wasn't it? Never likely to break, never likely to hurt,' she adds, and breathes in sharply.

There's no cynicism in her voice. She sounds hollow. Empty. 'He might not have known, Em,' I say gently. 'It's possible—'

'*No*. It's *not* possible,' she insists fiercely. 'They asked me if he took recreational drugs. They must think that he took something. Tom doesn't take *drugs*. He's too body conscious. He's only ever smoked cannabis, and that was years ago at uni. He's even careful about how much he drinks. He would never put anything into his body that's—'

'Why did they ask?' I stop her, my stomach twisting as I realise what she's implying. 'What did they say?'

'That's just it, they wouldn't say anything. I could tell by the look on that woman detective's face what she was thinking, though. It wasn't just a heart attack. Do you think it was?' She's talking fast now, the words gushing out. 'After Jodie dying? And Zoe? That poor man who worked for Richie? Do you think it was, Becky? Honestly?'

As I try to take it all in, I'm moving towards the lounge, where I glance carefully out of the window to scour the courtyard and the meadowland beyond it. There doesn't appear to be anyone out there now. But then, he – a man definitely – could be anywhere. 'I don't know, sweetheart,' I say cautiously, though I'm terrified that I do. It's Richie, isn't it? With Tom gone, it has to be. 'Em, where are you?'

'Home,' she whispers.

'Are you on your own?'

'No,' she replies after a pause. 'His mother's here. I had to call her. She came straight away. The police say they're sending a family liaison officer, but... I don't want to be here, Becks,' she says tearfully. 'Where are you? Are you still with Jack?'

'Yes, but—'

'I'm coming over there,' she says, a determined edge to her voice.

'But what about the children?' She can't leave them. Not now.

'His mum's taking them to her house. They'll be better there. Safer. We need to talk, Becky. Decide what to do. I'm setting off now. I'll be there soon.'

'Emelia, I don't think that's a good idea. You'll be in shock,' I warn her. 'You shouldn't be driving.'

'I'm coming, Becky. We need to stick together.'

'Wait.' I stop her before she hangs up. 'I think there was someone here, outside Jack's house.'

She hesitates. Then, 'Richie?' she asks.

I feel my heart go into freefall. She's thinking along the same lines I am. But who else could it be when members of our group had been picked off randomly? 'I... don't know.' I hear the defeated tone to my own voice.

'Is Jack there?' she asks warily.

'No. He's gone out. I'm in his house now. He's on his way back. I'm sure he'll be—'

'Make sure the doors are locked, Becky,' she says.

I'm about to try again to dissuade her, to tell her the children will need her, when I realise she's rung off. I curse myself for not thinking before opening my mouth. I shouldn't have mentioned anything. I should have called the police. Should I now? I've no idea where Jack is or how long he will be. But what if it is Richie out there and he has nothing to do with Tom's death? My stomach recoils as I picture Tom, lying still and cold, the life gone from his body. I'm doing it again, giving Richie the benefit of the doubt. I have to call the police. Reaching for the lounge curtains, I draw them tightly and flick the lights on. Then hurry back to the kitchen to double-check the back door and close the blinds in there, Jester following my every step.

As I go back across the kitchen, my eyes snag on the sharp

knives in the knife block. I hesitate for a second, then snatch one up. I'm back in the hall about to press 999 into my phone when I notice the envelopes sitting in the letter cage on the front door. Noting they're not addressed to Jack, something compels me to take them out. They're all addressed to the same man. Icy trepidation creeps through me as I recognise the surname. Thinking again of the lack of photographs in the house, I glance around the hall, then go to the lounge. I hadn't noticed it before, the absence of any personal touches and souvenirs from Jack's life. I should check the bedrooms but, recalling how meticulously tidy his study is, how devoid of visible signs of work, apart from the files, the top one of which was Emelia's, I run to that room. The files are gone, leaving the desk bare. Quickly I check the drawers. Finding them all locked, bar one, I take a breath and then rifle through it. There's nothing of significance, random bills mostly. Moving them aside, I waver as I come across a box of tablets, then take them out and read the label: Amitriptyline, prescribed for Jack Evans. Antidepressants. Also a painkiller and sedative. A sick feeling creeps through me as I recall how woozy I'd been the first morning I'd woken up in this house. When I find the photograph at the bottom of the drawer my stomach lurches violently. Carefully, I extract it. I'm studying it, seeing the likeness, when the office door opens – and my heart stalls, my mind shooting back to Pippa's funeral.

Richie is by my side, clutching my hand tightly as I stare not at the small coffin that holds her slim body, but at her mother approaching it, supported by a young man I assume to be Pippa's brother. Tears cascading down my face, I choke them back as the lyrics of Norah Jones' 'Come Away With Me', a moving mournful ballad, floats melodiously through the church. As her mother reaches tremblingly out, her fingers lightly brushing the box her daughter will be transported away from this earth in, I see her shoulders slump, a shudder shake through her. As she crumbles, the pain of her loss clearly too heavy to bear, the young man is there for her, threading an arm around her, his other hand gently easing hers away from the coffin. Leading her away, he holds her close, and slowly, stumblingly, they make their way down the aisle towards me. My urge is to go to her, tell her how sorry I am, more than she will ever know, but Richie tightens his hold on my hand, as if to still me.

The young man looks in my direction as he nears me, looking straight at me. I hear the bird that had flown into the church, soaring into the arched roof as the minister had performed his rite of committal. Its wings beat frantically as it becomes entangled in the elaborately carved cross beams. I sense all eyes swivel upwards towards it, but I'm transfixed by his gaze. His eyes – deep hazel with rich flecks of cinnamon – are awash with grief and tangible fury.

The breath leaves my body as I look at him now. He makes no move towards me. Simply stares at me, his eyes, deep hazel, dark and inscrutable, drilling unflinchingly into mine. How did I not recognise him?

SIXTY-TWO

ADAM MOORE

The Day of Jodie's Funeral

After watching a group of people walking sombrely away from a burial, Adam Moore stepped away from the side of the church and made his way to the path that would take him to another graveside. Once he reached it, he took a breath, then crouched to place a simple spray of carnations and posies in front of the headstone. 'Your favourites,' he said, swallowing back a knot of emotion as he recalled how surprised and delighted his mother had been the first time he'd bought her flowers. Finding her in the kitchen catching up on the housework, as she always seemed to be, he'd presented them awkwardly to her, as a kid his age would. He'd been fifteen. Twenty-one when she died. It had changed the course of his life.

He wasn't intending to buy flowers that day. He had his heart set on a CD, Evanescence's debut album, *Fallen*. He'd first heard their music in the Ben Affleck movie *Daredevil*. It had blown him away and he'd had to have it, taking a paper round at the local newsagents to pay for it. Seeing how down his mum was, though, how hard she was working, juggling two jobs, he figured he could buy it later. It was her birthday. After much soul-searching, he walked out of the HMV store leaving the CD at the till and went to the flower seller in the shopping precinct. It was ironic, he thought later, that the lyrics of the song centred on a loss of love and innocence.

The look on his mum's face had been worth the sacrifice. 'My favourites,' she said, tears pooling in her eyes. He shrugged as if it was no big deal and tried not to roll his eyes in despair when she ran her fingers through his carefully spiked hair. He doubted they really were her favourite flowers. He knew she was genuinely pleased, though. That was one of the rare times he'd seen her smile properly, a smile that reached her eyes. His old man had never brought her flowers, a tight-fisted, aggressive bastard, he'd never brought her anything but pain and heartache before he'd finally walked out, leaving her in debt up to her eyes. That's when she'd started working two jobs almost back to back, a nursing auxiliary during the day, a cleaning job at the tyre factory in the evening, which was gruelling.

'We're better off without him,' she would say, trying to sound upbeat as she prepared tea for him and his sister in between jobs. Adam guessed they were. There were no more arguments at least, but it killed him watching his mum working herself to death.

Doing his best to help out, he carried on working his paper round. Once he was at university, he got a part-time job stacking shelves alongside his studies. His hope was that his sister would be able to concentrate on her university course without the distraction of having to do a job alongside it. She was doing art and design, and she was good at it, creative and talented, if only she could have realised it.

She was so busy putting herself down, Adam didn't think she'd ever realised how unique and special she was. How much she was loved. He'd hoped her new environment alongside like-minded students might help bring her out of her shell. It didn't.

If anything she retreated further into herself. She tried to pretend everything was cool, that she was making new friends. He never saw any evidence she was. Eventually, when he pressed her, she broke down in tears. 'I just don't fit in,' she sobbed. 'I try, but whenever I go anywhere, the pub, or even the refectory, I always end up sitting on my own.'

Seeing her like that gutted him. They didn't know who she was. They were judging what they saw on the outside, someone shy and awkward precisely because she felt she didn't fit in. They didn't know the person inside, the girl who'd risked her life rescuing a litter of puppies zipped up in an overnight bag and chucked in the canal. The girl who helped the elderly neighbour out, fetching her pension or bringing her groceries, talking to her because she thought she was lonely, who helped her mum out with the housework without being nagged to like he was.

'So do something about it. Throw a party or something,' Adam suggested. 'I can invite some of my friends and get some drinks in. I doubt they'll turn down the offer of free booze.'

She shook her head hard, and he guessed it was because she dreaded the worst-case scenario: no one turning up. 'What about this beach party they're having?' he asked. 'They invited you, didn't they?'

It was him who'd persuaded her to go. She was miserable, it was obvious. Their mum was worrying herself sick about her, confiding that she thought she was bordering on anorexia. She had her own worst-case scenario: that her girl might end up trying to take her own life.

Adam couldn't remember his mum smiling again after the last birthday she had on this earth, the day her daughter died and her heart had broken completely. She'd become depressed, sunk further and further down until no one could reach her. Adam couldn't fix it. She would hardly notice the flowers he brought her in the weeks before her own death.

A deep rage that had ignited inside him on the dark day that he'd found her burned steadily inside him. He would bet his sister had never been brought flowers in her short life either, not even by the bastard who'd had sex with her. Closing his eyes, he pinched the bridge of his nose and waited for his anger to pass, then reached out to trace his fingers over the simple inscription he'd had engraved on the stone.

~ The hardest part of losing you is living without you.
Be safe. Be happy.
Save a place for me ~

Head bowed, he stayed where he was for a moment, reflecting on all the things he wished he'd said to his sister and his mother both, then got to his feet. As he walked away from the graveside, he ruminated about all his sister had missed in life, her graduation, a career doing something she was good at. Having children with someone who would love and care for her as she should have been loved, if she'd chosen to. She would be the same age now as the women who'd walked ashen faced away from the burial, had she lived. Instead, with her confidence destroyed, first by their father, and then by her peers, she'd died. It hadn't been at her own hand, or a tragic accident. Adam was as sure of that as he was that night gave way to day. It was at the hands of the animal who'd honed in on her vulnerability like a wolf stalking its prey. It was *him* who was responsible. The people who'd invited her to their exclusive party, pretending to be her friends, only then to humiliate her, *they'd* been responsible. He firmly believed that. She was on her own, alone on that beach, just like she'd been alone most of her life, because she'd been driven there by cowards, then left there to die.

Breathing in sharply again, he held it. Finally, with his

emotions sufficiently under control, he breathed out. 'You were beautiful, Pippa. You just didn't know it,' he whispered.

Kissing his forefingers, he pressed them to the stone, then went to find the path that would take him to another grave, that of the friend who'd grown from a boy into a man alongside him. Also snatched away from life by some sick bastard who'd ploughed into the back of his motorbike and just kept going. Adam never had found out who'd killed Jack Evans. He had found out the identity of the people who'd driven Pippa to her death, though. They were never held accountable. He supposed they'd consigned the sad little loner from their university days to history and moved on with their lives. Karma eventually catches up with you, though. Adam believed that too.

SIXTY-THREE

BECKY

Jack hesitates in the doorway, seemingly indecisive as he looks from me to the photograph in my hand. Then, smiling sadly, he moves into the room and extends his own hand. 'Adam,' he introduces himself. 'Adam Moore, Pippa's brother, but I'm guessing you know that now.'

I step away from him, terror gripping me like a vice as my gaze sweeps over the black hoodie he's wearing, the Adidas badge prominent on the breast of it.

'Jack Evans was a friend,' he goes on, as I stare at him bewildered. 'A good friend.' He smiles, a melancholic, reflective smile. 'He died. A hit-and-run accident.'

He loses the smile, and my heart freezes. It was *him* out there. He's the stalker. He's been stalking us all for years.

'He quite fancied Pippa,' he adds, 'but he never let on to her. I wish he had. Things might have been different. She might never have been at that beach party if they'd been together. She might never have been murdered.'

I stumble another step back. 'What do you want?' I ask, cold fear slicing through me as I realise that one by one he's caught up with us. Is that why I've heard nothing from Richie? *Emelia.* My stomach twists violently. Has he caught up with her?

He frowns contemplatively, then nods slowly, as if it's a fair question. 'I've been watching you, you will no doubt have gathered. All of you.' He smiles again, a short, tight smile. 'I wanted to know who was responsible for the death of my sister.' He pauses, studying me thoughtfully. 'I think you all were, to a degree.'

I can feel the anger emanating from him. It's palpable. It had obviously festered inside him, but to wait until now... *Why?*

'I saw you in Jodie's café,' he continues, no particular inflection in his voice, which is petrifying. 'I was sitting at a table across from yours when Jodie joined you. I overheard you talking, her self-pitying tears, you trying to reassure her. I recognised you immediately. It was a sharp reminder of my sister.'

Jodie? I close my eyes. I'd known it. Deep in my bones, I'd known it. She hadn't been contemplating taking her own life... until the day she'd met him.

'I went back to the café after a while, as Jack Evans, obviously. It's surprising how easily you can change your identity,' he goes on, almost as if he's casually chatting, which compounds my absolute terror. 'I helped Jack's mother go through his things. I kept his driving licence. He was over the moon when he got it. Little did he know his days were numbered from the moment he climbed on his first motorbike.' He glances down, his expression darkening. 'Oh, I am a qualified psychologist, by the way,' he adds, looking back at me. 'In case you were wondering.'

My terror intensifies. Does he imagine this information is reassuring?

'Jodie clearly needed someone to talk to,' he says, actually looking concerned. 'She opened up a little after a while. I had some new business cards printed, gave her one and, offered her my services. She was grateful, I think. Her guilt was eating her alive. He's watching me steadily, his dark eyes locked on mine, as if looking for a reaction. I try hard to give him none. 'The day I saw you in the café was the anniversary of Pippa's death, did you realise that?'

I swallow back the tight knot in my throat, which grows excruciatingly more painful every time I think of Pippa. 'I know. I'm sorry,' I whisper.

He considers, frowning pensively. 'I think you are. Possibly the only one of your delightful group of friends who has any remorse. Jodie struggled with her conscience, quite obviously, but her angst was more to do with the exams she'd failed after the event, the girlfriend she lost, her messed up life.' Smiling this time in wry amusement, he shakes his head. 'I don't think she could see the irony of that: the fact that she had a life while Pippa had had hers snatched away from her? Do you think that's fair, Becky, that people who would snub out a life as if they were crushing an insect should be allowed to continue to live theirs? To thrive? To have children, when the person they've robbed of their life will never have *any* of those things?'

He pauses for a long blood-freezing moment, kneads his forehead with his thumb and forefinger. Swallowing back the parched lump in my throat, I glance from him to the open door behind him. As I do, he snaps his gaze back to me, his eyes narrowed dangerously, and a sudden jolt of pure rage shoots through me. What I did to Pippa was wrong, unforgivable. I won't let him hurt my innocent baby, though. I tighten my grip around the knife I have pressed to my side. Somehow, I will fight him.

He continues to study me. 'My mother never got over losing her,' he speaks, after another long, loaded pause. 'She killed herself. You probably wouldn't know that either.'

Oh no. I squeeze my eyes closed, picturing her, him supporting her at her daughter's funeral and, though terror claws at my chest, my heart aches – for him.

'I found her hanging from the stairs,' he goes on, his voice now raw with obvious emotion. 'Have you ever seen a hanging corpse, Becky? It's not pretty. Suicidal hangings can cause a slow and horrific strangulation. The lips swell and turn purple, the protruding tongue blackens. The eyes, those are worst of all. You thought you were being haunted. I don't think you have any real idea what it's like to feel that way, though. When you see the bulging eyes of your own mother every night in your dreams and every day in your waking nightmares, *that's* being haunted.'

The seashells. The seaweed. The photo, the same one that had scared Emelia half to death, it was all him. I swallow back a sour taste in my throat, my gaze going again to the door, where I glimpse Jester panting and circling in the hall. The dog's distressed, clearly picking up on the sensory and auditory cues.

'The smell was unbearable,' Jack says throatily. 'I don't suppose I need to be too graphic about that, though, do I?'

'Stop,' I beg him shakily. 'Please stop.'

There's a flash of fury in his eyes. Then he blinks, as if trying to erase it. 'The tap was dripping, plop, plop, plop. It was enough to drive a person out of his mind.' He emits a short, cynical laugh. 'The body wasn't swinging, but I swear I could hear the rope creaking.'

'Stop!' I cry, pressing the heels of my hands to my ears. I'm still holding the knife in one hand. I drop it back to my side, my knuckles tensing as I clutch it more tightly.

'What my mother suffered was remorse.' He pays no heed to my pleas. '*Real* remorse, because she felt she'd let her daughter down. None of you could *ever* know how that felt.'

His face is tight, white. His eyes, boring steadily into mine, thunderous.

Deep visceral fear settles in the pit of my belly. 'What are you going to do?'

He glances down and back. Then, 'I've no idea,' he answers

with a shrug. 'I wanted to kill whoever was responsible for Pippa's death, for my mother's – because, make no mistake, what you all did killed her too, but...' He draws in a long breath, then steps towards me. 'It wasn't part of my plan to fall in love with you.'

What? I stare at him, shocked to the core.

'I'm sorry I wasn't truthful with you.' He takes another step. I take another step away, only to realise my back is almost to the wall. 'I lied out of necessity. I knew you wouldn't let me anywhere near you if you knew—'

'Get *back!*' I raise the knife. My hand shakes. My whole body trembles.

He tips his head to one side, his expression a mixture of confused and cautious. Then, 'Jesus.' He blows out an astonished breath. 'You think it was me who was responsible for the death of your friends, don't you?'

'I said get back!' I scream, as he moves again towards me.

'Woah.' He stops, holds his hands up. 'Becky, you need to put that thing down.'

'Back away,' I warn him.

'Christ, Becky, it wasn't *me*. You have this all wrong.' He shakes his head. 'It's not *me* you're in danger from. Don't you see?'

SIXTY-FOUR

'I don't believe you!' I thrust the knife out.

'Becky, please listen to me,' he begs, his panicked gaze travelling to the knife and back to my face. 'I was angry. I hated you all, I admit it, but you *have* to believe me, there's someone filled with far more hatred than me.'

'You're insane.' My gaze flicks to my phone on top of his desk. 'Don't!' I snap my gaze back to him as he risks another small step.

'You *have* to listen to me, Becky. She means you harm. It's been festering away inside her for years.'

'Listen? To you?' Tears spring from my eyes, tears of anger and almost paralysing fear. 'When you've done nothing but *lie* to me. When you're standing there *threatening* me?'

'I'm not threatening you.' He gasps out a surprised breath. 'Jesus. Becky, you need to wake *up*. Just think about it, her husband attacked my *sister*. You *know* he did. He's a serial womaniser, for Christ's sake. She turns a blind eye to it in exchange for a lavish lifestyle. When Jodie threatened to go to the police about him, she—'

'Jodie?' I eye him narrowly.

Jack – Adam – whoever he is, wipes a hand over his face. 'He decided to try his luck there too,' he says, astounding me.

What rubbish. Does he honestly think I'm going to believe anything he has to say when he's lied about everything, his wife, his parents, an awful, dreadful lie to gain my sympathy. Another sharp stab of guilt pierces me as I recall I'd lied about my parents too. But that was different. I lie to avoid questions, not to hurt and deceive people.

'He'd been drinking, I gather,' he goes on with a sneer of contempt. 'The man's scum. You know he is.'

My heart jolts. He's using present tense, as if he's unaware that Tom's dead. I search his face, my head a whirl of hopeless confusion. Is there a possibility he might be telling the truth?

'He really thought his sexual prowess could "convert" her.' He shakes his head in disdain. 'It beats me how anyone could stay with a man like that. And then when your husband rejected her, which I'm guessing he actually did…'

'Richie.' I struggle to keep up with him. Is he implying what I think he is? That it was *Emelia* who started the fires? That's preposterous. I try to dismiss it as the ravings of a madman, which he clearly is, but a new fear settles inside me. Where was Emelia when my house was set alight and my world and everything in it was ripped from beneath me? I scramble through my mind, trying to think back. She was at home. I spoke to her on the phone. She was sober. She asked me if everything was okay between Richie and me.

'It wasn't the other poor sod who was meant to burn, Becky,' he says as I look at him in bewildered astonishment. 'It was Richie.'

I stare hard at him. 'Are you saying that Emelia is responsible for all of this? That it's her who set fire to Richie's office? My *house*? Her who killed her own *husband*?'

He looks me over cautiously. 'Jealousy is one of the prime

motives for murder, Becky,' he repeats what he'd said once before.

'No,' I murmur shakily. 'You're lying.'

'I'm not lying, Becky, I promise you,' he says softly. 'I have lied to you, and I am truly sorry for that, for isolating you here, but I needed to for your own safety.'

My heart booms out a warning, *Don't trust him!* I lift the knife sharply. 'You *need* to let me *go*.'

'I *will*.' He holds out his hands again, urging me to calm down. 'I will, I swear. You're in no danger here, Becky, but you will be in danger if you trust Emelia. I'm begging you not to.'

'That's ridiculous. I don't *believe* it.' I choke back my tears. 'Any of it! Not for one minute. She's on her way over here.' I warn him. 'She doesn't trust you. She told me she didn't. She knows I saw someone prowling outside and...'

I falter as he looks me warily over, realising I've just as good as fed Emelia to him... if he hasn't already killed her. I breathe in hard, desperate to suppress my now undiluted terror, to protect my baby. To protect Emelia. 'We've agreed she'll call me before she arrives,' I tell him with every ounce of conviction I can muster. 'If she doesn't get an answer she'll call the police.'

'I see.' He nods slowly. 'And you're sure she means you no harm?'

'*Yes*.' I hold his gaze. 'I know her. She would never hurt anybody.'

'You mean, not intentionally?' He eyes me curiously. 'Is the notion it's her doing all of this really so ridiculous, Becky?' he asks, clearly seeing my uncertainty. 'You thought it was Richie doing these deplorable things. And while you were thinking that, she was happy to let you. She was waiting for an opportunity, surely you can see that? In telling her you were on your own here, you've given her one. Think about it, how does she know where I live? How is it she's capable of driving over here having learned her husband has just died?'

He's been edging towards me as he's been talking. I search his eyes as he stands just a foot away from me, well within striking distance of the knife. There's nothing there but the same earnestness and compassion I saw when I first spoke to him.

'We probably do need to alert the police,' he says, a sad smile curving his mouth. 'Let me have the knife, Becky, before someone gets badly injured. I'm not going to hurt you. I would never do that.'

He hesitates for a second, and then reaches to ease it from my trembling hand. Hopelessly confused, a part of me wanting to believe him, a bigger part desperate not to, I watch as he places it carefully on the desk, then slides an arm gently around me.

Am I wrong? About everything? Richie? Emelia? Tom?

'You can trust me, Becky,' he says, his gaze holding mine. 'I know that's impossible to believe right now, but I've only ever had your interests at heart. You know that, don't you?'

Tom. My insides tighten as it hits me like a thunderclap. He's just asked me how Emelia would be capable of driving over here having learned that Tom was dead. He *does* know. I stare at him, horrified. Though he still smiles, something behind his eyes shifts, growing impenetrably darker, and now I feel as if I'm staring into the abyss. I don't notice his other hand sliding towards my neck until his fingers are digging cruelly into my flesh.

'How does it feel to be friendless, Becky? To choke? To death?' he asks, his tone quiet and bone-chillingly calm. 'Unpleasant, I imagine.'

He squeezes slowly. My hands flying to his, I claw at his fingers, attempting to prise them away. Panic spirals inside me as I try to suck life-giving air into my lungs. My throat gags. My chest burns. My ears roar. My head screams, *My baby!*

No! Adrenaline surges through me, and with the primeval

instinct of a lion protecting her cub, I fight. I scratch and I claw; feel the warm blood that oozes from his cheek onto my fingertips, the soft resistance of his orbs as my thumbs gouge deep into his lying eyes.

'Fucking *hell!*' He lurches backwards, his hands pressed over his face, a roar of rage erupting from his mouth as I half crumple towards the floor. Disorientated, I glance feverishly towards the door and my heart stops dead – and then kicks back hard.

As Jester hurtles towards us, his fangs bared, snarling and spitting, a primeval instinct to survive, to live and breathe for my baby, fuels me and I lever myself up, scrambling, half-crawling towards the hall. I don't look back as I hear an agonised yelp, not that of an animal but that of a human, as a dog who clearly senses danger obeys his primeval instinct to attack the aggressor.

'*Fucking dog,*' I hear Jack's spat out blasphemy behind me, his bellowed, 'Stay!' followed by, 'Becky, don't you *dare* go out there!'

Reaching the front door, I release the chain it's secured with, fumble with the latch. He's almost on me. I can hear his laboured breathing, feel his breath on my neck. The searing pain through my cheekbone as he slams my face against the glass in the door.

'You should have trusted me, Becky,' he seethes, spittle wetting my face as he weaves a hand through my hair, yanking my head back and twisting me around to face him. 'I told you I wouldn't hurt you. We *had* something, you and me. I told you I *loved* you, for Christ's sake, but you just had to spoil it, didn't you, rating those selfish bastards you call friends over me? Your pathetic husband, who's so obsessed with self-preservation he *ran* rather than protect you.'

'Let me go,' I croak, looking into his eyes, which are red raw and filled with nothing now but hatred and disdain. '*Please.*'

He breathes in hard. 'Sorry, not an option.' He tightens his grip on my hair. 'You're going nowhere.'

Hope fades inside me as I see a ridiculous smile curve his mouth. And then resurges, leaping inside me as a woman much stronger than me quietly approaches.

'Nor are you, you bastard,' Emelia hisses as she plunges the knife deep into his back. 'You were right to hone in on Becky, you know. She's the caring sort. She's always been stuffed full of remorse,' she says, looking down on him with a mixture of fury and contempt as he slides to his knees. 'Me, on the other hand, I *am* a selfish cow, remember? If you die, I really don't give a shit.'

SIXTY-FIVE

Emelia and I wait in the lounge while the paramedics carry Adam through the hall to the waiting ambulance. The police believe our story, that he'd attacked me. The evidence is there, livid purple bruising on my neck, my voice a rasping croak. He'd intended to kill me. I'm sure of that. It was right there in his eyes.

Once the ambulance has gone, Detective Simons comes back into the room, her gaze sympathetic as she looks towards where I'm sitting on the sofa, Jester sitting at my feet, unharmed, thankfully, but panting worriedly. I'm not sure what will happen to him, but if his only option is a rescue centre, then I know I can't let that happen. 'It's okay, boy.' I stroke his head reassuringly. 'I'll look after you.'

Detective Simons smiles as Jester emits an emotional whine, his tail thumping on the floor next to me. 'He's hanging in there,' she informs me. 'He has an acute subdural haematoma according to the attending doctor. Unusual, apparently, for such an injury. Most likely caused by... What was it, Dev?' she asks PC Nayyar, who's busy scribbling notes.

He flicks back through his notepad. 'Rupturing of the small subdural veins in the spinal area,' he provides.

'That's the one.' Simons turns back to me. 'Do you know if he was taking any medication? Anticoagulants, possibly, which might help explain the excessive bleeding?'

A cold chill shivers through me and I glance down, rub at the congealed blood on the palm of my hand with my thumb. Emelia had wanted me to *let the bastard bleed to death*. I couldn't do that. Aside from the guilt I would carry with me to the grave, in part, I understood how grief and anger had driven Jack to the dark place he was in. I take a breath, look back at her. 'Amitriptyline,' I supply. 'The packet is in his study drawer.'

She nods towards Nayyar, who goes off to check. When she looks back at me, her expression is hesitant. 'I checked out your blood tests at the hospital,' she says, scanning my face carefully. 'They found traces of the drug in your system. Were you aware of that?'

'No. I didn't manage to get to my doctor's appointment, but I'm not surprised.' I swallow painfully.

Judging by her agitated expression, Simons clearly draws the same conclusion I had, that it was Jack – Adam – who'd fed them to me, probably to make me feel more vulnerable, more dependent on him to take care of me. 'I take it you're prepared to give us a statement about all of this?' she asks. 'Obviously any information you have regarding his motives would be helpful.'

I answer with a small nod. 'Will he be okay?'

Simons draws in a taut breath. 'He'll need major surgery, but he'll live to face charges,' she assures me.

'Pity,' Emelia mutters from where she's sitting next to me on the sofa. Her eyes are on her phone. She's photographed the family portrait Jack keeps on his mantelshelf and has been busy googling it. 'Found it,' she says, drawing in a terse breath and handing me the phone. As I stare down at the image, I realise the hopeless extent of my gullibility. The woman he claimed was his wife is an actress, the photo one from a magazine shoot of her at home with her family. Emelia had warned me not to trust him. I should have listened to her.

'He's Pippa Moore's brother,' I murmur. 'Adam Moore.'

'I guessed he wasn't all he claimed to be,' Detective Simons says with a sigh. 'We did a little digging. The information that came back was that Jack Evans is deceased, killed in a hit-and-run motorbike accident approximately twenty years ago. His photo didn't match the Jack Evans you've come to know.'

Again, I nod, a deep sadness enveloping me, even knowing all that I do. 'I think he killed Jodie,' I venture. 'He was counselling her. I can't know for sure, but...' My gaze flicks to Emelia. 'We couldn't understand why Jodie would have taken her own life when she seemed to have something to live for. I think he might have also been responsible for Zoe's death. She was one of the students who was there, years ago, at the beach party.'

Detective Simons draws in a breath. Her expression as she studies me tells me she's possibly reached a similar conclusion. 'We found flecks of paint on Zoe Cooper's clothing,' she confides. 'Forensics have yet to confirm it, but it looks to be similar to the metallic silver paintwork on Adam Moore's car.'

I feel that like a thud to my solar plexus. Still I'm struggling to believe that under Jack's kind exterior lurked a vengeful monster. 'And the fires?' I ask warily.

She takes another breath. 'The hoodie he's wearing and the scorch marks I saw on his arm when the paramedics cut it off would seem to corroborate it.'

'You don't think it was Richie then?'

'It would seem not,' she confirms, almost apologetically.

Overwhelming relief sweeps through me, followed quickly by remorse. I'd almost convinced myself it was all Richie. Yet he wasn't guilty of anything, other than handling his own finances badly and allowing his insurance to lapse. They had him in custody, Detective Simons had informed me when she arrived.

His car had been traced parked in a side road, apparently abandoned. On a hunch, they contacted local car hire firms. It hadn't taken them long to establish he'd hired a car, or to apprehend him when CCTV cameras picked him up, apparently on his way here. I imagine how scared he will be. Even still uncertain whether he had been with Pippa on that bleak, long ago night, even after all the awful things he'd accused me of, I care about what happens to him. How stupid does that make me? It was no wonder Jack honed in on me.

Emelia glances worriedly at me, and then she takes hold of my hand, a reassuring smile brushing her mouth. 'Tom killed his sister,' she says, turning back to DI Simons, a look of determination on her face. 'Pippa Moore, Tom killed her. That's what this is all about.'

I twist to stare at her, staggered. Why is she saying that? She can't possibly know.

A deep furrow forming in her brow, Simons scrutinises her carefully. 'You seem very certain. Do you have any evidence to back up your claim?'

'No, but I doubt he would have admitted he had if he hadn't. They had sex apparently.' Emelia shrugs defeatedly. 'Tom thought she was up for it – his words. Pippa wasn't, or else she changed her mind. I can't be sure of the actual details obviously.'

'Emelia?' The breath leaves my body. Shaken to the core, I squeeze her hand.

Emelia squeezes mine hard back, and then goes on, 'He said she was going to report him. She was distressed, he said. She ran off and fell apparently. When he reached her, he thought she was having an asthma attack. Her inhaler was lying next to her, fallen from her shorts pocket probably. He picked it up and tried to get her to take it. When he couldn't, and he saw she'd stopped breathing, he panicked and ran. That's it. That's what he told me. I should have reported it. But poor Pippa was dead and buried by then and... I didn't. I should have. I'm sorry.' She pauses, takes a shuddery breath and wipes her cheek with the back of her hand.

Detective Simons' eyes are wide with surprise. 'I see,' she says, composing herself. 'And can I take it you're prepared to give a sworn statement, confirming everything you've just told me?'

'I am.' Emelia nods firmly.

She doesn't look at me. She's lying. I know she is. Now that he's dead, she's giving them Tom to bring a close to it. A tumult of emotion washes over me, relief, gratitude. Guilt. That will always be there.

'Richie didn't have anything to do with what happened to Pippa, DI Simons,' Emelia goes on. 'It was Tom and Adam Moore who were responsible for so many deaths. So, you see, you really should let Richie go.'

SIXTY-SIX

'It's a mess.' Richie sighs as we survey the charred interior of the nursery.

'It's definitely that.' A cold hollowness settles inside me as I glance around, taking in the damage. The plaster will have to be stripped back to get rid of the smell of smoke. I walk across to the window, brush my fingers along the black film of dust that coats the shelf and wonder how we'll ever make the house habitable again. If there even is a 'we', a way forward for both of us, together. 'It will cost a fortune,' I murmur, exhaustion, bone-deep, settling inside me.

'I'll find the funding,' Richie says gruffly behind me. He comes across to me. I sense he wants to put his arm around me but he doesn't, resting his hand tentatively on my back instead. 'I'll take on an extra job. Work twenty-four hours a day if I have to. I'll put it right, Becks. I promise you.'

I look down at the scorched polka dot giraffe propped under the window, its big, embroidered eyes seeming to look pleadingly up at me, the burned rocking horse, and swallow back a hard lump of emotion. I wish dearly that it was that easy. We might be able to rebuild the house, but how will we rebuild the trust between us? He's lied to me, said things he can't take back, accused me of sleeping with Tom, with Adam Moore. What does that say about his trust in me? But then, I hadn't trusted him, not deep down. Ever since the beach party there'd been that insidious seed of doubt worming away inside me, and though I tried to deny it, I'd seen with my own eyes the way Richie's gaze would stray to Pippa, the way her cheeks would flush prettily whenever it did. The way she would gaze after him like a lovestruck teenager. I could almost feel her stomach turning to liquid whenever he smiled at her. No matter how hard I tried to push it down it would surface. I hadn't needed that photograph to remind me there was an attraction between them, one which would have grown had Pippa's untimely death not nipped it in the bud.

Can I trust him now? Up until I'd walked in on him and Emelia, he'd been everything a woman could want in a husband, in a man, steadfast and caring. Always careful to watch his alcohol intake, which he's aware, for him, is majorly mood-altering. How will I ever trust my instinct again though, after being sucked in so easily by Adam? Still the uncertainty lingers. I want to believe Emelia's story about Tom's confession, but even knowing all I did about him, I can't dismiss the fact that he's not here to defend himself.

'Do you think it's fixable?' Richie asks.

I face him. 'Do you mean the house, or our marriage?' I ask wearily.

He falls quiet for a moment. Then, 'It will take time,' he concedes. 'Can you give me that time, Becky?' His voice is wretched, laden with guilt, and I want to say yes and make everything all right, but I just can't. Not yet, if ever.

'Can we at least meet to talk about what happens next? The future? Our baby?' he asks hopefully.

'You do accept he's yours then?' I hear the acerbic edge to my tone. I can't help it.

Richie emits a heavy sigh. 'I know I hurt you.' He glances down. 'I didn't mean to. I was hurting so much myself after all the things you said, though. You were so quick to judge me and, knowing how little you trusted me, how ready you were not to... It gutted me, Becks. I love you. I've *always* loved you.' He looks earnestly back at me. 'There's no one else for me. There never will be.'

I don't respond. I need to process my emotions. I can't do that with him standing so close to me.

He takes a breath. 'Just tell me one thing. I need to know, do you still have doubts about me? I couldn't bear it if I thought you'd lived all these years imagining I'd deceived you,' he presses on, as I hesitate. 'I just wouldn't do that to you. You must know that?'

My heart falters as I glance at him. I don't think it's possible for a man to look more dejected. 'Do we have a future, Becky?' he asks. 'Can you forgive me?'

I hesitate. 'I don't know,' I answer honestly. 'I think we have to take it slowly. One step at a time. Meet on neutral territory. It is going to take time, Richie. We both have to learn to trust again.'

He nods. 'It's a start,' he says throatily. 'Maybe we could go for a coffee now, if you're...' He stops as my phone beeps.

I check it. 'It's Emelia,' I tell him. 'I have to call her back.' I've promised myself I will be a friend to her. She will need someone to help her through this, to be there for her and the children. She's trying so hard, seeking help with her addiction. She's taken me in, and I'm grateful for that. Truthfully, I think I'm going to need her support as much as she needs mine.

'How is she?' Richie asks.

I pause. 'Coping.'

'Did she give her statement to the police?' he asks. He's aware of what she'd said about Tom, which had helped secure his release from the police station, and I suppose he wants to be certain he's in the clear.

I nod. 'It couldn't have been easy for her.'

'No.' Richie sighs. 'She'll be in bits, I imagine, especially learning how he died.'

Someone had laced his whisky with one hundred per cent rubbing alcohol, according to DI Simons. She's investigating the possibility that Adam Moore might have paid someone to do it, someone who might have been desperate for money. Emelia's bitter response after the initial shock was to say it was a fitting ending. It was her anger talking. She was referring to his being with another woman. Once Detective Simons had gone, she sobbed until I thought her heart would break. When she was more composed, I slipped discreetly into the room she uses for her beauty makeover parlour. It didn't take me long to find and dispose of the Isopropyl rubbing alcohol she uses to sanitise her equipment. She was in my corner when I really needed her to be. Richie's too. I have to be there for her now.

'I'll leave you to call her back,' Richie says with a sad smile.

I watch him walk back to the landing, where he pauses, running his fingers through his hair in despair as he takes in the fire blackened walls.

Turning away to make my call, I glance back through the window, where everything looks normal, throwing the chaos my life has become into sharp focus.

'Hi, how's it going?' Emelia asks when she picks up. 'Have you two managed to sort anything out?' She knows I was meeting Richie here. She's apologised a thousand times for what happened on the day of Jodie's funeral, saying that when Richie hugged her, she'd been so desperate for affection, she'd drunkenly, stupidly, thrown herself at him. That it wasn't his fault. Do I believe her? I think I do. Even so, I don't think we can just pick up our relationship as if nothing's changed.

'Okay. We're talking at least,' I answer.

'Good.' Emelia breathes a sigh of relief. She doesn't pursue it. I'm guessing she realises I'm not ready to go into detail yet. 'I just wanted to say thanks,' she hesitates, 'for cleaning up the beauty room.'

I glean her meaning. 'No problem,' I assure her, and leave it at that. After checking she's okay I finish the call and go in search of Richie. Hearing a noise from the main bedroom, I head that way, pausing at the partially open door as I note him crouching down in front of the wardrobe, rooting around the wardrobe floor. 'Looking for something?' I ask him, pushing the door open and going in.

'Jesus.' He jumps. 'You nearly gave me heart failure.' Laughing nervously, he straightens up. 'I was just checking how much stuff is smoke damaged. Looks like it will all need intensive washing or dry cleaning.'

Including the shoes? My gaze drifts to the various pairs of trainers he's pulled out and is now kicking back in before closing the doors.

'So how's Emelia?' he asks, heading towards where I'm standing inside the door.

'Coping.' I eye him curiously. 'I already said.'

'Good,' he answers distractedly, and walks past me out onto the landing.

Hearing him going down the stairs, I turn to follow him, but waver. I want to ignore it. So badly. But it won't be ignored, the nagging little voice in my head that whispers, *Are you really going to accept that his priority right now is to check his trainers?*

I'm not sure what I'm looking for as I kneel in front of the open wardrobe doors and scoop the trainers back out, new trainers, old trainers. There's a rolled up pair of socks stuffed in one shoe. Puzzled, I pull them out and tip the shoe up. My heart freezes, blood crackling through my veins like ice as something falls silently to the carpet.

'Becky?' Richie calls from downstairs.

I don't move. I can't move. Frozen with shock, I stare down at the blue inhaler, which seems to stare mockingly back at me.

'Becks?' Richie says cautiously behind me.

I snatch the inhaler up, jump to my feet and whirl around to face him. 'It was you.' I gasp out a ragged breath. 'You were with her. You had sex with her.'

Richie's face blanches as he looks down at the evidence I hold in my outstretched hand. Then, 'Are you serious?' He emits a strangled laugh, his gaze shooting back to me. 'Don't be bloody ridiculous, Becky. I was never anywhere near—'

'You have her inhaler!' I scream. 'You killed her!'

'No way!' Richie yells. 'No fucking way. Whatever you're thinking, Becky, you're wrong. Completely wrong. I did *not* have sex with her. I did *not* kill her. I swear to God I didn't.'

I simply stare at him. I have no words. No ability to speak them.

'I *didn't*. I swear,' he repeats, panic flooding his features. 'It was in my rucksack. I found it after the police arrived. I didn't put it there. I didn't know what to do. I—'

'Then how did it *get* there?' I yell over him.

'I don't *know*.' He swipes a hand through his hair.

'So, are you saying someone *planted* it there?' My voice is filled with incredulity.

'Tom. It must have been Tom,' he gropes feverishly for some kind of explanation.

'Really?' I laugh in bewilderment. 'Is that the best you can do? I mean, it's pretty weak, isn't it, trying to shift the blame to someone who's not here to—'

'For Christ's sake! *Stop*! Just stop, Becky, will you?' Richie grates, his eyes drilling furiously into mine. 'It was *you*. You had the bloody inhaler. You hid it in *your* bag.'

SIXTY-SEVEN

'*What?*' I stare at him, staggered.

'You put it in your bag.' Richie's voice is less strident, defeated almost. 'I came into the tent as you were stuffing it in there. I *saw* you. I didn't know what to do. I asked you what was up? You said, "Nothing," and walked right past me. You wouldn't look at me. You were acting weirdly. Spaced out. I knew you hadn't drunk or smoked anything and... I didn't know what to do.'

'You're lying,' I murmur tremulously. 'You're trying to drive me bloody insane, that's what you're doing.'

'Becky, I'm not.' Richie's voice is soft as he moves towards me.

I back away from him. 'It was you Pippa fancied. *You*, not Tom. You who she was making eyes at. You who was making eyes at *her*. Even when you were dancing with her, you were eyeing her up, pulling her close. It wasn't Tom. It was *never* Tom.'

Richie tugs in a sharp breath, exhales slowly. 'I know what you did, Becky.' He eyes me steadily, watching me carefully.

'What do you mean?' My voice emerges a dry croak.

Richie draws in another deep breath. 'I should have said something. I just didn't know how to. You were pregnant with our baby. You walked off. I waited in case you'd gone to the loo. Looked for you.'

'This is wrong,' I murmur shakily. 'It's all lies.'

'Becky, for the love of God, I am *not* lying.' Richie's gaze doesn't flinch. His eyes are dark, troubled. Frightened. 'Half an hour after you put that inhaler in your bag, you were back to normal. Back to being you. Full of concern for Pippa. Worried about her. I could see it was genuine, and... I was *so* fucking confused, Becky. I had no idea what to do. I thought you'd blocked it out.'

I feel my world crumbling, the very foundations beneath me shifting.

'I knew about your mother. How worried you were her illness might be hereditary. I should have done something. I kept wanting to talk to you. I didn't. And then, after you lost the baby...' He stops, pressing his thumb and forefinger hard against his eyes.

He thinks I was in some state of fugue, that I *have* inherited my mother's madness. But her lapses in memory were exacerbated by the alcohol she swilled back her medications with. Her bipolar disorder was manageable. It was unbearable, for her, distressing for my father, who found her violent moods swings impossible, but it could have been managed. He'd defended her – he'd loved her. Even claiming that when she'd attacked him so badly he still bore the scars, she'd been unaware of what she was doing. I'd never known whether it was alcohol-fuelled psychosis or blind rage that caused her to lose all control that day. It was just hours after that, that she'd had her first stroke. My father was right, I knew from bitter experience she wouldn't remember what she'd done. She never did, even before she was rendered incapable of speech.

The thing is, I could remember. Now. In this moment,

though I'd buried it so deep it only ever visited me in my subconscious, in the nightmares I could never escape, I recall it in vivid detail. It was right there in front of me. The day of Pippa's death, the way she died, playing out in surreal slow motion right before my eyes.

EPILOGUE

PIPPA

Then

She was going to die here. A lurch of fear gripped her as she realised her rasping gasps for breath might be her last. The cruel irony was, just a short while ago, she'd wished she could die rather than suffer the humiliation she did at other people's hands. Their slings and arrows cut deep, yet they stood by and watched her bleed. Now, she wanted to take her wish back. She didn't want to die out here all on her own. She tried again to do the most simple thing in life of all and just breathe. It was impossible. As impossible as her trying to be part of their world. She didn't fit in. She was different. Not like them.

She was frightened.

Coarse sand and grit bit spitefully into her cheek as she lay there like a stranded fish, her mouth gaping open as she attempted to suck in life-giving oxygen. Blinking salty tears from her eyes, she crawled a hand towards where her inhaler lay on the beach just out of her reach, where she'd dropped it after fumbling it from her shorts pocket. *Please help me.* She begged silently.

Hopelessness settled like a stone inside her as the person who might save her made no move to retrieve it. A yard or so off, she simply stood there instead, quietly watching her. Pippa guessed why. She couldn't have her live to tell the tale. Becky had too much to lose. A life worth living. She was pregnant. She was going to marry Richie. She wasn't going to let Pippa come between them. Had she seen him following her down here? What happened once he'd found her? If she had seen, Pippa realised that she would be struggling with her conscience. Did she help her, in so doing throw away her own future with the father of her child, or did she use this perfect opportunity to silence her?

Pippa tried again to speak. Nothing emerged but a rasping gurgle. Her chest whistled as her breaths became shorter, stopping partway down her trachea. Minimal air reached her lungs, and, though it felt like an eternity, she knew it wouldn't take long. She was growing cold. Couldn't feel her fingers or toes. Desperately, she tried again to reach the inhaler. It was useless. She was useless. Weak and clumsy. Inarticulate. Body conscious, with no sense of self-worth.

No sense. She shouldn't have come here, opened herself up to this. She should have kept her head down, paled into the background. Gone unnoticed. Overlooked was safer. She'd so wanted to be accepted as one of their circle. Liked, if not popular. She was never going to be that.

Deprived of air, she felt her organs beginning to shut down. Her vision blurred, fading to pulsating liquid red, and she squeezed her eyes closed. Her ears hurt so badly, she wanted to press her fingers against them to stop the itchy burning, but she couldn't even do that. Her limbs felt like they didn't belong to her and the compression on the centre of her chest was growing so heavy she felt her ribs would crack. She could hear her blood pumping, a slow, sluggish pulse at the base of her neck. Her throat tightened. Pressure, like something pushing inward against her oesophagus, closed her airway completely, and she guessed it would soon be over. The water was only yards away. The tide was coming in. Would it wash her away? She wondered. Obliterate any evidence of her insignificant existence? She'd always liked the sound of the sea – softly ebbing and flowing, it sounded like the earth breathing. It was mocking her. If she could have, she might have smiled at that sad irony.

As the waves quieted to a soft whisper, she heard her speak, finally. Felt a soft thud through the ground as she dropped down beside her. 'I'm sorry. So sorry. Please don't die.' It was a wretched, hopeless apology. Too late. Could she forgive? Would Becky be able to forgive herself as her life moved forward while she'd been robbed of hers? Pippa hoped not.

A LETTER FROM SHERYL

Thank you so much for choosing to read *One More Lie*. I can't believe this is my sixteenth book published with fabulous Bookouture! I really hope you enjoy reading it as much as I enjoyed writing it. If you would like to keep up to date with my new releases, please do sign up at the link below where you can grab my FREE short story, *The Ceremony*. You can unsubscribe at any time and your details will never be shared.

www.bookouture.com/sheryl-browne

Because of my own experiences, I'm fascinated by toxic relationships and the subtleties at play within, say, manipulative behaviour, where one partner will employ manipulation to undermine the other person's sense of reality, leaving them doubting their memory, sanity, and ultimately their sense of self. Why would someone do this? Could it be that the manipulator themself might be terrified of exposing their own vulnerability? People who lie, pathological liars, narcissistic personalities, will often go to terrifying extremes to avoid having their lies exposed and the truth coming out. They might try to deflect blame if they feel caught out, saying you are 'this' or 'that' in an argument in order to deflect blame from themselves.

What happens, though, if the blame they're trying to deflect is for an act too heinous to contemplate? A secret you're complicit in burying because you couldn't make yourself believe your partner could possibly be guilty of it? What if in working to deny that truth, you end up snarled in such a tangled web of lies there's no hope of extricating yourself without implicating other people and ultimately destroying their relationships?

The question I'm posing is: Can we forgive a likeable character who does something that is morally wrong?

I'm really keen to know what you, my lovely readers, think.

If you have enjoyed the book, I would love it if you could share your thoughts and write a brief review. Reviews mean the world to an author and will help a book find its wings. I would also love to hear from you via social media or my website.

Happy reading all!

Sheryl x

facebook.com/SherylBrowne.Author

x.com/SherylBrowne

ACKNOWLEDGEMENTS

Heartfelt thanks to the fabulous team at Bookouture, whose support of their authors is phenomenal. Special thanks to Helen Jenner, who has magic eyes. She just knows when a story isn't quite working and has an incredible ability to steer it in the right direction. To everyone in our wonderful editorial team, too, who work so hard for all their authors. Huge thanks also to our fantastic marketing and publicity teams. Kim Nash, Noelle Holten, Sarah Hardy and Jess Readett are always enthusiastically behind us and are just amazing. We could not do this without you! To the other authors at Bookouture, thank you for your support, which is always there when one of us might need it.

I owe a huge debt of gratitude to all the fantastically hardworking bloggers and reviewers who have taken time to read and review my books. It's truly appreciated. You do a phenomenal job shouting out to the world when we might be too shy to. Yes, I am, really. Thank you. Special thanks to Coombs Wood Book Club who invited me along to give an author talk and were so welcoming and enthusiastic the nerves didn't even have time to surface.

Final thanks to every single reader out there for buying and reading our books. Knowing you have enjoyed our stories and care enough about our characters to want to share them with other readers is the best incentive ever for us to keep writing.

PUBLISHING TEAM

Turning a manuscript into a book requires the efforts of many people. The publishing team at Bookouture would like to acknowledge everyone who contributed to this publication.

Audio
Alba Proko
Sinead O'Connor
Melissa Tran

Commercial
Lauren Morrissette
Hannah Richmond
Imogen Allport

Cover design
Lisa Horton

Data and analysis
Mark Alder
Mohamed Bussuri

Editorial
Helen Jenner
Ria Clare

www.ingramcontent.com/pod-product-compliance
Ingram Content Group UK Ltd.
Pitfield, Milton Keynes, MK11 3LW, UK
UKHW041300140225
4603UKWH00012B/52

9 781835 259641